DEVOID
OF
LIGHT

Nick Campanella

Devoid of Light
Copyright 2024 by Nick Campanella
ISBN: 978-1-970153-47-7
Library of Congress Control Number: 2024901655

Devoid of Light is a work of fiction. Names, places, and incidents are either products of the author's imagination or are coincidences.

Parental advisory: Violence, explicit language, and strong sexual innuendos.

La Maison Publishing, Inc.

Maison
Vero Beach, Florida
The Hibiscus City
lamaisonpublishing@gmail.com

A Special Thank You to My Friends and Family

My girlfriend and my daughter. My mom and dad. Step-parents and in-laws. My coaches and teachers. My lawyers, accountants, and employers. I am also grateful to my professional support: editors, graphic designers, and marketing experts. My website designer. My publisher. My manager. And my launch team. Thank you!

My biggest thank you goes to the readers—past, present, and future. Without you, there would be no reason to write. Your opinions matter so much. Please leave a short review on Amazon.com and Barnesandnoble.com.

Oh, one more thank you to God, for guiding me away from the path of affliction I was running toward twenty-five ago.

There is no peace, there is only passion.
                                              — Darth Bane

Author's Note

Devoid of Light is a stand-alone book, but does take place in the same world as my other books.

Devoid of Light is a **nonlinear story.** Because of this, it will be important to pay attention to the dates at the beginning of each chapter. ***Dates in italics represent the past.***

Thank you for reading. Enjoy!

Nick Campanella

INTRODUCTION

Two Harbors, Minnesota
March 4, 2026

Dr. Randy Beaumont curled his fingers on the lid of the storage freezer and lifted. A cool chill wafted upward. Screaming in his short-term memory was the pleading voice of the crumpled-up man before him. Permafrost was now covering the body. Glancing sideways at the over-sized man standing next to him, he saw a smirk hiding under his thick beard.

"We should tip it over," Beaumont said to his associate in the dimly lit basement. "Yank him out." The large tarp was crinkling under their feet.

Rick Gaytan's eyes shifted from the Sawzall on the workbench to his short and thin boss. "Nah, we can lift him out," he said with a low monotone voice. Reaching inside the freezer, he grabbed the corpse by the belt with his muscular hands.

The out-of-work doctor pulled a pair of surgical gloves out of his black Carhartt jacket and snapped them on. "Hold up," he said to a man almost twice his size. "You just left your fingerprints on the belt. You need to smarten up. I need you on top of your game." His black rectangular glasses magnified his dark eyes that were wide open.

"I'll burn the belt," Gaytan said, receiving the gloves from his boss. After pulling them on, he re-gripped the leather.

Dr. Beaumont reached underneath the dead man's armpit. "Lift," he said, grunting with an upward jerk. Another grunt and the victim tumbled over the edge and crashed on the tarp.

A thousand tiny pieces of frost broke off and tapped on the wrinkled plastic.

Both men stood silent. A man was frozen solid in the fetal position, lying on his side. He was frozen in time. The result of their direct actions. Gaytan lifted his head and the two men shared a cold, muted look before hard labor.

"You still haven't told me what this guy did to you." Gaytan's gaze was locked on the dead man on the tarp. He looked athletic size. Black hair slicked back with a few hard clumps out of place. He wore a cheap black suit. No shoes. Thin black socks.

"Go get the Sawzall," Beaumont said stiffly, his freshly shaved face made of stone. No smile. No emotion. Low thin eyebrows that matched his gel-parted black hair.

Gaytan fetched the reciprocating saw and hurried back. As he stood there, the corner of his mouth hoisted upward.

Dr. Beaumont held out his hand for the cutting machine. At Gaytan's pointed look, he said: "Yeah, I know. Normally, you would amputate. But this time, it's personal."

"Here ya go, Doc." He handed off the cutting machine like they were carpenters on the job. Surgeons in the operating room.

"They'll be plenty of work for you to do," Beaumont said with a nod to follow. "Plenty of money to be made." Squeezing the trigger of the saw produced a sharp loud whine that proved the battery had juice.

"What are you gonna do with the body parts?" Gaytan's voice was slow and deep. Face fully bearded and pale. Long and dark sandy-blond hair in a ponytail that rested in the hood of his duck-canvas work jacket.

The good doctor shifted the saw blade at Gayton's chest. "I decide," he said slowly and deliberately, "what you need to know. And when *you* need to know it. It's a peace of mind. If something goes wrong, it's on me. And you don't want *me* pointing my finger... at *you*. Understand?"

Gaytan swallowed hard. "M-my bad. I know you don't like questions." He let out a heavy breath. "It...It just popped out of my head." He shoved his right hand into his jacket pocket.

"One step at a time, Rick." He shook his head. "I don't pay you to ask questions."

"I know, I know," Gaytan said, nodding with his fist clenched in the black void of his pocket.

The self-proclaimed doctor dropped to one knee. Lowering the saw blade just above the neck of the dead man, he placed one hand on top of the front grip and let out a breath. Beaumont's olive oil skin was darkening with each passing second as he flexed every muscle in his little body.

Gaytan took a few steps backward. Now off the tarp, his eyes lowered to the gray scruffy face of the victim. Some of the frost had melted away and revealed the oval handsome countenance of a man named Blake. That's all he knew. His name and address. Time of death. Cause of death.

Gaytan wondered, as he watched his boss squeeze the trigger of the saw, his body precise as it slowly cut into the corpse's neck, how these two men knew one another.

What had Blake done to make things so personal for Dr. Randy Beaumont?

The saw's high-pitched scream was muffled by frozen flesh. Pink saw dust was shooting down on the tarp. Shiny partials were glinting in the air.

1

Caleb Hunt's dark eyes were raking over the ballroom full of Duluth Kennedy High School alumni. Bountiful dresses, nice suits, and drinks in their hands were all he saw. Smiles, too. After twenty years, he could still recognize everyone at the reunion. Except for one guy who stuck out like a sore thumb.

Spinning on his bar stool, Caleb faced his drunk friend who was chugging a beer. "Who's the short guy in the fancy suit?" he asked, gesturing at a person mingling in the crowd.

Blake Connor set his beer on the granite bar top. "Probably some broad's rich ass husband," he said, slurring his words. "W-why? Why you worried about that chump?" Blake itched his designer scruff and then reclaimed his beer.

"I ain't worried, bro," Caleb said, running his fingers through his gel-streaked short brown hair. "Just curious. I thought he looked familiar." He adjusted the collar of his navy blue Oxford shirt. Tucked into dark gray slacks, the outfit was smart but casual. No blazer. No tie. But at least his face was freshly shaved for the occasion.

"I've never seen that pussy in my life." Blake shrugged in a black and bulky suit jacket. "That would suck to be that short." He chuckled and then adjusted the collar of his white V-neck shirt underneath the blazer. Stepping off his stool, he stood a full six feet tall.

When Caleb stood up, he hit the shoulder of Blake's hand-me-down suit. "His suit makes your shit look like a dishrag," he said in the shadow of his taller but thinner friend. "I'm gonna get another pop and mingle a bit. The twenty-year reunion only comes once in a lifetime."

"Make it a whiskey." Blake's smile widened. "Pop ain't gonna win over your high school crush. I'll tell ya that much. A shy guy like you needs some liquid courage."

Caleb squinted his brown eyes. "Who you talkin' about, Mars Sundean?"

"Yeah, I noticed you eyeballing her thick ass all night. Too timid to even say hi."

"Why don't you watch your own bobber?"

"That's what I'm gonna do." Blake smiled. "Just sayin', you've been in love with that girl since ninth grade. It's now or never. Time to man up."

"Whatever."

"Good luck." Blake playfully shoved Caleb. "I'll come find you in a bit. Don't get abducted by Rich Boy in the pimp suit." He laughed shortly. "I saw him staring at you earlier. Seriously."

Caleb only shook his head and watched Blake strut into the crowd of the ballroom with two beers in his hands. One halfway to his lips. "What a lush." He crept toward the punch bar.

The music from the turn of the century was pounding in his ears. Every person in his path wore the same electric pulse of bliss on their face. Heads were bobbing to the beat of the music. Not at the punch bar. It was just Caleb by himself with an empty Styrofoam cup in his hand. Setting it underneath the soft drink dispenser, he pulled the lever until his cup was full of orange fizz.

Aimlessly weaving around people in the friendly crowd, Caleb caught a glimpse of red hair and then lost it in the sea of people. He felt a flutter in his chest. Stepping aside, he exchanged a hi to an old acquaintance, but kept moving steadily forward. *There she is,* he thought, stopping in his tracks. His mouth cracked open and he sucked in some air.

Mars Sundean was laughing with her friends, smacking her hand on her tight maroon dress. Swallowing his doubt with a sip of pop, he smiled at the beacon pulsating in his mind's eye. From a distance, Caleb watched Mars laugh. Her flaming locks of dark auburn hair were dancing in slow motion just above her shoulders. Her smile must have been contagious. Because everyone around her was smiling, too. Guys and gals.

She's gorgeous, Caleb thought with widening eyes. The flutter in his heart had progressed into a buzz that was shooting throughout his entire body.

Caleb's eyes met hers. Locked. Squeezing his cup tighter, he smiled and then advanced toward her—his feet finding direction at last. Cutting through the crowd of well-dressed alums, Caleb heard a familiar voice, and his feet planted against protest from his thoughts. *Can't snub Bob,* he thought, whipping his head around. In annoyance to being waylaid from Mars, he pursed his lips.

"What's up, Hunt?" Bob Sturgis said with his usual sly grin.

"Bob," Caleb said, sticking out his hand. "I thought Tarik said you weren't coming?" He shook his large hand firmly, meeting the eyes of an old friend who had grown distant over the years.

"I changed my mind." Bob gestured to the line of women in low-cut dresses at the bar. "I hope it pays off." Bob stood over six feet tall and had a menacing presence in his black-on-black suit. To make up for his balding hair that was combed over to one side, Bob wore a thick but clean beard that was a shade darker than his light brown hair.

Caleb offered a curt nod. "Speaking of that, I was just about to go say hi to Mars."

"Me too." Bob smiled, grabbing Caleb by the shoulder for a playful shake. "Just kidding, bro." He let go and continued. "I smoked a cigarette with her earlier. She was asking all about you." Bob tilted his beer for a chug.

"What'd she say?"

"I told her you went sober," Bob said. "How you've been in construction for a long time." He glanced at Blake on the dance floor grinding on a curvy brunette. "I didn't tell her how your best friend is a degenerate gambler. I heard he owes Derek Bane, big time."

"Thanks for reminding me, bro." Caleb patted him on the shoulder. "I'll talk to ya soon." Caleb took two steps and bumped into another old friend he couldn't snub. *Fuck,* he thought. *All I wanna do is talk to Mars.*

"Well, if it isn't my man, Lee Wallis?" Caleb said, thumping his old school friend on the back. He was so painfully thin, Caleb hoped it didn't hurt him.

"What's up, man?" Lee stuck his hand out and exposed the head of a dragon on his wrist. He was dressed up more than Caleb. A dark blue tailored suit with a fat red tie. Fancy leather shoes that were pointed at the toe. But his sun-kissed face and horseshoe hairline threw off the elegance of his attire.

Caleb excitedly shook his hand. "It must have been like fifteen years," he said with a growing smile. "Where ya been, man?"

"Cali," Lee said, adjusting his wireframe glasses. "You still live in this shithole?"

"Duluth ain't no shithole." Caleb shot back, his dark eyebrows lowering.

"Defensive." Lee laughed shortly. "I like it. I guess some things never change." He flashed a nodding smile.

"To me, California is a shithole. Nothing but commies and gangbangers."

Lee smiled. "I make a hundred thousand a year to work on a weed farm. The women are beautiful out there. Easy pickins. I've never even seen any gangbangers in the mountains. But, yeah, everyone *is* progressive out there. Including me." He poked himself in the chest a few times.

"Hey, I'm glad it worked out for you." Caleb gave a half shrug. "Just not for me." He flashed a smile. "How long you in town for? I'd love to catch up."

"I'm hopping on the next flight tomorrow," Lee said. "I just wanted to see everyone one last time."

Caleb nodded, his eyes skirting to a moving flash of red hair just twenty feet behind Lee. Returning to Lee's squinting eyes, he felt a sudden thirst for Mars. "Well, shit…we should keep in touch."

Lee nodded. "Yeah, great to see you, bro. It's been a long time. You're welcome to come visit sometime. It's paradise. My treat. Just don't bring Blake." He handed him a business card.

Caleb stuck the card in his pocket. "You still holding a grudge against Blake, eh?"

"No. I just wouldn't invite him to my house. Sicilians never forgive." Lee shook his head. "We never forget."

"Great to see you, Lee." Caleb shook his hand and broke away only to realize that Mars was watching him. As he stepped forward with a suppressed smile, his fluttering buzz of adrenaline returned.

His gaze once again locked with hers. *Those eyes,* Caleb thought, placing one foot in front of the other. *Holy shit.*

She wore a growing smile. The corners of his mouth shot upward to reciprocate. Mars inched toward him, her tattooed hand rising. He could feel that buzz under the skin.

A few more steps and his compressed lips sounded the letter M — and then the little man with a fancy black suit cut in front of him. He hugged Mars. It was the same little guy Caleb had been assessing earlier. He had black gel-parted hair and black rectangular glasses. No facial hair. Olive oil skin. And a clear underbite grin.

No way, Caleb thought. Stopping his advance, his head jerked backward. Dropping his eyebrows, his mind flashed back to the high school Sweetheart Dance. The moment he caught Mars dancing in the quarterback's muscular arms. *I was too slow.*

Just like that night, he turned around in defeat. A sting in his chest. *It's all Bob's fault,* he thought harder. *Nah, she's probably married to that little chump.* To hide his contorted face, Caleb took a sip of his orange drink and retreated with a lowered gaze.

His steps were slow and dragging. The loner table in the corner of the next room was calling his name. The one o'clock bar close couldn't come fast enough. *I should just grab Blake and bounce.*

Feeling pressure on his elbow, Caleb spun around. His eyes widened, a puff of breath bursting out of his mouth as his eyes raked over the woman standing opposite of him.

"Mars!"

"Caleb," she said, reaching her arms around his back.

Taken aback, Caleb's spine stiffened until he smelt her perfume. Closing his eyes, he melted into her warm embrace and felt her dark red hair on his brow.

"I was starting to think you didn't remember me," Mars said, grabbing his muscular upper arm while stepping back.

He smiled, eyebrows arching. "Mars, *you*...are unforgettable." Caleb gestured to the short guy on the dance floor who was spying on them. "No, I just figured, your husband might not be cool with me swooping in like that. He doesn't look too happy."

Mars laughed out loud. "Uh, God no." She patted her chest and let out a sweet giggle. "You really think I'd marry that weirdo?"

"Who was that, anyways?"

"Uh, I'm not sure. He said his name was Dr. Beaumont." Mars shrugged. "He mentioned a song I sang in choir class." Her head shook tightly. "I don't remember him."

"Why do you think he's so weird?"

"I don't know. Something about him gave me the creeps. For one: He forced a hug on me. And two: he stood way too close once he finally let go. His beady little eyes were at tit level." She gestured with a flat hand near the tanned skin on her bulging chest and cleavage. "Anyways, enough about that guy. I want to hear about you. Tell me something interesting about yourself."

Caleb took a sip of his pop as a defense mechanism to his nerves and anxiety. "I've been grinding my back in construction," he said. "Pays the bills, ya know? How 'bout you?"

"I need a cigarette." Mars tilted her beer back. "If you join me, I'll tell you all about it."

"I quit smoking, but I'd love to listen to what you have to say."

Mars met his eyes. "That's what I liked best about you." She slipped her arm under his and locked it tight. "You always made me feel important. You used to let me vent for hours on the phone when we were kids."

*****

Mars sparked up a cigarette on the snowy patio. "What kind of construction are you in?"

"Mostly siding and windows," Caleb said. "But me and Blake do just about everything."

"Yeah, I saw you guys talking," Mars said. "You two are still pretty close, huh?"

Caleb nodded. "He's my best friend, but outside of work, we don't hang out as much as in the old days. I try to avoid the party scene."

"That's what I heard." She took a drag from her cigarette and tucked her head in between her shoulders to hide from the icy wind.

Caleb shook his head. "We used to party pretty hard," he said. "And then I went to prison. You didn't hear about that?"

"No way? Prison?"

"Just for a few years after high school."

"Shit, I haven't talked to anyone in Duluth since eleventh grade. When my parents moved us to Germany, I never looked back." She reached for his upper arm and felt rock-hard muscle. "What the heck happened?"

"Wait, you don't know what happened to me?"

She shrugged. "No, last I remember you stood me up on the day we moved." She took the last sip of her beer and set it down. "Remember, you were supposed to meet me and say good bye?"

"Mars. That's the day I got shot." His eyebrows were raised.

"Oh my God." She covered her mouth with her hand. "That was you? I'm so sorry. I totally thought you stood me up. That's why I never reached out to you. I thought you hated me for moving."

"Just the opposite. I could never hate you." Caleb smiled. "You're the great Mars Sundean."

She pursed her plump red lips. "Aww... still too kind." Smiling. "So, I see you survived. But how bad was it?" "I actually got stabbed first," Caleb said, pausing to meet her light green eyes. "Then I got shot in the back. All flesh wounds, but I was less than an inch away from being paralyzed. Lucky, I guess. Had it been a .40 caliber I'd be dead."

"Getting shot and stabbed and going to prison doesn't sound too lucky to me."

"It's all in the eye of the beholder," he said. "For me, seeing that white light and coming back, really woke me up. Made me feel alive after. But it took prison to calm me down. Sobriety, too."

"What did you go to prison for?" Mars was shivering in her dress.

Caleb put his arm around her side and lowered his tone. "What do you think?"

*****

Caleb paid the bartender, grabbed the ice-cold bottle of beer, and handed it to Mars.

"Thanks," Mars said, tilting the beer to her lips. "I'm thirsty tonight." She smiled.

"Me, too," he said. "But I've had like ten orange pops. Feels like I got a sugar high."

Mars laughed, leaning into Caleb's space. He propped her up as she staggered slightly. She could feel his muscular hands gripping her back and arm.

"Oh, shit, I'm sorry." The corner of Mars' mouth curled upward. "I'm all drunk and shit. Showing bad form."

"No, I don't mind." He shook his head. "Everyone drinks. I'm fine with it. Just not for me."

"I don't drink much either. Special occasions. Once in a while, alone."

"Why does a woman as cool as you drink alone?"

"Thirty-eight years old. No kids. No want for kids. Retired from the Airforce." She let out a breath. "No clue what to do next. Sometimes I drink to just let go. Forget about everything."

"I see. I'm kinda in the same boat. No wife, no kids yet. No way out of manual labor. Without alcohol, I have to read books to let go."

"Do you have a girlfriend?" Mars took a swig.

"No." Caleb shook his head slowly. "You? Boyfriend?"

"Nope. Got engaged to a guy I met in the Air Force." She showed him the small tattoo on her pinky finger of Air Force wings flying in dark blue ink. "Didn't work out. Too controlling for my liking." She let out a short breathy laugh.

He tilted a hand. "What do you mean by that?"

Mars took a sip of her beer. "A story for another time." She beamed a smile. "I'm still waiting for you to tell me how pretty I look."

"Mars, you look like a million bucks." His chest was buzzing with nerves. "Prettiest girl here by far."

"That's better. How bad do you miss me?"

Caleb stuck out his arm and gently placed his hand on her waist. The dress was thin as silk and he could feel her warmth. "You have no idea."

"Prove it."

Looking into her eyes, his gaze lowered to her lips. When Mars tilted her head, he pulled her close, locking his lips on hers. With his eyes closed, he melted in ultimate bliss. In the darkness of the moment, he heard a few cheers, and then an eruption that over powered the Y2K pop music.

When Mars released her lips and opened her eyes, the class of 2006 was surrounding them with smiles and jubilance.

2

Duluth, Minnesota
March 2, 2026

After the high school reunion, Caleb parked his Crew-Cab Chevy truck in front of Blake's tiny house. It was tucked in the back-end of a wooded lot. Mars was in the passenger seat looking at Caleb. Blake snoring in the cab. Snow was falling from the dark sky. And the street was packed with parked cars and trucks. No lights were on in any house on the dead-end street.

"Game over," Caleb said, craning his neck to face his inebriated best friend. "Blake!"

Blake jerked back into consciousness and unbuckled his seatbelt. "All right, bro," he said slowly, coughing to clear his scratchy voice. "See ya at work, Monday. You two have a good night." Blake shook Caleb's hand with a clasp and hook. Two hard pats on the shoulder. "She must be blind... to be kickin' it with you." He then opened the back passenger-side door, laughing and coughing at the same time.

"Hold on, Blake," Mars slurred her words, swinging the door open. "It was really good to see you." She climbed herself down to the slushy road wearing Caleb's jacket.

Blake slammed the back door shut. "Mars Sundean," he said with a robust smile. "Goddess of the red planet." Blake opened his arms.

"It's been a lifetime." She moved in for a quick hug then let go. "I hope to see you again sometime. You take care now."

"I'll be around," Blake said, gently touching her shoulder. "Just take care of my boy." When Mars climbed back in the truck and shut the door, he gave a staggering Richard Nixon salute. And then he turned for his driveway.

The truck idled. Blake edged toward his one-story house.

Inside the pick-up, Caleb's head was cocked out the passenger-side window. "Let's make sure he gets inside," he said, watching Blake Connor saunter up the snowy driveway. "Some drunk girl froze to death back in the day." His brow lowered. "Her friends dropped her off and didn't look back. That's a bad way to die."

Blake weaved a crooked footpath, his steps winding along the trees and bushes heavily dotting his property line. After dropping his keys in the snow, he swooped them up, patted the snow off on his pants, and then unlocked the door. Shouldering it open, he stomped the snow off his shoes.

As he closed the door and locked it, he could still hear the departing growl of Caleb's truck. "Lucky mother fucker."

*****

Down the block from Blake's house, Richard Gaytan pulled a dolly from the back of a short moving truck. Dr. Beaumont's head was on a swivel. It was almost two o'clock in the morning, and the neighborhood was empty. Dark. Both men were wearing black.

"Don't roll it," Beaumont whispered sharply. "Carry it."

Gaytan lifted the heavy dolly and held it in the middle so that it hung horizontally as they followed Blake's crooked footprints up the long driveway. Coming to a stop at the side door, Gaytan set the dolly down and turned toward his boss who was holding a high-tech lock-pick device in his gloved hands.

Beaumont inserted the needle of the device in the keyhole. After pressing a button, something clicked, and then he turned the knob. Slowly pushing in the creaky door, he led the way through the pitch-black kitchen with covert movements, his eyes stretched for sound. He knew the layout. They'd been there before.

Stopping at the entrance of the dining room, Dr. Beaumont heard a low fluttering noise. Bending his ear, he took in the sound of a man snoring on the couch in the living room. Carefully gliding around furniture, his eyes started to focus in the darkness. A man was lying on his side with his back facing him.

Beaumont pulled a small plastic case out of his jacket pocket. Silently snapping it open, he grabbed the syringe and slipped the case back to where it came from. Inching forward, his breaths coming more and more forcefully out of his mouth. But his hands were steady. *This should keep him sleeping for a while,* he thought, his mind on his plan for when Blake wakes up.

Lifting the palm of his gloved hand, the mad doctor indicated for his accomplice to stay put. Slow and steady, he drew closer to the inebriated man. With each fluttering snore, Beaumont's heart jumped. Leaning forward, his eyes widened as the dripping needle poked Blake in the neck. He pressed down on the syringe and pulled back.

Blake's shoulder twitched, a mumble coughed out, and then his body went limp.

"Get the dolly." Dr. Beaumont pulled out two heavy-duty zip ties.

3

Duluth, Minnesota
March 4, 2026

In the snowy yard of a customer's two-story house, Caleb Hunt climbed to the top rung of the scaffolding ladder. The cold wind gave him a boost; the extended hand of his boss did the rest. Once on his feet, Denzel smacked him on the back of his shoulder twice. Since Blake was absent, Boss Man filled the void.

"Thanks," Caleb said, letting out a heavy breath. Glancing twenty-five feet down with anxiety, he saw snow and bushes and long boxes of composite siding.

"I know you don't like that last step," said Denzel, zipping up his black Carhartt jacket with no hood. As the icy wind blew, he ducked his bald black head in between his shoulders.

"This job never gets easier for me," Caleb said, tugging his knit cap lower to cover his ears. "The only thing in the whole world I'm afraid of is heights. Other than that, I ain't scared of shit."

"I still remember your first time on the ladder." Denzel laughed shortly. No hat, no gloves. Just a trimmed beard to protect him from the elements Caleb endured every day while he sat in the office signing contracts.

Caleb shook his head. "Don't remind me."

"All right, all right," Denzel said. "Let's get to work." Dropping to a knee, he reached for a stack of long composite siding.

Caleb did the same. "Thanks for filling in for Blake."

Denzel lifted his end just about level with Caleb's side. "So, what's Blake's story?" He kneeled closer to the house in his thermal black pants. "No call no show? What's up with that?"

"I have no idea," Caleb said, pressing the strip of siding against the wall where they left off on Friday. "It's not like him." He snapped it into place. "His phone goes straight to voicemail. Sent him a few texts, too. Crickets." He shook his head. With his air-power nail-gun, he blasted three nails in a row on the top of the piece of siding.

"It's not the first time, but it will be the last."

"He must be pretty sick," Caleb said. "I know he needs that money."

"I don't like it." Denzel pounded his second nail in the siding with a regular hammer. "It's disrespectful. I might have to shit can his a—"

"I'll stop over there after work," Caleb exclaimed. "You got to give him one more chance. He'll be here tomorrow if I have to drag him."

*****

After a long and cold day at work, Caleb drove to Blake's house and pulled his truck into the empty driveway. The sun was hiding low behind the garage and tall evergreen trees. "His car ain't here?" he said, throwing the shifter in park. "What the hell?"

Craning his neck, he scanned the darkening street for a twenty-year-old Ford Mustang with meaty tires. "Where could he be?" He got out of the truck, thinking in his head the possibilities as he approached the front door.

Probably sick and went to the ER, he thought. *Maybe he relapsed?* "Nah...." Caleb pounded on the door with the side of his fist at least five times. Reaching for the door knob, he tried to twist it and found out it was locked.

As he waited, he peeked in the window but it was dark inside. No light. *He's probably feeling better. That's it. He called Denzel and went out for dinner and a beer with one of his ladies.*

Pulling out his phone, he called Blake. It went straight to voicemail. "Hey, I'm at your house. Just checking on ya. If you want your job, you gotta call Denzel. Alright? Hit me back."

Caleb let out a heavy breath, and then angled for the rundown garage. Twisting the doorknob, he pushed it open. It was dark and cluttered, but he could see there was no car. A buzz from his pocket received the attention of his hand. *Blake,* he thought, whipping out the phone.

"Mars." He read the name on the screen and swiped to answer the call. "Hello."

"Hi!" she said. "Anything good happen to you today?"

"Nope, not until now," Caleb said, pressing the receiver to his ear. "We still on for tonight?"

"Um actually," Mars paused dramatically. "Something came up."

Caleb shut the garage door and headed for his truck. "Yeah, what's that?"

"Hot date with Dr. Beaumont." She giggled.

"Ha, ha, you think that's funny?" He smiled. "I should destroy you."

"What? I'm just kidding," she said with a breathy laugh. "Can you meet me soon? I'm homeless. I checked out of the hotel this morning."

"After the last few nights," he said, hopping in his truck, "trust me, I ain't kicking you out of my bed. Ever. Unless of course, I catch you talking to that Beaumont chump."

Mars laughed shortly. "When ya going home? I'm getting hungry."

"Soon. I'm at Blake's house right now." Caleb dropped the shifter in gear. "He didn't show up for work. Boss Man wanted me to check on him. But he's not here."

"Huh. Does he play hooky often?"

"Not for a long time." He turned on the road and hit the gas. "I call in sick more than him. But that's the thing... he didn't call in."

*****

The next morning, before the crack of dawn, Caleb stood in his work jacket watching Mars fill his thermos with coffee. She was wearing the T-shirt he wore the day before. Just the shirt. *She's perfect,* he thought. *Ten times more perfect than I ever imagined in high school.*

Mars spun around on her bare heel and handed him the steaming thermos. "I put a little extra sugar in there." She smiled, looking up to meet his eyes.

"Thanks," Caleb said. "This will wake me up." He took a small sip.

"Be careful. Super-hot." She fell into his arms.

"I hope you have a good day," he said, kissing her softly, pulling her closer. "Make yourself at home."

"Drive safe," Mars said. When she let go, she rubbed her eyes. "I'll hold down the fort. Maybe I'll have dinner ready for when you get home." A fleeting smile skated across her face.

"I'd really like that." Caleb grabbed his lunch box and thermos. "Surprise me. I ain't picky."

"I will." She touched his arm and disappeared into the long dark hallway. Thudded up the steps to the bedroom.

Caleb strolled to the foyer. Opening the front door, he was on the point of leaving when he spied a cardboard box resting on his ice-encrusted doorstep. Footprints in the snow were walking away.

"What the...?" Caleb muttered. "I didn't order anything?" Squinting, he scooped up the medium-sized box, closing the door with his boot. *Kinda heavy,* he thought, turning for the dining room table. *What could it be?* He set it down and gave it a full spin. Scratching his head, he peered down at the tape-sealed box.

Mars came back into the room in a tank top and yoga pants for her daily work out session. "I thought you were leaving?"

Caleb turned the mysterious package. "I am," he said with a puzzled look on his face. "Just found this box on the doorstep. It's addressed to me, but no stamp. No return address." He shrugged. "That means someone dropped it off. Don't you find that odd?"

"Don't open it." Mars shook her head. "People don't just leave boxes on steps."

"Why not find out what it is?"

Mars raised her eyebrows. "Because we just watched the same damn thing happen on *Forensic Files* last night. Remember?"

"Yeah, but in the show, it blew up when the guy moved it." Caleb shook the box and something shuffled around inside.

"Stop that!"

He set the box down on the floor. "I'm curious." He took a knee and whipped out the razor blade he kept in his jacket pocket for work. With his thumb, he clicked the blade out of its case.

"I wouldn't open it if I was you."

"Look, it's addressed to me. Might be a gift." His lips raised enough to show his teeth.

Mars let out a heavy sigh. "You're probably right," she said sarcastically. "Maybe it's filled with cash." She shot him a look and left the room.

"If it explodes, call 911." Caleb chuckled and then slit the tape as she hid in the other room. Flipping up one flap triggered a sniffle from his nose. A crude odor jumped out of the box and attacked his nostrils like a dead rat. His head jerked backward and he immediately stood up, backpedaling with a scrunched-up face. "What the hell is that?" The open flaps were still covering the contents in question.

Pulling his shirt over his mouth and nose, he took a cautious step forward and hovered over the box with an elevated heart rate. Breathing heavily, he reached out a trembling hand and quickly unfolded all four flaps. Squinting briefly as he studied the pale object, his eyes then exploded. "No," he cried, his face contorting as he gazed down into the discolored face of a man whom he knows and loves deeply.

The cardboard box was holding a white container with bags of dry ice that cradled Blake Connor's face so grotesquely within its depths. His pale, grayish face looked like a doll with pennies in his eyes. "It's got to be a prank." He let go of his shirt and inhaled the offensive stale taste of death.

Shooting bolt upright, he staggered back into the fridge. His right hand propped him up and his left hand shot to cover his open mouth. His panicked breaths became fast and sharp. His heart had plunged into his gut. Drowning in a mud puddle of crushing anguish, he could feel it continuing to sink. The sharp pain in his chest felt like he was on the top of Building 7, free-falling to the pits of hell.

"Blake," Caleb said under his breath, slowly dropping to his butt. Sobbing with his hand on his overflowing eyes, his head bobbed. "This isn't happening." He slammed his fist against the cupboard he was leaning against.

Mars peeked her head around the corner. "What is it?" She saw her Caleb on the floor, weeping with a beet-red face and lines on his forehead. She ran to him, gently wiping his tears and running her fingers through his hair. "Are you okay?"

"No," he said softly with a remote look on his pinched face. "Blake's dead."

*****

In less than twenty minutes, the city's top detective was in Caleb's living room. A clipboard in his pale, meaty hands. His mouth was flapping, but Caleb had a blank look on his face. While sinking into his out-of-date couch, his fingers pinched the bridge of his nose. Detective Fred Reid was talking to him but his mind was somewhere else. Somewhere far away from his house and yard and street filled with cops and nosy neighbors who were outside snickering and passing judgment.

"Caleb," Detective Reid said, snapping his hairy fingers from a chair directly in front of Caleb. "I need you to pay attention." His voice was husky. And so was the frame he hid under a black wool trench coat.

Caleb crossed his arms and pressed his lips together. His bloodshot eyes were now studying the gray-haired detective with a sky-blue tie and wireframed glasses.

"I want you to tell me every single person in Blake Connor's life," the detective ordered, "And tell me anyone who might have a reason to hurt him."

"With all due respect," Caleb said, shaking his head, "no one I know is capable of this. A killer is out there. I think you're wasting your time here." He relaxed his arms but continued sitting there, trying to take it all in. The horror, the shock, the confusion of the moment. He couldn't wrap his mind around why anyone would do such a thing. Or why anyone would involve him?

"Why would it be a waste of time?" Reid opened his hands. "You're a valued witness. This doesn't happen every day. In fact, in my twenty-five years on the job, it's *never* happened."

"I'm just saying, I have no idea who did this." Caleb's squinty eyes shifted. "I just lost my best friend. And I just want to be left alone. Okay?" His last word held a touch of irritation.

"Caleb, I don't like your tone." The detective shook his head tightly. "I'm here to help you." He paused, and then continued with much slower voice. "Look, I can tell you're not telling me everything you know. Because of that, I have to ask you: Caleb, did you kill Blake Connor?"

"Fuck no!" Caleb's voice came out in a bark that he hadn't heard for many years. "How 'bout that?" When he heard his voice raise, he took a deep breath—as he's learned to do, especially when dealing with police.

Reid stood up and pointed at Caleb. "Don't get hostile with me, buster. We can have this interview downtown if you want."

"I called 911 for help." Caleb's throat thickened. "Not to get interrogated."

"Look, Mr. Hunt," the detective said, lowering his voice. "I got the box, the shoe prints out front…and whatever you write down on this paper. That's it." He paused to sit down on the sofa. "Caleb, this box was sent to *you*. That means *you* could be next. I'd start writing down names so we can find this guy quick."

Caleb nodded. "I got a...." He caught himself before he admitted the crime of a convicted felon possessing a firearm. So, he lied. "I-I got a compound bow for home protection. He comes around here, he—"

"Be careful with that thing, son." Reid offered a faint smile while reading the chip on Caleb's shoulder. "Don't shoot me when I come back here tomorrow."

"I won't. But if he steps foot on my property, I got something waiting for him."

"Protect yourself by all means." Reid handed him the clipboard and a pen. "But, do yourself a favor—write down a list of Blake's potential enemies. Love interests. Friends. The odds are you know this guy. Someone who knows both of you. Someone you least expect. I want to rule everyone out one by one."

Caleb pressed one hand against his face. Finally letting go of his defensive resistance, he decided to level with the cop. His words had sunk in. "Blake had a lot of people who didn't like him."

"What do you mean?"

Caleb let out a heavy breath. "Well, for starters, he slept with a lot of married women over the years. That could have generated some hate. What else? He treats his girlfriend Nicole like shit. *She's* nuts. But why would she drop the box off on my front step? Hmm..." His eyes wandered up toward the ceiling then came back down to meet the detective's eyes. "And yah, he's been in dozens of bar fights. Alley brawls. Beef with small gangs around town." Caleb offered a shrug. "Happy?"

"I need names. Why didn't you tell me this earlier?"

Caleb's eyes averted. "I don't know. I'm not used to airing my friend's dirty laundry." He covered his face with his hand. Let out an audible breath.

"Who'd he have beef with?" Reid opened one hand in a welcoming gesture.

"I'm not giving out names right now." He shook his head. "I'm not trying to get dead like Blake."

"Why won't you give up the names?"

Caleb shook his head. "I don't think you understand. I give up names, I might end up dead."

"Mr. Hunt, the box was a clear message. You're next. What type of shit are you guys into?"

"I'm clean, sir. I changed my life. But Blake didn't."

"What *were* you into?"

"Nothing. I just used to run with a rough crowd. I'm out of that circle. But I'm not gonna be a rat."

"Fine. You're on your own then."

Caleb's hands rose briefly. "Sir, you don't understand, these people don't play games. They do not tolerate snitches."

"Okay. Give me a hint. Where do they party at?"

"Hell. I don't...." Caleb shook his head and let out a sigh. "Ever heard of Sharks' Pool Hall?"

"Pool hall across the bridge in Superior. Yeah, I know it."

"Honestly, I don't think they did it. But..." Caleb sighed again, looking off to the side. "Blake owes them some money."

"How much money?"

Caleb shrugged. "A couple thousand bucks. Give or take."

"Drugs?"

"No, gambling."

"I'm definitely going to check this out. What do they look like?"

"White dudes with tattoos. Flat brim hats. You know, the gangsta look."

"What gang are they in?"

Caleb pursed his lips and squirmed in his seat. "They're not in a gang," he said. "They just do gangster shit."

"Like what?"

Caleb shrugged. "They beat people who owe them money. Intimidate rivals. Make money any way they can."

"But they don't kill people?"

Caleb's eyes shifted. "I don't think so. But if they were to kill someone, the person would probably just disappear. Or get shot in their car. They don't seem like the type to…" He offered a half-shrug. "I just can't see it. They're lazy."

"Mr. Hunt, what type of business was Blake in?"

"I've already told you too much as it is." Caleb plopped his hand on his face. "I just want justice for my best friend." His voice cracked. "It hurts. I can barely think." He rubbed his eyes and sniffled, but if he was crying, he didn't show a tear.

Detective Reid looked at his watch. "That's it for now."

Caleb rose and wiped his hand on his pants. "If I think of anything else I'll let you know."

"Thanks for your cooperation." Reid shook Caleb's hand, meeting his dark, menacing eyes. "I'll be in touch."

4

In the back of the dimly lit pool hall, Derek Bane bit into a fat cheeseburger. Bane's top man, Sam Lugo was sitting across from him with a bottle of beer in his hands.

"I didn't believe it when I heard it," Sam said, tilting his beer back.

"Me neither," Bane said. "I mean, who the hell would chop a guy's head off and...." He was interrupted by the front door opening. His bloodshot eyes, half hidden beneath the brim of his hat, narrowed in suspicion. At the sight of one of his underlings, his tattooed hands momentarily tensed around his food. "Tell Aiden I don't like being disturbed when I'm eating." He gestured to the scrawny young man with a baby face who was striding purposefully forward in baggy clothes.

"He'll do anything I tell him," Sam said, nodding his head.

"And bulk him up. He looks weak." Bane took a big sip of his drink as the kid got closer to the table.

"Bane!" Aiden said with rosy cheeks and a manufactured southern accent. "Some cracker in a tie out there be taking pictures of yo fuckin' ride." His wiry arm was pointing toward the front door.

"What?" Bane sprung out of his seat. Rushing past the line of pool tables, he beelined toward the entrance with a low growl that was rumbling in his throat. "Fucking pigs," he said under his breath as he shouldered the glass door open. His boys were trailing behind him.

Detective Reid was squatting with his camera phone aimed at the rear license plate of Derek Bane's midnight blue BMW M3 sports car. At the sound of cursing, he rose tall, turning the camera to Bane and his roughneck friends.

"What the fuck are you doing?" Bane barked, his hand rising to block out his chiseled face and etched jawline from the camera.

"Taking pictures." The detective snapped off three more, and then stuffed his phone inside the breast pocket of his wool coat.

Bane stood still about ten feet away. "Why are you taking pictures?" he asked, folding his bulky tattooed arms across the chest of his light gray Polo shirt.

"That's a good question," Detective Reid said. "A better question would be: Do you have a lawyer?"

"What the fuck for? You ain't got shit on me!" Bane held his arms out wide. "I'm clean as fuck." He lied, his baggy jeans were loaded with a fat sack of pot, a wad of cash, and a handgun in the small of his back.

"Mr. Bane, we've been watching you for years," Reid said. "Every cop in town knows you sell meth to kids." His head shifted to Aiden, the skinny nineteen-year-old drug mule whom Bane groomed for a life of crime. And then his eyes landed back on Bane with disgust. "Why don't you come with me downtown? I want to ask you a few questions."

"Am I under arrest?"

"Not yet."

Bane turned to Sam and laughed shortly. "This prick thinks I'm stupid." He shifted back to the cop. "Come get me when you have something. I'm gonna go finish my dinner while it's still hot." He turned for the door.

"I get the DNA back tomorrow!" Reid said loudly.

Bane stopped, spinning around with a puzzled look on his squinting face. "DNA for what?"

Reid took a few steps forward. "The murder of Blake Connor."

"You think I killed Blake?" He tapped his well-defined chest.

"I know you killed him." The detective's eyebrows twitched with the bluff. "Connor got in too deep. I have a witness, but I want your DNA to match." He laughed shortly, holding his rotund belly. "Oh…and I *have* your DNA in the data base from last time you hurt one of your friends. Fingerprints, too. And I'm going to take you down." He pointed his finger at the threesome of white street thugs. "Your accomplices, too."

*****

Under a dark starless sky, Richard Gaytan loaded a long cardboard box in the trunk of a black Chevy Cruze. Dr. Beaumont closed the trunk and the sound shattered the early morning silence.

"So, why are we driving all the way to California to drop off a box?" Gaytan asked. "We could just send it in the mail with the other boxes."

Dr. Beaumont raised his hand sharply and the big man flinched. "How many times do I got to warn you?" he asked, dropping his hand with his voice. "Do not ask stupid questions. I don't want to have to smack you again. I pay you enough, right?"

"Uh, yeah." Gaytan bowed his head, curled his shoulders. "Of course, Boss."

"You trust my judgment, right?"

"You're right. I'm sorry. My mind's always crankin', ya know. In Afghanistan, I was always aware of every angle of each mission. I just want to be a part of the planning."

"Rick, I don't pay you to make plans or think." Beaumont softened his tone. "I pay you to follow orders to a tee. Just like in the military. You cannot divert from the plan." He swiped his hand. "Get in the car. You're driving."

Gaytan thumped his heavy frame into the driver seat and turned the key. The four-cylinder engine hummed softly, its lights cutting through the approaching twilight.

Dr. Beaumont opened the passenger side door and dropped into the shotgun seat of his own car. "Go to the post office. We're on a deadline."

5

Duluth, Minnesota
March 10, 2026

Caleb leaned back against his couch, his legs kicked up on the coffee table before him. "Look at that," he murmured, his voice a low rumble as he glanced from the news reporter on the television to Mars. "Biological weapons seized? In Pakistan? A high-value target killed in the mountains?"

"Unnamed source," Mars said, snuggling closer to him on the outdated piece of furniture. "Probably fake news."

A chime sounded and the screen suddenly switched. A big red BREAKING NEWS appeared with yellow highlights. The subtitle widened his eyes. "Holy shit," Caleb said, jerking forward, pointing at the small flatscreen TV. "That's Lee Wallis!"

Mars's eyes snapped wide open, locked on the TV. The familiar face and the news heading: BOX ON DOORSTEP gave her a shock of memory and pain. Leaning on the edge of the seat, her hand covered her mouth.

Grabbing the remote, Caleb turned up the volume. Felt his heartbeat thumping in his ears.

The female anchor held the microphone close to her lips. "...in Cypress California, a man by the name of Lee Wallis found a box on his doorstep." She paused dramatically. "The box contained the amputated arm of a man he identified as Blake Connor, a thirty-eight-year-old construction worker he went to high school with. He said he recognized the pitbull tattoo on the upper arm and notified police right away. The last time he saw Blake Connor was at the high school reunion the previous weekend...."

Caleb dropped a hand on Mars' thigh. "This is like a nightmare." He used her knee to help lift himself up. "I got to call Lee." Running upstairs to his bedroom, he found Lee's business card on his dresser. When he came back to the living room, he was holding it in his fingertips. After dialing Lee's number on his cellphone, he pressed it to his ear. It rang four times.

"Hello," said the man on the other end of the phone.

"Lee," Caleb said with a raspy voice. "I saw your name on the news." He cleared his throat. "I'm sorry, man. I know exactly what you're going through. I've been sick ever since I opened the box I found." He was pacing back and forth between his living room and dining room.

Mars was watching him intently. She was listening to his conversation, trying to put some sense to it all.

"Yeah, the cops just told me what you found on your doorstep," Lee said. "I know that was your boy. I'm sorry, Caleb. This shit is fucked up. I haven't talked to Blake for years. And I get his arm on my doorstep? What the fuck is going on here?"

"At first, I thought Bane took him out. Gave me the head to send a message. But why would he send *you* his arm?"

"It just doesn't make sense."

"The cops are clueless." Caleb sighed heavily. "They actually thought I might have something to do with it." Caleb let out a short breathy laugh. "We should put our brains together and figure this shit out."

"I've already started writing down a list of people who know that me and Blake used to be tight. I've been in California for almost fifteen years. Must be someone from the old school."

"It's gotta be. Probably someone who doesn't know you and Blake got in a big fight after our senior year."

Lee coughed. "Yeah, the prick was fucking my girl behind my back for like a year. Why the hell would anyone send *me* his arm?"

"That's the million-dollar question. Can't be Bane and his crew. They wouldn't send you a box."

"It was delivered in person," Lee said. "No return address or stamp. The gangsters at the pool hall wouldn't drive across the country. No way. Got to be someone else."

"What about the Asians we had beef with in high school?"

"I heard Kong Zang got killed in prison."

"And I think his cousins moved away," Caleb said, the distant thought of past threats gave him pause. "But they did hate us. All of us."

Lee shared his heavy sigh through the receiver. "Hmmm. I just hope we ain't next."

6

Cyprus, California
March 12, 2026

Dr. Beaumont turned off the light and climbed into his motel bed. Preparing to fall asleep, he stretched his arms and let out a deep breath. His heart was thumping too fast to sleep. Tossing and turning, his thoughts rewind back to a dank cinder block basement—the smell of alcohol and sweat invaded him. He smiled at the memory, chuckled into the silence of the dark room and let himself relive the pinnacle moment of his life.

"The fuck?" Beaumont remembered Blake saying when he first woke up from the medication he injected in his neck. A puzzled look was on his squinting face. He tried to buck his restraints, but the wide canvas ratchet straps were tight against his ankles, torso, and neck. "Who the fuck are you?" Blake's face bloomed red. His eyes bouncing from Beaumont to Richard Gaytan with short audible breaths.

"Oh, Blake," Dr. Beaumont said, glancing over his shoulder where Gaytan was hovering behind him with a large red book in his hands. "Calm down." He stared down at Blake's dark eyes and continued. "I'll tell you who I am. I'm your worst nightmare."

"Tell me what you want." Blake's breaths slowed down but his chest was still rising and falling. "I'll make it right."

"Ya know, I'm not surprised you don't remember me, but I *am* disappointed. I was... so much looking forward to the expression on your face the moment you saw me and realized…." He remembered letting out a breath and taking a step closer to the man on the bench. "But, I guess I'll get that enjoyment now." He turned and gestured to his subordinate.

Gaytan handed him the book. "Here ya go, Doc." He stepped back to the wall and leaned against a large storage freezer.

"I bet you recognize this book, Blake," Dr. Beaumont said, smacking the book on Blake's chest. "My mom took out a credit card to buy it back then. My dad was too stingy to get me one. Oh, and she got beat for it. So did I." He sighed again, opening the book. "Let me flip to the... oh, there it is. Look on the bottom left." He held the open book just above Blake's scruffy face.

"L-Lerch Black," Blake said, snapping his head from the picture of the scrawny zit-faced kid to the little man bending before him. "Fuck." He muttered softly with widening eyes. "Um, uh, you know that wasn't me, right? I didn't do nothing to you. I was just there."

"Don't insult my memory."

"Okay. I'm sorry. Please don't hurt me."

Beaumont twitched his finger and clicked his tongue a few times. "Oh, I forgot to tell you the name of the game." He pursed his lips. "Consequences and repercussions. You lie, you get the consequences. Understand?"

"What?" Blake crunched up his face, his eyes averting to Gaytan who had a hammer dangling at his side and a face made of stone and beard.

"This is a game," Beaumont said. "You lied to my face. You said you didn't do nothing to me. Now, my beast is about to break a bone in your body. Don't lie again."

"W-what do you want from me? What are you trying to prove?"

"Blake, I usually don't tolerate any questions, but in your case." Beaumont dropped the book on the floor like it was nothing. "I want this conversation." He leaned closer to Blake, his voice lowering, smoothing out in giddy anticipation. "I need it. I've been craving it for more than twenty years."

Blake was shrinking away from Lerch's hot breath. "What, are you gonna kill me?" His words sped up. "Because I kicked your ass a few times when we were little kids?"

Beaumont stood tall and let out a sigh. "Blake, I want to see you cry. I want you to beg for your life."

"You know what? Fuck you, Lerch. You better kill me. Cuz—"

"Ah," Beaumont zipped a thumb across his lips. "I'll stop you right there." He slammed his hand around Blake's neck. Gripping as tight as he could, he could feel Blake's muscles fighting the pressure, he could see his face changing colors, contorting. "The last time someone said that to me, I hit him across the face with my favorite sword."

A panicked gagging noise emanated from Blake's throat.

Beaumont let go and stood tall, shaking his head. "Wrong words. Just wrong words." His right hand balled into a fist. "You used the same words my dad did."

Blake gagged, coughed, and gasped for air.

"You're going to get the worst possible death imaginable." He nodded his head. With his lips pressed together, he snapped his fingers and Gaytan stepped forward with the hammer.

"Just say the word." Gaytan slowly approached with the weapon swaying at his side.

Pursing his lips, Beaumont looked at the hammer and then Blake before slowly shaking his head. "No, I want worse. I want him to suffer." Lerch met Blake's eyes. "I want him to think about his life before he dies. In the freezer."

"Yes, sir." Gaytan dropped the hammer on the concrete floor.

"What the fuck is wrong with you?" Blake's voice was low and fast. "Why don't you just put a bullet in my head and get it over with?"

"That would be a waste of a good bullet. Too messy. Too loud."

"Lerch." Blake's tone softened, his eyes darting, pleading helplessly. His hands shaking in their holds. "Look, I-I'm sorry for what we did to you. It was wrong, but we were—"

"Stop!" Beaumont cut him off with a soft tone and smile. "I accept your apology, Blake. Thank you. Seriously. It does mean a lot, but it's too late. The damage has been done. There has to be consequences. My honor depends on it."

Beaumont lifted the lid of the freezer. A big Rambo knife was resting at the bottom. Reaching inside and pulling it out, he gripped it in his right hand. With a sharp turn, he approached Blake. "You're gonna get in that freezer as soon as I release your restraints." He gently poked Blake in the side of the neck with the tip of the knife, just hard enough to break skin.

Blake cried out, flinching when it had nicked him.

When Beaumont pulled back with a snap, a drop of blood rolled down Blake's skin. "You try anything, I'm gonna stick this knife in your gut."

"Come on, man," Blake said. "You don't want to do this. It's not right."

Dr. Beaumont laughed shortly. "There's no talking your way out of this, Blake." He nodded his head. "This is happening. Right now."

"Remember, don't try nothing." Gaytan unbuckled the legs first.

Beaumont lowered the knife to his side. "You freeze either way. Bleeding or not. You choose."

Gaytan unbuckled the neck strap. "One more. Don't be stupid."

"I won't resist," Blake said, his head lifting slightly.

"Last one. Here we go." Gaytan unbuckled the final strap and it clunked on the ancient concrete floor.

Blake swung his feet off the side of the bench and sat upright.

Beaumont studied Blake's dark glaring eyes and gripped his fingers tighter on the leather handle of the knife. "Step down," he said sharply. "Slowly... put your hands on your head." With his heart thudding in his chest, he could feel a surge of hot adrenaline building.

Blake dropped to his feet. "What about money?" He shrugged. "I own my house. I could sell it, give you all the cash."

"Walk to the freezer," Beaumont said, eyes wide. Knife at hip level. "Slow."

Blake nodded. "Okay." His lower lip was quivering. "What the fuck is that?" He pointed to the stairs but only Gaytan looked. Blake charged at Lerch full bore. Roaring like a beast.

Dr. Beaumont remembered extending his arm and plunging the knife into Blake's mid-section. He heard Blake cry out. Felt his flailing body go limp as he twisted the blade and wrapped his free arm around his back like a bro hug.

When Beaumont pulled out the knife, Blake crumpled to the floor. Face down, he squealed softly, cowering in the shadow of a person he only knew as Lerch Black.

"Stay the fuck down!" Dr. Beaumont hollered. "Get ready to freeze, bitch." He bent over, stuck him in the back and pulled out fast. Standing tall with his jaw set, he watched blood pooling around Blake. Heard his agonized groans.

Hunched in the fetal position, Blake rolled on the cold basement floor, his fingers reaching to put pressure on his back wound. His suit was drenched with blood and leaking on the slab of concrete. Gasping for more life, his mouth was opening and closing, but no words were coming out.

"Blake!" Beaumont barked. "I'm going to do the same exact thing to Caleb."

"No!" he cried almost soundlessly. "Leave him alone."

"I can't. But I promise not to hurt him until he sees your head in a box."

Blake's voice was ragged. "He never did anything to you."

"It's not all about Caleb, it's about you," Beaumont said. "You were the ring leader of your pitiful little gang. And you'll die, knowing firsthand what your best friend will go through. All because of your actions. Your orders." Beaumont snapped his fingers twice. "Rick, grab his arms. I'll take his legs."

"No!" Blake wailed with clattering teeth. "P-please. Don't."

Both men grabbed the wounded Blake Connor and dragged him to the freezer that was up against a brick wall. Dr. Beaumont propped up the lid, and then re-gripped Blake's legs. Heaving his thrashing body up, they dropped him in the freezer. Gaytan punched his head until he was in.

Blake's blood-drenched fingers were reaching for the top. His sharp howls of anguish were reverberating throughout the basement and probably outside. But no one heard his screams because the closest house was half a mile down the road.

"Help!"

"Scream all you want," Beaumont said, his voice riding roughshod over Blake's muffled cries for help. "No one's coming to save you."

"You're not going to get away with this." Blake wept and trembled.

"Oh, yes I will," Dr. Beaumont said. "I have a few tricks up my sleeve." He pulled out a zip lock bag full of short and curly hairs. "Distractions." he paused, shifting toward Gaytan. "I'm gonna toss the knife in there. Give you the option to slit your own throat."

"Lerch! Please! Don't!"

When he quickly slid the knife into the freezer, Blake's hands rose, trying desperately to grab at Lerch, trying to find purchase in anything. Even a scratch. But it only got his fingers cut.

Beaumont leaned closer, peering down on Blake's scrunched-up face and bloody hand that was clinging to the rim of the freezer. "See you in forty-eight hours!" He locked eyes with Blake for a long moment before slamming the lid shut.

Gaytan snapped a padlock on the hinge. "Chill out," he said in monotone.

"Help!" Blake screamed but only a muffled sound was audible. "Get me out of here!" He was pounding on the wall and kicking the top. The thuds were loud but did no damage to the freezer.

"Plug that thing in."

7

Duluth, Minnesota
March 14, 2026

Fred Reid's eyes jumped from the computer screen on his desk to the sound of three knocks on his office door. "It's open."

The door swung inward and a thin, well-dressed black man in his forties stepped inside. "Good afternoon," he said, closing the door behind him. He was holding two large manila envelopes in his hands. "I got the autopsy and forensic reports for you, sir." He gently set the envelopes on the shiny oak desk between them.

"Thanks, Ford," Reid said as he adjusted his glasses. "The moment of truth." He emptied the contents onto his paperwork-cluttered desk. Lifting the first page to his face, he read the report out loud. "Blake Connor died as a result of a homicide. Without the rest of the body, the cause of death is unknown. Alcohol and pain killers were in his system. CT Scan revealed he had brain cancer. The white eyes can be a result of being frozen alive, but we cannot be certain." The detective paused to swallow hard with low eyebrows.

"No other cuts, marks, or damage was found on Mr. Connor's head. But there was dried blood on his face and hair." Reid set that paper down and picked the page with the DNA results. "The blood came back as his. The victim has black hair, but we found a single sandy blond hair on the back of his head. An auburn dark red hair was also found. No match in the database. Multiple black pubic hairs were found in the mouth of the victim. One was stuck in his front teeth. DNA was also found on the victim's chin." The detective shifted to see the reaction of his partner.

"DNA on his chin?" Detective Jerome Ford asked with a scrunched-up face. "Does it say who?"

Reid lowered his head to the paper and squinted his eyes. "When we ran the DNA in the database, Caleb Hunt came up as a match. 99.92 percent. He was in the system for a felony in 2007. First Degree Arson." Clapping his hands together, the detective sprang out of his seat. "We got our man!"

"I'll send a squad to Hunt's house right now," Ford said, pulling out his phone. "Let's go get this sick fucker."

"I knew it was him." Detective Reid shook his head. "I should have taken him downtown right away. Once a piece of shit, always a piece of shit."

*****

Mars Sundean did her twentieth push-up, then popped up to her feet, throwing quick jabs in the air. Shadow punches at an invisible enemy who had been haunting her dreams.

Five loud knocks at the door spun her around in her yoga pants and sweaty tank top. Breathing heavily from her workout regiment, she crept up to the window and peeked out the blinds. "Holy shit," she said, raising her eyebrows at the squadron of police officers lining up at the front door. Behind them were at least a dozen squad cars and trucks clogging up the street in front of the house.

Bringing her hand to her heart, she felt a rush of nerves and adrenaline. "Caleb." Her lip started quivering and her eyes became wet. "Please be okay. Please be okay."

"Police! Open up!" A heavy voice traveled through the wall.

She trotted to the door, swinging it open with her wet green eyes shifting from cop to cop, landing on the husky man in a suit and wool trench coat.

"We have a search warrant," Detective Reid said, document in hand. "Where's Caleb Hunt?"

Mars shook her head in confusion. "He's at work," she said, blocking the doorway. "Is he okay?"

"Who are you?" Reid took a step closer.

"Mars Sundean." Her eyes narrowed suspiciously. "I'm his girlfriend. Is he okay?"

"Come with me," Reid said, grabbing her by the arm.

"What did I do?" Mars' voice was high-pitched. "Let go!"

Reid yanked her out of the way and a flow of officers entered the house. Leading her to his black Dodge Challenger, he spoke sternly. "You're not under arrest, but I am detaining you for questioning."

"Why?" Her face pinched in frustration. "What do you want?"

"Get in the car." He opened the back door.

Mars regarded him with a look of contempt. "This is ridiculous."

"Get in. Or I'll charge you with obstruction."

She set her jaw and slid inside. He slammed the door shut.

When Reid got in the warm car, a mug shot of Caleb was displayed on the computer screen on his dash. "Caleb is wanted for the murder of Blake Connor."

"What?" Mars' eyes narrowed. "That's impossible." Her face was flushed with red-hot anger, and her tone was sharp.

"Calm down," Reid barked, meeting her eyes in the rear-view mirror. "Sorry to break it to ya, sweetheart, but your boyfriend is a sadistic killer. We got a ton of evidence." He paused, craning his neck to read her eyes. "The question is: what was your role?"

"My role?" She laughed shortly. "That's crazy. Do you know who my uncle is?"

"Let me guess, the honorable Keith Sundean?" He chuckled.

Mars nodded, and then swiped a lock of hair out of her face. "That's right. And he's my attorney. If I were you, I'd let me go right now."

"I'm not you," he said, sitting back in his seat. "And until you answer some questions, you're a person of interest. That means... I can detain you for at least two hours."

"I plead the fifth. I'm not saying another word."

"Hmm. Maybe you are in on it." He nodded his head. "We did find a red hair, by the way. You hang tight. I'm going to help with the search. I'll question *you* later." He got out and slammed the door shut.

*****

High on a scaffolding platform with a nail gun in his hand, Caleb fastened the last piece of cedar shake siding with two squeezes of the trigger. A sigh of satisfaction escaped his lips. *Finally done,* he thought. *Can't wait to see Mars.*

At the loud bark of his name, Caleb's shoulders jerked. Twisting his neck, he looked down to the snowy backyard and saw Detective Reid and at least a dozen policemen with guns drawn. His heart immediately rose to his throat. Mouth half-open for air.

"We need you to get down from there!" Detective Reid yelled, and a cloud of condensation followed his words. "Now!"

"What do you want?" Caleb raised his voice.

"Toss down the weapon!" Detective Reid shouted. "Do it now!"

Caleb glanced at the nail gun in his hand. "Fuck." He dropped it off the side of the scaffolding. It splashed in the icy snow bank against the back of the house.

"Now climb down. Slow!"

"Okay!" Caleb raised his hands briefly and then glanced down at the first rung of the ladder part of the scaffolding. Hesitating to exhale a heavy breath, he bent his knees and slowly lowered his legs until he found the rung with the toe of his boot. He stalled for a long moment, his arms shaking as he gripped the top rung. As he descended, his mind cranked and his heart pounded.

I bet the cops are trying to pin it on me, Caleb thought, lowering himself one rung at a time until his boots were on the snow. He turned around to face the wall of cops.

"Hands up!" Detective Reid yelled.

Caleb obeyed. "What'd I do?"

"On your fucking knees, asshole!" Detective Ford ordered. He was in plain clothes, but the armed policemen behind him were all wearing black uniforms. Bullet proof vests. Some had camouflage pants.

The cops inched closer. Spreading outward in a half-circle, all guns were on Caleb Hunt.

Caleb's eyebrows lowered in fear. "I am not resisting!" He put his hands on top of his head. "I just want to know what this is about."

Looking past the police officers, Caleb saw his boss on the sidewalk with the homeowners. Their arms were crossed. Wrinkles in their foreheads.

"On the ground!" Detective Reid yelled.

The voice pierced Caleb's chest, and his veins filled with hot adrenaline. "What'd I do?" He barked with raw anger burning inside him. His hands spreading apart with resentment for authority.

Reid nodded to Detective Ford who pulled out a yellow taser gun.

Caleb felt the shock of electricity before he heard the crackle. Dropping to the crunchy snow, his body quaked until Ford let go of the trigger.

"Stay down!" Ford shouted.

"What's wrong with you guys?" Caleb's boss, Denzel yelled from the sidewalk. "He wasn't resisting!"

Three cops dropped their knees on Caleb's legs and back. One had his knee and weight on his neck. A female cop twisted his arms and locked handcuffs on his wrists. The cuffs were so tight that he winced as they lifted him to his feet. Humiliated, he buried his chin in his chest, growling with snow clumps falling from his face.

Head down, Caleb got roughly escorted by two bulky cops. One gripping each arm, yanking him forward faster than his legs wanted to go.

Caleb didn't see Denzel, but his deep powerful voice gave him calm in the storm.

"You're gonna be okay, Caleb!" Denzel shouted. "I'll get your truck to your house."

Detective Ford stepped in front of Denzel. "Which truck is his?" he asked. "We have a search warrant. It's getting seized."

"Let's see the warrant," Denzel said, tilting one hand.

"You in charge here?" Detective Reid asked.

"Yes, I am." Denzel nodded. "Caleb works for me. What'd he do?"

*****

Detective Reid dropped into his unmarked Dodge Challenger and shut the door. The V8 engine was grumbling as it idled. The sound of heavy breathing from the back seat reminded him of victory. Looking in the rear-view mirror, he smirked. "It's days like this that make it all worthwhile." He paused briefly to let out an exasperated sigh. "I'm just glad I got you off the street." Glaring at Caleb's reflection in the mirror made his blood boil. He could feel it underneath his skin. A murderer was in the back seat.

"Sir," Caleb said firmly. "You got to tell me what I did."

"You know what you did." Reid threw the shifter in drive and stomped on the gas pedal. The high torque engine growled as it raced down the wet street. He flicked on the cherries but not the siren.

"I don't know shit." Caleb's voice was low and raspy. A hint of a tremble because he was scared—of being wrongly accused and unjustly convicted. "Tell me."

"You murdered your best friend." Reid hit the door panel with the outside of his fist. "You killed Blake Connor. And then you chopped him up in pieces. And then you dropped them off for your friends to find. But you kept one for yourself to throw us off." Reid cursed under his breath. "Unfortunately for you... we found DNA. Hairs, too." Reid slowed down, took a hard right, and then pounded on the gas. The car roared as it opened up on the two-lane road.

"Bullshit!" Caleb sprayed desperation as if a gun was in his face. "This is a set-up. I didn't do shit and you know it!"

Reid let off the gas and coasted at sixty miles per hour. "Caleb, we got your DNA on file. Arson, 2007. I remember you now. You were the little punk who tried to burn a house full of little Asian kids."

"You got *my* DNA on Blake?" Caleb said, his eyebrows arching. "That's crazy."

"Keep telling yourself that, Mr. Hunt. I bet the jury will convict you in five minutes."

"Get fucked. Call my lawyer."

8

Duluth, Minnesota
July 4, 1998

In his tiny backyard filled with dirt, a ten-year-old Lerch Black was playing by himself in his make-shift sandbox. After hours in direct sunshine, his sweaty black shirt stuck to his back as he stood up. A small garden scoop was in his hands. Dropping the tool in the sand, he peered down on his death trap. One starting place but two potential ends — dependent upon which path one chooses to take — the one to salvation, at the end of the sandbox, or the one to death, at the bottom of the pit.

Lerch giggled. "I need supplies."

Jumping to his feet, the skinny kid with bruises on his arms turned and carelessly ran over countless armyworms all the way to his front porch. Taking his shoes off, he tip-toed inside the house. Bathroom. Kitchen. Basement. In two minutes flat, Lerch came running out with a bulging plastic bag. His long black mullet flowing behind him in the warm summer breeze.

"Time to fill the pit," Lerch said, trotting up to the sandbox. Just to the right, he emptied the bag in the dirt and released the empty bag to float in the humid air. Looking down, he saw a round jug of laundry detergent, a can of lighter fluid, and a bottle of shampoo. One by one, he drained each bottle into the pit at the base of the second path. The pit of despair.

"Time for the trials to begin." Lerch grinned.

Earlier that day, Lerch had collected a bucket of armyworms from his front porch, and now he was dumping them at the beginning of the maze of doom. "Choose wisely."

At the start of the maze, the dark green little insects began their trek. Lerch stood impatiently with his hands on his hips. "Hurry up," he said. "Or I'll choose for you."

After twenty minutes, Lerch's mouth widened. "Uh oh," he said to the first worm that chose path number one. "Tisk, tisk. Almost time to suffer."

As the majority of worms followed the leader toward the pit of goo, Lerch clapped his hands giddily. "Almost there, guys! Don't give up."

In no time at all, the first armyworm plopped into the thick liquid mix of pink and blue swirls. Lerch jumped up and down. "Die!" he pointed at the pit with three little insects trying to swim or crawl to safety. Laughing hysterically, he dropped to his knees and assisted several more worms into the toxic pit. "Nothing can save you now. You stupid little bugs."

Lerch marveled at his creation. Glancing at the worms who were traveling down path number two, he reached over and grabbed a few and tossed them in the pit.

"There is no escape." He pointed at the worm closest to freedom. "Except for you." He allowed the last armyworm to keep inching toward safety. "I'll let you live to tell your friends. Don't ever come on my porch."

Lerch pulled out a box of matches and rose. "You guys aren't fun anymore." He struck a match on the side of the box. "Game over." He dropped it in the pit of flammable toxins, and it burst into a large fireball. Feeling the heat, he stepped back, beaming at the tall flames and the sound of living beings crackling in the fire.

"Lerch!" his dad screamed from the balcony of their house. "What that fuck are you doing, boy? Put that shit out and get your ass in the house! I got the belt waiting for you."

9

From inside a small brick visitation room in the county jail, Mars pressed the big black phone closer to her ear. "I just don't get it," she said, staring at Caleb and his low eyebrows through the thick glass window. "Why would the cops blame you for Blake's murder?"

"Mars, they're not blaming me," Caleb said with new lines of frustration on his forehead. "They *charged* me with first-degree murder, mayhem, dismemberment, and a long list of other charges." He let out an audible sigh. "I'm fucked." He plopped his free hand on his face.

"That's impossible," Mars said, looking warm in a light gray fleece zip-up. "You were with *me* that entire weekend. You didn't leave my sight. Best weekend of my life."

Caleb pursed his lips. "Ditto." His eyebrows lifted. "But they don't care. They said they found forensic evidence on the body. And my fingerprints put me at the scene of the crime. They said I was the last person to touch Blake's doorknob."

"You went to his house to check on him." Her face pinched tightly. "A lawyer can make that point. But how the hell is your DNA involved? Does that mean semen?"

Caleb sunk his head, let it bob, and then leveled it off to look into her squinting eyes. "Mars, someone is obviously trying to frame me." His voice choked up, and the tears started flowing down his cheeks. "They got my DNA. They got it somehow." Giving a sideways glance, he started to feel hot. Taking a deep breath, he returned his eyes to hers at the sound of her elevated pitch.

"What do you mean, DNA? Hair?" She gave a half shrug. "He was your best friend. Of course, he'd have your hair on him."

"No, you don't understand." He slowed his words down. "They're trying to say... me and Blake were gay lovers. And that we must have got in a fight. They think I killed him, Mars. They say there's more evidence, but I ended the interrogation. I need a lawyer to help me with this."

"Hold on." She lifted the palm of her hand. "They found your DNA on his head?"

"Yeah, and they said they found pubic hairs in his teeth." Caleb's head shook. "It's absurd." His closed fist dropped down on the desk, but not too hard or loud to draw any attention from anyone other than Mars. He glanced up to the security cameras.

Mars' mouth opened but no words came out for a long moment. At first, she couldn't think of what exactly to say, but then a tremor in her body took hold and she began to panic. "Look at me." She leaned closer toward the glass barrier. "Don't lie to me, Caleb. Please tell me you didn't sneak out in the middle of the night. Tell me you didn't do it."

He was looking directly into her big green eyes. "God, no." He flung his free hand in abject frustration. "Come on, Mars. You're my alibi. You're all I got. Please believe me." He opened his left hand. "I'm not gay, and I didn't kill my best friend. I'm losing my mind in here. I lost Blake. I lost my freedom. And now I lost you."

"You didn't lose me. And I'm not going to let you lose your freedom. You need a good lawyer."

"I don't have any money."

"You own your house, right?"

"Yeah. Are you still staying there?"

She shook her head. "The cops kicked me out. They got yellow tape all around it. I can't even get my things. Been staying at a hotel."

"I'm sorry." He clenched his fist and his jaw. "What are you gonna do?"

"Don't worry about me. I'm a survivor. You need to worry about yourself."

"Okay, so what? Should I sell my house?"

"No, you'll have to refinance," Mars said. "You'll need a lot of cash for legal fees. My uncle is a crafty lawyer. He'll give you a good price." She flashed a smile. "Since you're my boyfriend."

Caleb nodded, his mouth widening for the first time. "You mean, you're going to stand by my side?"

"Of course, dummy," Her nod was continuous. "But if I find out you lied to me... I'm gone. I'll run so fast, you won't even see it coming."

"Give me a lie detector test. Anything. I mean, if I killed Blake and dismembered his body, where's the saw? Where's the mess? Where are the witnesses? How 'bout the GPS on my truck insurance? There's got to be a street light with a camera or something. Don't you think I'd be on camera coming and going?"

"I trust you, Caleb. How 'bout this: I'll talk to my uncle. He's got some banking friends. He might be able to help with your refinance."

"Thank you so much. I owe you my life."

"You'll owe me more than that."

After watching the jailhouse visit between Caleb and Mars, Detective Reid turned off the computer screen, frowning at his partner. "He's guilty as sin."

"I know he's guilty," Detective Ford said. "But his facial expressions seem real. Those were real tears. Most killers only get the crocodile tears."

"His entire world is crashing down," Reid said. "He didn't think he'd get caught. Now, his pretty little piece of ass is just out of reach. I'd be crying, too."

"I'm just saying, he's gonna fight the charges. And if he retains Keith Sundean, the prosecutor will have his hands full."

Reid laughed shortly. "Caleb Hunt is dead to rights. He's drawing dead into a straight flush. DNA never lies."

"You're right. But let's search his house again. I think we rushed the search because of the DNA match. There's got to be more evidence."

Detective Reid popped out of his seat. "You go search the residence. I'll check his phone records and social media history."

*****

Caleb was sitting in a small white room with cinder block walls and a metal desk. His hands and feet were shackled together. At the sound of creaking, his head snapped to the opening door. A tall and large man in a dark blue suit was holding a briefcase. His thick eyebrows were gray but his head was bald. Glasses black.

"Mr. Hunt, I hear you're in some trouble," his new lawyer said, reaching out his hand. "My name is Keith Sundean. I'll be representing you in court."

Caleb rose to shake his hand. "Thank you, sir." His chains were jangling. "I appreciate your time."

"Don't thank me yet," Keith said, opening his briefcase on the desk. "We got an uphill battle ahead of us." He sat down and scooted the chair closer.

"You came fast," Caleb said, returning to his seat. "I'm just saying...I appreciate that. This place is crazy. One dude called me a gay psycho-killer at lunch yesterday. I've been getting nasty looks and comments ever since. I'm just sitting here waiting to get it like Jeffrey Dahmer."

Sundean winced at the thought. "Mars spoke highly of you, Mr. Hunt," he said, fixing his blue eyes on Caleb's solemn mug. "And I trust her judgment. She represents truth. Served twenty years in the Air Force. In my view, a good judge of character." He opened a folder, and set a pen on the first page of the Caleb Hunt file. His criminal profile. One felony for aggravated arson twenty years ago. Time served. Clean record ever since.

Caleb let out a heavy breath. "I'm lucky to have such a strong alibi."

"I took an hour and looked over your file." Keith shook his head. "If you're telling the truth, I can understand your frustration. It looks like a setup. I don't believe a killer who sent a box to himself would be so sloppy to leave DNA and hairs. But you should know, that a third extremity was found this afternoon. It came in the mail, so this doesn't exonerate you."

"What? Who found it?"

"Bob Sturgis."

"Holy crap. Bob? Really?"

"Caleb, I'm sorry, to be the bearer of bad news here, but as of right now, I believe they have enough evidence to convict. DNA and motive. Violent criminal record." He sighed. "The good news is—"

"Enough to convict?" Caleb interrupted with a shrug restrained by shackles. "What are you talking about? This is clearly a setup. You said it yourself."

"Calm down, Caleb," Keith said. "I believe you; Mars believes you, but the jury has to look at the facts laid before them by the prosecution."

"What facts?" Caleb raised his voice a notch. "What motive?"

"Life insurance," Keith said. "Motive, fingerprints, hair, and DNA is enough to convict."

Caleb dropped his jaw. Swallowing a proverbial blade of reality felt sharp going down his windpipe. He stared off into space, searching for a distant memory of any life insurance talk with Blake. After a few deep breaths, he met Sundean's eyes. "I don't know nothing about any life insurance."

"That doesn't matter," Keith said. "It's a matter of fact. One more piece to the puzzle. Do you see what I'm saying?"

Caleb was massaging his throbbing temples and breathing heavily. Audibly.

"It gets worse. I want you to know your violent criminal history matters as well. The jury will be confused with a solid alibi, but they *will* convict you with the evidence I listed. *Unless* we can build a mountain of truth and fact to dispute the planted DNA. That's your only play, Mr. Hunt. I believe you were framed. But who would want to frame you? That's the question."

Caleb's head bobbed as he let out a long-exasperated breath. "That's what I was trying to tell the cops." His neck stiffened. "I've been framed. Pubes in the teeth. Come on."

"That was your first mistake," Keith said. "Never talk to authorities without the presence of legal representation. You may have hurt yourself, but if you are indeed telling the truth, I can fix that." His large head was nodding confidently.

"I'm definitely telling the truth. Check my phone records. My car insurance tracker. Check anything. Give me a lie detector test. Please, sir. Help me."

"Caleb. Calm down. We have time. Without bail, you might be stuck in here for a year or two before the trial begins. Now tell me: when was the last time you saw Mr. Connor?" He pulled a notepad out of his briefcase. Picked up the pen.

"Last Saturday night." Caleb swallowed the lump in his throat. "I-I mean the Saturday before. The second or third of March. Me and Mars dropped him off at his house around 1:30 in the morning. After the high school reunion."

"Did anybody see you leave with him?"

"No, but everyone at the reunion saw us together all night. They know he's my best friend."

"Did you see him talking to anyone suspicious?"

"No. But he was drinking heavily. He was talking to everyone."

Keith let out a breath. "Does he have any enemies?"

"I'll tell you the same thing I told Detective Reid. He's lived a wild life. I love him like a brother, but he's wronged a lot of people. Slept with many married women. Got in bar fights with dozens of people. But he owed a shady guy money. I know the guy. He's a common street thug. A crooked meth dealer. The guy is capable of that, but it's not his style. He's known for breaking legs, not dismemberment."

"Who is this person?"

Caleb sighed. Dropping his gaze, his teeth clenched together.

"Caleb?"

"I don't want a murder charge, but I don't want to be murdered either."

Keith nodded in sudden understanding. "Look, I'm here to help you. If you have a one percent inclination that this guy killed your friend and framed you, I need to know so I can get an investigator on him right away."

"Well, the guy doesn't exactly like me too much. Maybe he was sending me a message?"

"Who?"

"His name is Derek Bane. He hangs out at the pool hall all the time. He's got a lot of tattoos, and always wears a flat-brim hat. He drives a fancy blue BMW."

Sundean wrote fast then lifted his head to face Caleb. "Good, that's a start. Any other threats against him?"

"Well. Actually, there is something else. But it doesn't make sense."

"What's that?"

"In eleventh grade, I got stabbed in the bathroom. Then they shot me in the back. An inch away from my spine."

"Oh my God." Mouth gaped, Sundean continued. "I'm glad you survived. Who was it?"

"An Asian kid named Kong Zang shot me," Caleb said. "He went to prison and his two cousins got off because they testified against Kong. Back then, me, Blake, and Bane grew tight. I wanted revenge, so they helped me set a fire at Kong's cousin's house. They were the ones who stabbed me." He shrugged. "Maybe they want revenge?"

Sundean set the notebook down. "Caleb, that's important you told me that. I need names."

"I heard Kong Zang died in prison," Caleb said with low eyebrows. "I don't know the other kid's names. Something Zang. American sounding. Like Brian or Kevin. You could find out in my file."

"I can get the details," Sundean said. "Now, how about the life insurance? As of four weeks ago, your name was added as the primary beneficiary. What's that about?"

Caleb shook his head. "I have no idea. Other than his mom, I'm the only family he's got. He never said anything about it."

Sundean was holding the notepad again. "Okay. Moving along, your car insurance tracker helps, but you could have walked to Blake's house or got a ride. See what I'm saying? I need more conclusive evidence to clear your name."

"What about my phone records? Internet activity?"

"That helps, too. But same thing there. Someone else could potentially have used it for you. We need exculpatory evidence, otherwise...."

"What about a lie detector test?"

Sundean tilted his head an inch. "I've never recommended that before. Could go bad, but if you're positive, you didn't do it. It might be a feather in your hat. Shows confidence."

"Set it up." Caleb nodded and then rocked his body back and forth. "I'll answer any possible question they can think of."

"Good. I'll come back tomorrow with more knowledge on your case. I'll look into this Zang family. And we'll look into the other body parts that keep popping up, too. Three now, including yours. I believe you, Caleb. Someone framed you good. Do you have any other enemies you want me to look into?"

"No. I'm pretty sure I've righted all my wrongs."

"Good."

"By the way, how's Mars? She was staying at my place, but—"

"That's not an option now," Keith informed him as he stood up. "She's staying at one of my rentals. She'll be safer there."

*****

Detective Ford opened Caleb Hunt's garage door with gloved hands. Scanning the room, he saw storage bins lining the left wall, a lawn mower in the center, and a cluttered workbench up against the right wall. Stepping around the mower, he approached the bench. Underneath it were several large tool cases neatly pressed together.

"Search 'em again," Ford said softly to himself. "Maybe we missed something."

Pulling out a random case, Ford opened it. A Skilsaw for cutting boards. He closed the case. The next one was an angle grinder for cutting pipes. Closed it. But the third box was red. Rectangular. The opened box revealed a reciprocating saw for cutting anything.

Leaning closer, Ford's eyes are squinting even as his heart jerks. "What the????" A tiny amount of red material was caked on the teeth of the white saw blade in a small compartment underneath the machine. "That's blood!"

Ford's eyes snapped open. "Bingo!" He closed the case. "I can't believe we didn't find this before."

Hopping to his feet, he peeled off the latex gloves and tossed them on the floor. Excited to tell his boss the news, he whipped out his phone and called Detective Reid. The phone rang twice.

"What is it, Sergeant?" the man on the other end of the line said.

"Sir, I found something over here," Ford said, pressing the phone to his ear.

"What's that?"

"I found a power saw in the garage," Ford said. "It's got blood on the blade. Well, looks like blood anyways."

"That's good news…because his computer history shows activity during the dates in question. His truck never left his house on Saturday or Sunday. His phone was active at his residence those days as well. His story is checking out. But the DNA points to him."

"Maybe his girlfriend is an accomplice. There was that red hair on the body."

Reid laughed shortly. "He probably thinks he's smart. I bet he had Mars Sundean use his phone while he killed his best friend."

"And he probably borrowed her car, too."

"Get off the phone. Bring me that saw. We need to match that blood."

10

From behind an oak alter, a black-clad Alice Connor was choking down tears as she eulogized her son in front of a packed funeral home. "…w-wasn't perfect, but he…he had a good heart." She sniffled, leveling her head full of gray hair that was rolled into a bun. "He didn't deserve this. No one deserves what happened to him. I-I feel the pain he felt when he died. I hear his screams, echoing all day and night. It never stops." She paused, grabbing on to the lectern for comfort. "I-I love him. I only wish… I told him more." She let out a quivering audible sigh and then continued. "Please…hug your loved ones. Tell them you love them. Because…one day they're here, and the next day they're gone." She sobbed, bobbing her head as she sucked in air. "And one more thing… I know my son. He loved women. He was *not* a homosexual—" She was interrupted by gasps in the audience. A soft rumble that only lasted a few seconds.

"Those lies are insulting!" Strength grew in Alice's voice. Her finger was shaking in the air. "The real killer is still out there. Mark my words: He will kill again. And there is *no* way… his best friend killed him. Caleb Hunt straightened up his life a long time ago. That boy was so gentle, so sweet, so caring. He calls me on my birthday every year. Since his mom died, he calls me mom. What kind of killer does that?" She broke down and started balling, her hand covering her wrinkled face full of tears and emotion. "If Caleb goes to prison, I lose two sons."

The priest escorted Alice off the stage, guiding her to a seat in the front row. He returned to the alter and gave his words of wisdom and prayer.

*****

Outside in the parking lot of the funeral home, four men stood in an imperfect circle as the snow fell from the gray sky. Two black men and two white. One of each race smoking.

"When I talked to him on the phone," Lee Wallis said, shaking his head, "he seemed pretty fucking innocent to me."

"I can't believe you don't trust the science," Bob Sturgis said, ashing his cigarette in the crisp air. "Caleb did it. And he sent me, Tarik, and Lee the body parts to cover up his tracks. I should get thrown in jail, so I can fuck him up. That's how fucking mad I am." He stuck his cigarette in his lips and then punched the palm of his hand. Then he did it again making a louder smack.

Lee shook his head. "So, you think them two were gay?" He laughed shortly. "Impossible." He shook his head tightly. "No way. Someone planted that shit."

"I'll second that," Denzel said in a black sweater with a shirt and tie underneath. "Caleb got set up. A hundred percent. And I'm gonna do everything I can to help get him free."

"I'm with you guys," Tarik Brownridge said, loosening his fancy tie with a cigarette in his lips. "Blake was the biggest anti-homo I've ever met." He removed the cig from his mouth and blew out a stream of smoke. "He told me he dumped a hotty once because she wanted it in the ass." Tarik was a hefty black man in a sharp suit and tie. His super short hair matched his finely trimmed goatee.

"Homophobes are usually the gay ones," Bob said, puffing on his cigarette. He wore no tie but his black Oxford shirt and gray slacks looked respectable.

"Not Blake," Tarik said, shaking his head and diamond studded ears. "Never."

"So, what are you guys saying?" Bob asked. "You think the science is wrong?"

"No, I think someone planted the evidence." Denzel spread apart his hands. "Maybe they stole condoms from the trash can? I don't know."

Bob flicked his cigarette on the ice-crusted tarmac. "I doubt it." He threw his hands in the air. "Who? And how would a killer get Caleb's pubes? What about the life insurance? I read the article online twice. Caleb was going to gain three hundred thousand."

"If it is a setup, that means the real killer's been watching all of us," Lee said. "Keep your eyes open. I don't want to go to any more funerals."

"That's a good idea," Tarik said. "I'm keeping a gun on me at all times." He tossed his cigarette into the tall outdoor ashtray. "One more thing about Caleb. Other than Denzel, I'm the only one who actually still talks to him on a regular basis. Trust me, he wouldn't hurt a fly. His new life is so peaceful. I just can't see him cutting Blake to pieces. Plus, he watches *Forensic Files* all the time. He'd know not to leave DNA like that. He ain't a stupid dude."

"Watch out for the smart ones." Bob pointed his finger, shifting from Tarik to Lee. "I think he snapped." He spun his finger in a circle by his head. "Caleb went cuckoo."

11

Rick Gaytan checked as they sidled up to the secluded house: "When's he due back from the funeral?"

Dr. Beaumont pushed the lock-pick needle into the deadbolt, not bothering to glance up. "Don't worry about it. We got plenty of time."

Gaytan nodded, turning his head to the gravel driveway and the wall of trees it cut through. Hearing the click of the lock snapping open, he returned his gaze to the door swinging inward.

"Hurry up. Install those cameras," Beaumont said, adjusting his surgical gloves. "Just the bedroom." He then carried his small duffel bag into the stone and granite kitchen. "Nice place, Lee," he said, remembering twenty-some years back when the skinny fourteen-year-old Lee Wallis participated in cruelty against him. "You went from trolling the gutter with Blake, to living large in the Sunshine State."

Gaytan thumped up the steps.

Setting the bag on the kitchen counter, Beaumont pulled out a small rectangular container. Snapping it open, he grinned at the vial of medicine nestled inside of it. "Hello, pretty," he mumbled to himself, and then turned to the fridge with the vial in his hand. "It's time we find you a new home."

Dr. Beaumont reached for the handle and yanked open the door, propping it open with his hip. It was packed with food and drink. Beaumont scanned the bottom shelf, grabbing the half-full carton of orange juice. After giving the carton a quick shake, he twisted the cap and let the door close shut.

While hovering over the orange juice container with the tube half tilted, loud footsteps broke his concentration.

"All set, Boss," Gaytan said, his right hand clutching a small black duffel bag.

"Good," Beaumont said, nodding toward the outlet on the wall. "Put a camera directly in front of the fridge." Eyes back on the OJ, he poured the unknown substance inside. After another good shake, he screwed on the cap and placed it back in the fridge.

"How do you know he's gonna drink the orange juice?"

Beaumont pointed at Gaytan. "No more questions. Last warning."

*****

When Mars got home to her new apartment after the funeral, she poured a short glass of whiskey and sat down on her leather couch in a near-dark room. Silent. No TV. No social media. Just her and her painkiller.

"Why is this happening?" Mars said softly, and then took a gulp. "I come back home and my life becomes a shitstorm." She closed her eyes briefly.

Tilting the glass to her lips, she made a face as the burning alcohol drained down her throat. After a few deep breaths, the burn in her mouth was gone, but her pain and fear were still there. Her life was turned upside-down. Why couldn't she just have that one thing—being happy?

"A killer's on the loose." She leaned back in her seat, thinking about the unknown threat locked inside her head.

"And I'm all alone. No one to talk to. No one to protect me. I'm gonna have to get a gun."

Setting the glass down, she lit up a cigarette and began to cry. Her failed attempts to sniffle couldn't stop the mellow downpour of tears. With the back of her hand, she wiped her cheeks. As the drumbeat sound of time was ticking on the clock behind the sofa, her mind's eye tried to shy away mentally from the picture of Blake's head in that box. And the memory of how strained and stressed Caleb looked when she found him sitting on the floor with the box by his feet.

Mars' wet face was crumpling with anguish. Her friend got butchered. Sent out like mail. And her man was locked up in a cage, looking at life without parole. "I just can't believe it."

After the last gulp, Mars poured another glass. Sipping it slowly, she collected her thoughts and plotted of what she would do if the killer knocked on her door. And then she drank another. Smoked another. She continued this pattern until the bottle was half gone and a steak knife was under her pillow.

*****

One day after the funeral, Lee Wallis was back home in California. Sitting down at the kitchen table, he took a sip of orange juice and then set his glass down. He popped a small strawberry in his mouth and chewed it to mush. Washed it down with another sip. Looking at the digital clock on his phone, he slammed the rest of the OJ and grabbed a fig bar that he stuffed in the breast pocket of his sky-blue guide shirt. Unbuttoned. Bare hairy chest underneath.

The doorbell rang, and Lee's head snapped to the living room. "Who the hell could this be?"

It rang again. "I'm coming." Lee crossed the room and opened the front door without even looking out the window. Frowning, his lips tugged down as he stared across the doorway at two straight-faced men, neither of whom he recognized. Both wearing equally ominous expressions.

The short one was biting back a smile while the big one glanced quickly over his shoulder toward a black Chevy Cruze.

"Can I help you?" Lee's eyes bounced from the short man to the large grizzly man with a low brow.

The shorter of the two men lifted the corner of his mouth. "How was the orange juice, Lee?"

"What?" Lee's face was scrunching up in confusion. Who are these strangers? Orange juice? *Wait. I feel dizzy....*

The taller man pulled out a pistol from inside his jacket. "The poison hasn't kicked in yet, huh?" Gaytan asked amusedly. A short laugh followed.

"Whoa!" Lee tried to shut the door.

The short man blocked it with his foot. "Let us in if you want to live to see another day."

The big man shouldered the door hard.

A spike of adrenalin lifted Lee's arm to block the charging man, but his raw force flattened him like a truck on a deer. The thud was followed by cries. Grunts. Screams.

"Help!"

12

Blake Connor followed Caleb Hunt off the yellow school bus. Side by side, they joined dozens of other boys and girls walking slowly toward the entrance of Kennedy High School. The gray brick building with black windows crowned the top of the huge hill, overlooking the skyscrapers of the city and Lake Superior.

As the herd of kids bottlenecked at the double door, Blake and Caleb stood still in oversized plaid jackets and baggy blue jeans. Ball caps set low on their heads.

"You better show up for try outs next week," Caleb said, shoving him off his step. "Junior varsity hockey, bro. One more year and we'll be varsity."

"I'm straight."

"What?" Caleb's eyes narrowed. "Come on, man. I need you, bro. You've been my linemate for like five years."

Blake shifted to meet Caleb's eyes. "Not gonna happen," he said. "I heard the new coach is a prick. Banned earrings and all jewelry." He showed him the palm of his hand. "Fuck that. Fuck him. I heard he likes watching boys in the shower."

The line started moving at a steady pace. "What do you need an earring for anyway?" Caleb shoved him hard enough to make him stumble a bit. "You some sort of funny boy or what?"

Blake regained his footing and playfully tipped Caleb's hat off his head. "Hell no, the ladies love me," he said with a sly smile. "Watch this."

"You think you a Mack Daddy, huh?" Caleb laughed shortly.

"Correction. I am the Mack Daddy." He took a few steps off to the side and gently touched a young girl on the elbow. She had dark wavy hair and an athletic body. "Hey, girl. What's your name?"

"Nicole. Why?"

"I saw you from afar," Blake winked one eye. "And I wanted to get closer. A lot closer."

"What?" she asked with a repulsed look on her face. Clutching her backpack tightly, her shoulders curled inward but she didn't turn away. "Stay away."

"I'm just sayin' ... you sexy, girl." Blake snuck his arm around her waist, pulling her tight. "You're gonna be my girl, right?"

She laughed shortly, pushing him off her. "I got a man." She swung her backpack and crushed him in the arm before darting into the crowd.

Caleb bent over laughing hard.

"Laugh now, but cry much later," Blake said. "That ho will be mine before Christmas break."

As the 8:15 bell rang, hundreds of kids trampled over the shiny black and white checker tile floor. Blake and Caleb were the only two not rushing to class. They were both planted in front of the trophy display case.

"Don't you want that trophy?" Caleb asked, pointing at the picture of the Great Frank Buccetti and his team holding up the championship hockey trophy. The plaque was dark oak with gold letters. It read: STATE CHAMPIONS.

Blake smiled. "We have no chance—"

Denzel, the muscle-bound security guard interrupted Blake's thought with a bark. "Hey, you got a pass?" His deep voice gained immediate respect.

Caleb shook his head slowly at the African American bouncer with a meaty bald head.

"Then you gots to go." Denzel's thumb was pointing over his shoulder and behind him. "You get one warning. Take them hats off, too. Have some respect. Then you get respect."

Caleb shifted to face the man. "We're out of here." He removed his hat and held it in his hand. "We were just checking out the trophy."

"Get out of my sight." Denzel snapped his fingers and pointed down the hall. "Now!" The last word came out in a loud bark that made them both flinch.

Caleb nodded sharply, and the two friends speed-walked down the hall and around the corner where their locker was. "What class do you got?"

"English. Room 101. Old bag, Ms. Sanger. She sucks."

"I got history and health class," Caleb said. "Then lunch. Meet me here at noon." He extended his knuckle as a token of love and respect.

Blake pounded it with his fist. "For shizzle."

A sharp voice turned them around. It was a tenth grader who already had a driver's license and a black Ford Mustang 5.0 with twenty-inch chrome rims. "Whud up, Blake?" Derek Bane said, walking up to shake his hand and pat his shoulder.

"Shiiiit, cracker," Blake said to his friend from the other side of the tracks. "I'm late for class."

"Fuck class." Derek pulled a fat cigar out of the breast pocket of his black leather jacket. "I got a blunt of dank and a full tank of gas."

Blake's eyes twitched.

"Dude, put that shit away," Caleb said. "Denzel is on the creep. He already warned us once."

"Fuck Denzel." Derek chuckled. "Dat dog ain't shit."

"That dude could squish all three of us at the same time." Caleb shrugged.

"This is what I'm talking about, right here," Derek said, looking at Blake. "Ain't no one ever gonna squish us." He shifted back to face Caleb. "We a three-man team, right? It's either you're down...or not. What's it gonna be, Caleb? I got your back, I just wanna make sure you got mine."

"I'm still down for whatever." Caleb lowered his brow. "But not gonna fight Denzel over being late for class."

"You're missing the point, bro." Derek clasped Caleb's shoulder. "If he ever lays a finger on you, I'd fight to the death to protect you. That's called loyalty. And I expect the same from you. Now, leave your books in the locker and come with us."

Caleb's head shifted to the hand that was touching him. "Nah, I got a test today."

"Pussy."

"Whatever, Bane." Caleb shoved Derek harder than he expected, and then he made a beeline down the hall.

Bane shook his head. "He's lucky he's your boy."

"Bro, Caleb's down. But school and hockey are his main priorities right now. He thinks he's gonna get a scholarship or some-shit."

"And what's your priority?"

"Smokin' that fat ass blunt." He chuckled.

Derek cracked a smile. "Good, let's bounce."

*****

Parked in his mustang on the skyline of the city, Bane ashed his cigar out the window. "What are we gonna do about Caleb?" The panoramic view of skyscrapers, the Aerial Lift Bridge, and the bay of the Great Lake meant nothing to the stoned youth.

"What do you mean?" Blake asked.

"I mean, he's soft." Derek passed the blunt to Blake who was sitting in the passenger seat. "A fuckin' school boy."

"I wouldn't underestimate Caleb," Blake said with squinty eyes. "He's a pure athlete. Tough as fuck. You should see him on the ice. He's a beast."

"I've wrestled him before. He's physically strong, but he's scared to get in trouble. I need you to condition him a little bit. Teach him the glory of livin' that thug life. Give him a taste of adrenaline. Break some shit and run. Beat down a dork. Something."

"How am I gonna do that? He's not like us. He's a different breed. He thinks he's gonna play college hockey for Pete's sake."

"Wrong. He just needs to grow some hair on his balls. He's bitch made. No hard discipline."

"Don't ever tell him that. He *will* fight you."

"Just toughen him up. We need to be ready to defend ourselves. Everyone's clickin' up. The blacks are bad ass, but they split in two or three factions. Don't ever cross the Natives. They play for keeps. The Asians are killers, too. Quick to pull a gun or a knife. Not to mention the hicks and the westside whiteys. They don't like us cuz we talk to the blacks. This school is like a fucking prison. We either stick together or get eaten up. You understand?"

"Yeah." Blake nodded. "Maybe we should recruit a few more guys."

"Now you're thinking, brother," Derek smiled. "We'll both get a few more guys. I'll think of an initiation. It ain't gonna be easy to be a member of the Dangerous Crew."

14

Duluth, Minnesota
March 21, 2026

Sitting in front of a desk with two computers and a lie detector machine, Caleb Hunt sat bolt upright with sensors taped to his wrists, temples, and underneath his blue prison garb where a sensor was taped to his rapidly thumping heart.

"Mr. Hunt, are you a homosexual?" The female interviewer asked from across the table in an intimidating black pantsuit. Her gray hair was tide back in a neat bun and her lips were forming a thin line.

"No, ma'am." Caleb's eyebrows were low.

"Have you ever had sexual relations with Blake Connor?"

Caleb rolled his eyes. "No," he said, his head cocking to the left.

"Are you married?"

"No." He shook his head.

The interviewer cleared her throat. "Are you in a romantic relationship?"

"Uh, yes, ma'am."

"With Mars Sundean?"

"Yes."

"Did you drop Blake Connor off at his residence on March 2, 2026?"

Wiping the sweat from his forehead he flicked his glance upward. "Uh, I believe so."

"Yes or no?"

"Uh, yes." With sweat rolling down his sides, he squirmed in his seat.

"The last time you saw Mr. Connor, was he alive?"

"Yes." He nodded slowly.

"Did you... at any time in the next three days go to his house?"

Caleb looked off to the right. *Wait, what day did I stop by there?* he thought. "Uh. Um... I stopped by there after work on—" His hands were gripping his legs under the table.

The interviewer cut him off. "Yes or no?"

"Um, yes." He shook his head in disgust, an audible sigh expelling his mouth.

"Mr. Hunt, did you kill Blake Connor?"

A sudden flash of heat took hold of his body. "No," he barked. Feeling a rise of guilt and grief, he secretly strangled his clammy hands to comfort himself from the big lie surrounding the allegations against him.

"Did you hurt Mr. Connor?"

He shook his head slowly. "No, ma'am."

"Have you ever hit Mr. Connor?"

Caleb paused briefly. "We got in a fight once in seventh..."

"Yes or no?"

He let out a heavy sigh. "Yes."

"Did you have anything to do with his murder?"

"No.....ma'am." Caleb rubbed his head briefly.

"Do you know who did kill Mr. Connor?"

"No, ma'am."

"Mr. Hunt, this is the last question," she said. "Law enforcement found a reciprocating saw in your garage with Blake Connor's blood on it. Did the saw belong to you?"

Caleb's chest rose and then he let out a heavy breath. His heart sped up and he could feel the thumping in his chest and ears. "I don't know, but if it was, it must have been stolen. I was framed!"

*****

In a small garage, Derek Bane popped the trunk of his midnight blue BMW M3 and gestured to the large cardboard box inside. "It came in the mail," he said softly. "It's addressed to me. No return address."

"When was this?" His second in command, Sam Lugo asked. He was standing about two feet away with his gaze set on the opened box. Snapping his eyes wide, he shifted to face his boss who was fidgety and looking over his shoulder.

"Yesterday," Bane said, pointing at the box. "That's Blake's fucking torso in there. And his hairy fucking leg. It's packed with dry ice, but it fucking stinks. I want it out of here."

"Did you call the cops?" Sam's eyes narrowed.

Bane snorted. "I ain't no cop caller," he said. "Out of sight, out of mind. I like to keep pigs as far away from me as possible. Our business is too important."

"True that." Sam nodded.

"I need you to bury it in the boonies... or buy a bag of concrete. Make a tote brick. Toss it in Lake Superior."

"When?"

"Right now." Bane's head rolled to meet Sam's eyes. "We can't take a chance. With my luck, that fat ass detective would shift the blame to me. I got a violent record. And Blake owes me money."

"Caleb knows Blake owed us money," Sam said. "I'm pretty sure he squealed to the cops by now."

"Yeah, he sent the first box to himself," Bane said. "Probably paid someone to send out the rest of the boxes later.

He's trying to throw the cops off his track. Throw us under the bus."

Sam nodded with his lower lip stuck out a little bit.

"Caleb knows too much," Bane said. "Who knows how much he told them. We should lay low for a while. If they raid us, they'll get nothing."

"I think you're right." Sam was nodding. "Too hot right now. Better safe than sorry."

"Prison changed Caleb back in the day," Bane said, plopping a hand on the top of the shiny car. "I noticed when he got free way back then. He acts like he's too good to hang out with us."

Sam let out a breath. "I think he's a punk."

"He's not a punk at all." Bane shook his head. "He served hard time for me. Never said a word. But he is a quitter. And he can't be trusted. He just shows up when Blake gets in over his head. He seriously paid off Blake's gambling debt at least three times in the last year."

"Maybe they were gay?" Sam shrugged. "Caleb the sugar daddy." He laughed shortly.

"I wouldn't go that far." Bane folded his arms across his chest. "Blake was a degenerate gambler. But he ain't no homo. Fuck that. It's Caleb that can't be trusted. He thinks he's better than us. Like he's some sort of puritan." He paused dramatically. "I think he'd rat us out in a heart-beat. You got to get this box out of here, bro."

Sam shrugged. "I'm on it," he said. "What after that? You want me to reach out to the boys in the clink? Maybe we could have someone kick his ass?"

"Nah, just get rid of the box. Come straight back here."

15

Caleb Hunt spread apart his arms. "But I didn't do it," he said. "I wouldn't do it. Ever."

"Look, here's our case," Keith Sundean said. "It was a setup. They planted evidence. How else do you explain the cops missing the cutting tool during their first sweep? Because it wasn't there. Either way, DNA and the three-hundred-thousand-dollar life insurance plan gives motive. It doesn't look good, Caleb. I've yet to find the exculpatory evidence you need to clear your name."

"Keith, please, help me. I passed the lie detector test. I have an alibi. My digital footprint confirms Mars' statement. What else do you need?"

"All that helps your cause, but in my experience, I've found... *every* jury leans toward DNA over a digital footprint. I need you to give me a new list of people who don't like you. We have to find the killer to clear your name." He let out a breath. "My investigators found that Zang family. They alibied out. Nothing there."

Caleb buried his head in his hands. "I'm fucked."

"I'm going to hire a second private invest—" Mr. Sundean's hand snapped to his pocket because his phone was ringing. "Excuse me." He answered it. "Yes." He listened for a long moment. "Okay. Thank you." He hung up the phone and looked at Caleb with wide eyes.

"What?" Caleb's face was contorting.

"Lee Wallis is missing." His eyebrows were high. "Detective Garrison in California said there was a struggle in the residence. Blood in the floor."

"What? Nooo...."

Keith smiled as he leaned forward, clasping his hand on Caleb's shoulder. "Don't you get it, son? It can't be you. You're here. You're innocent."

*****

In a rusty old shed, Rick Gaytan ripped the duct tape from Lee's mouth and dropped it to the dirt floor belonging to the Beaumont family property. It was located in southern Oregon. Not much, just a hunting shack with land in the middle of nowhere. Handed down from generation to generation.

Lee let out a series of sharp breaths, his dilated eyes spinning around the room. "Let me go!" He was strapped down to an old work bench, the canvas lines pulled taut around his neck, arms, and legs; so taut, they carved deep grooves in the skin. His body was wet with perspiration. He could smell foul body odor coming from himself and the grizzly man hovering above him.

"The good doctor will be right with you, Lee," Gaytan said. "Calm down. Relax."

"Doctor?" Lee's face was scrunched up and beet red. "What? What kind of doctor? Who the fuck are you?"

"It's best... you don't ask questions." Gaytan's voice was slower and deeper than usual. "Trust me."

The door creaked open just then. Lee's head swung toward the sound, his eyes following the sharp movements of the silhouetted man who had just stepped inside. He was short with a white lab coat that hung around the knees of his black pants. "Who the fuck are you?"

"Good afternoon, Mr. Wallis." Dr. Beaumont stopped just short of the bench Lee was strapped to. "We have a few tests to take. And then you're free to go."

"What are you talking about?" His chest was raising and falling with each fast breath. "I'm not taking any tests."

"Oh, I am certain of it." Dr. Beaumont flashed a brief smile.

"You got the wrong guy."

"Lee Wallis," Beaumont said. "Class of 2006. I got the right guy."

Lee was squinting at the clean-cut little man with the crooked smile. "Who the fuck are you?"

"I'll give you another hint." Dr. Beaumont paused, glaring down on Lee who was breathing rapidly. He saw a vivid memory of Lee in ninth grade, slapping the sign on his back, and then laughing while all the Dangerous Crew kicked him repetitively.

"Cut the games!" Lee's eyes bounced from Beaumont to Gaytan and then back. "Who the hell are you guys?"

"As I was saying: I'll give you a hint." Beaumont leaned closer to Lee. "In high school, you put a "Kick Me" sign on my back. And then everyone kicked the shit out of me. And then everyone started laughing at my expense."

Lee's eyes grew big. Cracking his mouth open, he intently studied the baby-faced man hovering above him. Small frame. Black glasses. Under-bite smile. *Oh no,* he thought with a sharp pain shooting down his throat and into his gut. "You're Lerch Black."

"Bingo!" He clapped his hands together. "But these days I go by Dr. Beaumont. My mom's maiden name."

"L-look, I'm sorry. We were kids." Lee's voice raised to a high-pitched octave. "We were stupid. Trying to look cool in front of the other guys."

Beaumont's smile tightened as he thought back to when his dad beat him with his belt for not standing up for himself. "I was left ashamed in ways you cannot imagine," he said, remembering the pain and blood and tears throughout his childhood. "But in ways... you created a monster."

"I'm sorry." Lee's breaths and words sped up. "N-no kid deserves to get treated like that. It's not fair. Life isn't fair, Lerch. But that doesn't give you the right to —"

"No. It doesn't. But just because I don't have the right to do something, doesn't mean I can't. It doesn't mean I won't."

"I got money. How much is it gonna cost?"

"I don't want your money, Lee. I want to see you cry. I want to see how you react to pain."

Lee jerked his body, scratching the strap deeper into his already broken skin. "You don't have to do it. Just let me go. I won't say shit."

"Actually, I do have to do it." Beaumont flashed a quick smirk. "See, it's not all about revenge. Did you know I fought in Afghanistan?"

"No. What does that have to do with this?"

"It has everything to do with this. A man spared my life, under one condition...I bring pain and suffering to the American people. I just thought I'd start with you... and your pathetic friends. It will prove to be a meaningful distraction." Beaumont reached into a black canvas tool bag. When his hand came out, he was holding a yellow cordless power drill. "Consider yourself lucky. You won't have to see what happens to your nation."

Lee's body was thrashing as much as the restraints would allow. His eyes were bulging out of their sockets. Spittle was shooting out of his lips.

Squeezing the trigger, Beaumont angled the medium-sized drill bit down near Lee's forearm.

"No! Please! Don't."

"Stay calm or you're getting it in the head," Dr. Beaumont said and then squeezed the trigger while slowly pressing into Lee's muscle tissue and bone. Blood sprayed. The sound of the drill was overpowered by Lee's screams.

Dr. Beaumont slowly pulled out. With the drill hanging at his side, he smiled thinly as Lee thrashed helplessly against his restraints. Crying. Bleeding.

"Your turn." Beaumont handed Gaytan the drill. "Not in the head until I say."

16

Detective Reid was pressing his phone to his ear. "Just to be clear, you found two sets of bloody footprints in Lee Wallis' living room?"

"Yeah, either Caleb Hunt is part of a wider conspiracy," the detective from California said, "or...you're holding an innocent man."

"I'll interrogate Mr. Hunt again." Reid sighed heavily. "He's got to be part of this. His DNA is all over it."

"Let me know what he says," Detective Garrison said. "I'm gonna keep digging."

"You thinking what I'm thinking?" Reid asked.

"I think we have a team of serial killers out there. And they're not gonna stop."

Reid took a deep breath. "I hate to say it, but I think you're right," he said. "I got two other people in town who received body parts in the mail after Mr. Hunt got arrested."

"I'd get them protection right now," Garrison said. "This maniac is motivated, and he has at least one person helping him. I wish I offered Wallis protection after he found that box. I have to live with that."

"I better get on it."

"I'll be in contact."

"Good Luck." Reid hung up the phone, his head snapping to his partner, Detective Ford. "Let's go have a little talk with Mr. Hunt."

*****

Dr. Beaumont tossed a second suitcase in the back of a beat-to-shit Ford pick-up truck. They had bought the rusty thing for five hundred bucks. "Straight to Cali," he said. "Hit the dump and come back." There was other junk in the back of the truck. Half-full of stuff from the hunting shack in southern Oregon. Chairs. Clothes. Junk tools. A cleaned off broken drill.

"You sure you don't want me to get any supplies on the way back?" Rick Gaytan asked, slamming the back gate shut.

"Nah, just come right back." Beaumont's face tightened. "We need to go back to Minnesota. Duty calls."

"All right," Gaytan said. "I'll be back in two hours."

Beaumont nodded and then turned back toward the ancient cabin, his mind on his childhood stash spot in the woods where he had some digging to do.

Gaytan hopped in the truck, shifted into drive, and then drove down the road. "Always got me doing the dirty work," he muttered to himself. "I take all the risks. Always putting my neck out there. Little prick better learn to appreciate me." He hit the steering wheel with the palm of his hand. Twice. "He better show some respect, or *he'll* end up in the dump someday."

He turned the radio on and let his mind fester as he drove to town. When *Riders on the Storm*, by the Doors came on, he turned up the volume and chilled out. After a few more songs, he made it to a small town he never heard of. Flying through a green light, he passed a car with a young girl inside. He craned his neck to gawk at her. *There's only one way I'd get a girl like that,* he thought. *I'd have to take her.* The girl didn't even look in his direction.

Gaytan drove for another forty miles through a thick forest until the border between Oregon and California was before him. When he arrived at the landfill, he pulled behind a line of three heaping trucks full of junk. Waiting for his turn, he felt a bead of sweat rolling down his forehead and wiped it with the back of his hand.

Pulling up to the dump worker with a yellow vest and white helmet, Gaytan rolled down the window. "First time here," he said. "How much?"

"What do you got?" the dump worker asked, holding his yellow receipt book in his dirt-caked hands.

"Just some shit that had to go," Gaytan said, his wallet tight in his hands.

The scruffy worker stepped to the side and glanced at the bed of the truck. "Do you have any paint or light bulbs?"

"No." Gaytan shook his head.

"Any goodies under the rug?" the man asked, his eyes piercing Gaytan's.

Rick's lower lip puffed out. "No." He lied through his teeth with a tremor of fear rumbling in his chest, arms, and jaw. His eyes skirted off to the side as a failed attempt to push out the memory of Lee's dead body getting cut up into pieces and stuffed in suitcases.

"Seventeen bucks."

Gaytan nodded his head. "Not a bad price." He handed him a twenty. "Keep the change."

*****

Later that afternoon, Caleb was sitting in a conference room at the county jail with Keith Sundean and Detective Reid. "I told you, I'm not the killer," Caleb said, glaring across the table at the smug detective. "And I have no idea who is." He spread apart his arms.

"Maybe, "Detective Reid said. "Or maybe you got help."

Keith Sundean nudged Caleb who was about to blurt something out. And then he tilted his left hand. "You're wrong, sir," Keith said. "Caleb is an innocent man. I know it's hard to let go of your only suspect. But he's going free. Now or later. You decide."

"Mr. Sundean, your client could turn out to be a pathological killer." Detective Reid shifted to point at Caleb. "And I want *you* to tell *me* who your accomplices are. If you give up your friends, and it saves lives, I will personally talk to the prosecutor about reducing your sentence. I just want to stop the killing."

"I passed your stupid lie detector test," Caleb blurted. "What more do you want from me?"

Keith touched Caleb's arm. "That's enough. Let me do the talking."

"No, I have nothing to hide. I've done nothing wrong."

"Just give up your friends, Caleb." Reid was leaning forward in his seat, staring directly at the inmate.

"Lee and Blake are both my friends." Caleb's chains rattled when he tried to shrug. "Why would I kill them? How would I kill Lee from in here?"

"Mr. Hunt, my patience is running thin. I know you're part of this. Lee Wallis is missing, and we're going find him one way or another." His head cocked to the left. "With or without your help."

"Someone is setting me up." Caleb's voice raised a notch in volume and octave. "I told you—I was with my *girlfriend* that weekend. That evidence was planted. Because I'm straight, you idiot. I like women. Not men."

Keith turned and literally covered Caleb's mouth.

"Yeah, because people are just climbing through your windows looking for the tissue you jerked off in? Right?"

Keith Sundean stood up. "That's it." His hands both swiped across at chest level. "This interview is over. My client is not going to take this abuse. We thought—"

"Fine! Enjoy the next hundred years behind bars, Mr. Hunt."

17

Duluth, Minnesota
October 17, 2002

"What are you gonna do with a bag of rotten apples?" Caleb asked Blake who was standing on the inside ledge of a steep wooded ravine. Orange, red, and yellow leaves littered the landscape around them.

"We're gonna bomb some cars," Blake said with a shit grin on his face. A black hood pulled over his head. His thumb gesturing to the crumbly road over his shoulder.

"What?" Caleb scrunched up his face. "Why would you do that?"

"It will be fun." Blake was peeking his head above the bushes at the narrow ridge on the shoulder of the road. A car was cruising past them.

"What do you do when they stop?"

"Fight or flight." He grabbed an apple out of the sack.

"Why would you want to fight a guy for nothing?" Caleb was shaking his head. "Or worse, what if it caused an accident? I'm straight."

Blake stood tall, looking up and down the road. "Don't be a little pussy."

"You sound like Bane. That dude is shady."

"Just throw one apple. He tossed the apple at Caleb's chest, but he caught it with ease. "Every kid does it once. You need to embrace the adrenaline, bro. It's dope."

"I don't think so, man," Caleb said, discarding the apple. It bounced and rolled and hopped down the steep ravine. When he lost track of it, he lifted his gaze defiantly back to Blake. He shrugged his shoulders at the narrow-eyed glare of his friend. "These people live in my neighborhood. They probably know my mom."

Blake was holding another apple in his hand. "Fine, I'll do it. All you got to do is run. Be careful on the way down. Swing from tree to tree. You don't want to fall."

Caleb shook his head. "This is stupid, bro. I can't be a part of it."

"You don't have a choice." Blake's gaze was set on a black car coming down the road.

"What do you mean? I always have a—"

Blake whipped an apple at a black and white car that was rolling down the hill.

Caleb's eyes bulged. "Oh no!" he squeaked out in a horrified plea.

Blake eagerly watched the apple fly through the open window and crack the police officer in the side of the head. The squad car screeched to a stop. "It's a cop! Go! Go! Go!"

Caleb looked over the ledge. A husky traffic cop with dark hair and thick eyebrows was screaming. Lumbering across the road with mirror-finish aviator sunglasses. Pointing at him.

"Stop! In the name of the law!" Officer Reid hollered with his billy club drawn. "I saw your face!"

Blake was already skidding down the super steep ravine on his heels. One hand back just in case. Caleb descended after him. He was shuffling and barely keeping his balance as he flew down the uneven rocky ground. Sharp tree branches were scraping his face despite his best attempts to block each whip. He slowed his speed by bouncing from tree to tree. Coming to a halt, he studied a huge dead tree trunk lying flat. It was blocking his escape path.

"Stop right there!" Officer Reid yelled from the top of the ravine but closing the gap.

Blake had just crawled under the tree.

Caleb craned his neck to see the middle of the hill. The cop was still yelling. Turning back, he decided to climb over the fat tree and hop down to the dirt trail where Blake was huffing and puffing.

"Which way?" Blake asked, still breathing heavily.

"Stop!" the cop yelled from the bottom of the hill where the dead was resting.

Caleb's shoulders jerked. Within two rapid beats of his pounding heart, Caleb bolted down the trail.

"Fuck you!" Blake screamed at the cop, and then followed Caleb down the winding narrow path. A glance to the right offered a hundred-foot drop off into the rocky creek.

Caleb sprinted down the path. He didn't look back to see Blake way behind him jogging half- speed. Slowing down, Caleb angled off into thick bushes. The path was at first thorny and intricate, but led them to a secret pond and beach surrounded by massive rocks and trees.

Caleb stopped with his hands on his knees as he coughed for air.

"You see what I'm saying, dawg?" Blake was gasping for air. "Adrenaline is the shit!"

Caleb was huffing and puffing, trying to hold back his smile. "Let's do it again tomorrow."

*****

Leaning against his locker at break, Blake Connor playfully hit Caleb who was staring at a thin classy girl who had long reddish-auburn hair. "Dude, that girl is way out of your league," he said. "You need to find something easier than that."

Caleb ignored him and kept watching her walk down the hall with books in her hands. Her swaying hips and unique hair color had Caleb in a trance. A spell.

Blake snapped his fingers twice. "Hunt! You in there? You have no chance, bro."

"I hear ya," Caleb said, shifting to Blake. "Of course, Mars Sundean is out of my league. I just want to talk to her. Be her friend. I've been waiting for the right moment to spark up a conversation with her."

Blake held his belly and started laughing. "You just want to talk to her?" He reached for Caleb's arm, still laughing as Tarik Brownridge, Lee Wallis, and Bob Sturgis walked up and joined them.

"What's so funny?" Lee asked. His skinny frame looked like he was drowning in his double extra-large baggy clothes.

Blake perked up. "None of your business," he said. "You have to earn that privilege."

"Fine, don't tell us." Bob's head tilted slightly. "We don't care."

"What, you don't want to be in our crew?" Blake shrugged. "You don't want to be a made guy?"

Tarik chimed in. "What's it take to get in?" He was the biggest of the bunch, and had the darkest skin by far. He was a linebacker with Bob on the JV football team. All four had been tight since seventh grade. Lee had just met them at the beginning of the year as a freshman.

Blake looked to the other side of the hall for a target, past the sea of boys and girls gathering their books and belongings from the lockers stretching up and down the corridor. He smiled as his gaze zeroed in on one. A black-haired kid was grabbing book after book and holding them in his arms. *A perfect mark,* he thought. *The kid's got Velcro shoes. And a mullet.*

"You expect us to do an initiation or something?" Bob's eyebrows dropped low.

Blake pointed at the small dirty kid with black greasy hair. "First one to drop Lerch's books gets a free sack of weed."

Lee nodded his head. "I got this."

"Wait till the bell rings," Blake said. "He usually carries at least four books at a time. His parents probably can't afford a backpack."

"Dude, leave the nerd alone," Caleb said. "What'd he do to you?"

"It's a dare," Lee said, nodding his head. "With a prize. I want that bag of weed."

"What? Is that your boy?" Blake teased Caleb with his hand covering his mouth. "Oh, that's right, he used to be your locker partner." He laughed.

"So what?" Caleb shrugged. "Locker partner in seventh grade. The kid never did me wrong. I ain't dropping his books."

Tarik clapped his hands and rubbed them together. "You guys talk about seventh grade, I'm gonna drop his shit."

Blake smiled. "Live a little, Caleb. The kid's a dirt ball. Who gives a shit? You ain't got to do it. Just sit back and watch the show."

"Whatever, man."

The loud bell rang and all the kids in the hallway jumped toward their next class. Lerch Black closed his locker, adjusted his thick black glasses, and then started walking with the torrent of kids. He was shorter than all of them.

"Watch this," Lee said and speed walked behind Lerch. "Boom!" he dropped his open hand on the stack of books Lerch was holding. It made a clap noise. The books flew out of the kid's hands and scattered on the floor. Black folders full of homework assignments spread out in every direction. The steady flow of dozens of kids was stomping all over them, dragging them down the long and wide hallway.

"What the fuck!" Lerch screamed with his hands shaking by his ears, his face the color of a beet. Clenching his fists, he began to snarl with his head shaking.

Lee pushed Lerch into the lockers. "What's up, bitch?"

Bob kicked one of his books across the floor. "What you gonna do, fagget?"

Lerch lowered to a knee and started gathering as many papers as he could. "Leave me alone!"

Tarik, Lee, and Bob high-fived, and then tried to catch up to Blake and Caleb who were walking fast down the emptying hallway.

18

Detective Garrison and Detective Hopkins parked in front of the office at the dump. A frail old man was standing outside waiting for them with his arms folded across his chest. Both detectives got out.

"Where's it at?" Detective Garrison asked.

"In the dozer," the old man said in a raspy voice. "Right this way." He waved inward.

Garrison followed the dump manager to the yellow bulldozer parked next to a huge mound of debris. "Who found it?"

"One of my workers came across it this morning," the old man grumbled. "He said he smelled an extremely foul odor."

"Did he open it?" Garrison asked with a frown on his face.

"No," the old man said. "I did. I wanted to be sure before I called 911."

"Next time just call," Detective Garrison snapped. "You may have contaminated the evidence."

"Look around, pal," the old man said. "Everything here is contaminated."

*****

Inside a crime scene laboratory at the police station, Detective Garrison unzipped the first suitcase found in the dump. "Oh, my God," he said. Lifting the flap open, he swallowed thickly as he peered inside. Taking a step back, he covered his nose with the crook of his arm and looked down at four long objects wrapped in wet contractor bags. "You got a knife?"

Detective Hopkins pulled a scalpel from the toolbox on the table. "I'll open it up," he said, stepping forward, reaching for one of the objects wrapped in black plastic. Gripping the small knife, he poked a hole, and then slit the first bag open. A pale human arm was exposed. He quickly cut open the remaining three bags and set all the pieces on the stainless-steel workspace.

"Look at that," Garrison said, pointing at the discolored and bloated sawed-off limbs. "The dragon tattoo on the arm matches Lee Wallis."

"I wasn't looking at the tattoo." Hopkins shook his head. "All I see is body parts with holes in the flesh."

"Mr. Wallis got tortured to death." Garrison let out a deep breath. "I hate to see it." He snapped a few pictures of the arm with his phone.

"How sick could someone be?"

"Let's find out," Garrison said. "Open the other suitcase and count the holes. I'm going to call Detective Reid in Minnesota."

"I'm on it."

Garrison pulled out his phone and speed-dialed Reid. The phone rang twice.

"Detective Reid," the man on the other end of the line said.

"A suitcase was found in the dump," Garrison said. "I've identified the body. It's him. Lee Wallis."

"How do you know?"

"We haven't run any tests yet, but the dragon tattoo warranted the call." Garrison let out a breath. "I'm going to send you some pictures of the dismembered body."

Reid's sigh blew through the phone line. "What's the cause of death?"

"Homicide, but I'll let the Medical Examiner make that call." Garrison's gaze was on the full body that now lie on the workstation. Hopkins had put the pieces together like an archaeologist would with dinosaur bones. "I called to inform you we've made a match. I'll call you back when I have more info."

*****

Two days later, Detective Reid's fax machine buzzed. Springing out of his seat, he peeled off the first page. "It's the preliminary report of the autopsy."

"What's it say?" Detective Ford shot up and joined him at the printer.

"Homicide, obviously. But it says the cause of death was a drill hole in top of the skull. In addition, there were two holes in each arm and leg. Three in the abdomen. One in the left eye."

"Thirteen." Ford's hands were rubbing together. "That's evil. Who does such a thing?"

"Mr. Hunt's henchmen."

The fax machine buzzed again. Reid rushed to the fresh hot papers. "Forensic analysis!"

"Damn that's quick."

"Ours took much longer."

Reid dropped his jaw.

"Won't have Mr. Hunt's DNA this time." Ford shook his head.

"Wrong!" Reid's eyes dart down the page. "Same thing. Hunt's pubic hairs in the teeth. DNA on the chin...*and* rectal cavity."

Ford cocked his head. "No way?"

"There's more: Plastic shavings consistent with composite house siding."

"Hunt works for a construction company. He's a sider."

"That's right. This asshole—"

"Wait. Hunt has been in jail for a month now. Something isn't adding up."

"Fuck!" Reid slammed his fist on the desk. "The killer is fucking with us. Hunt can't rape Wallis in California. He's in jail. Here."

"Holy shit. We better release him."

19

Deep into the next semester, Lee Wallis burst into English class and took a seat in the back row right next to Blake Connor. Lerch Black was sitting in front of them in a black T-shirt with dandruff flakes collecting on his hunched, bony shoulders.

"Whud up, Son?" Blake hit him playfully in the shoulder. "You're late."

"I know," Lee said softly. "My girl wouldn't shut up. Bitching about some stupid rumor."

"Who's your girl?"

"Nicole Lorcani."

Blake nodded his head. "Damn, Son, that girl is bangin'."

"Stay away from her. She's mine."

Blake chuckled. "Just take it as a compliment."

Lee started to respond only to be interrupted by the teacher who was standing behind the podium. Ms. Sanger gave a brief lecture and then passed out a stack of tests. When she left the room, Blake passed a small folded-up sheet of paper to Lee.

Opening the note, Lee read the words softly: KICK ME. He shifted to face Blake who was pointing forward. And then he handed him a small roll of duct tape. Lee took the tape but shrugged in question.

"Do it after class." Blake whispered. "You'll earn your stripes."

*****

When the bell rang, Blake nudged Lee hard. "Do it."

Lee nodded and then walked up behind Lerch Black who was standing in the back of the line of kids funneling out the door. With a gentle smack, he plopped the KICK ME sign on his back, rubbing it in slowly so the tape would stick to the fabric. "Lerch," he said, moving his hand to the shoulder of a scrawny ninth grader. He patted twice then let go. "What class you got next?"

"Don't touch me," Lerch said, his upper lip curling upward.

"Woah, slow down, Lerch," Lee said, patting him on the back twice more. "I don't want to have to take your lunch money."

"I don't have any lunch money."

The line shrunk as they drew closer to the door.

"Then I'll take your food stamps."

"Leave me alone. Or you'll wish you did."

Lee playfully smacked him in the shoulder. "All right, Black. Peace out."

"There is no peace. Only death." Lerch snorted. Once he made it out the door, he accelerated his pace to get away from Lee. Right as he was about to climb the stairs, he felt a kick in his ass. Stumbling slightly, he turned to see Bob, Lee, Blake, Bane, and Caleb in the distance.

"What's up, faggot!" Blake said. "You got a kick me sign on your back, punk."

Lerch held up his hands in defense.

Tarik crept down the steps. He kicked Lerch in the ass as hard as he could.

Lerch fell to the floor, shrieking as he dropped his books and folders.

Bane kicked him in the back. "Take a shower, scrub."

Lerch was on all fours. Cowering.

Bob kicked him in the butt, and then Lee kicked him twice when he was down. An audience was accumulating. Most were snickering.

"Leave me alone!" Lerch screamed, jumping up to his feet. "Don't make me get my lice start jumping!" He bowed his head and shook it with vigor.

Caleb was laughing from a safe distance.

Lee and Bob jumped backward.

Blake put his fists up in a fighting position. "One more step and you're done."

"Just leave me alone." Lerch's arms were curled up around his face in the corner. Defeated with a crack his voice. "That's all I want."

Blake looked into the dark eyes of a zit-faced young man who was showing his stained teeth like a cornered animal. Behind him was a brick wall. They had him surrounded. Five on one.

Blake drew back his fist, ready to drop bombs when they all heard the sound of rushing feet advancing on them.

"Break it up!" Denzel the bouncer barked. "You ain't got no pass, you gots to go."

*****

Lerch Black's face was buried in his pillow as he cried and wailed. His clenched fists were pounding on his bed when a series of gentle knocks on the bedroom door interrupted his self-pity. "Leave me alone!"

"Lerch, it's time for dinner." His mother raised her voice. "Hot dogs and crawfish."

"I'm not hungry, Mom." Lerch returned his head to his wet pillow. The family cat meowed from the foot of the bed. It was black and bony with a crooked tail.

"Unlock the door!" She pounded louder. "Dad will be home soon. If you're not at the kitchen table, he's gonna open up a can of whoop-ass."

Lerch leaped out of bed in a black T-shirt and faded black jeans. On the way to the door, he moped past his dresser, reaching out his fingers to wipe the dust off his only possession of value: A black and red three-tier samurai sword rack his mother got him for Christmas.

He took a deep breath and wiped his eyes as he opened the door. But when he met his mother's gaze, the tears burst again. His hold on the door eased, and then he retreated to his bed and pillow. "Just let me be!"

The cat meowed.

"Shut up, Void! You stupid cat!" Lerch was thrashing about, his emotions pouring out of him unchecked as he pounded his fists impotently on the bed. When the cat jumped to the floor, the temper tantrum came to a halt.

As his mother got closer, he curled up in a ball and trembled with emotion.

"Oh, what's wrong, Lerch?" She rested a tender hand on his back. "I'm here for you." Her hand massaged his shoulders until his body went limp.

"I'm fine," Lerch said, turning onto his back and wiping his tears with the back of his hand. His eyes were bloodshot and squinty. His face blushed.

"Come on, Lerch. Something is obviously bothering you." Despite the thrift store clothes and the deep lines on her face attesting to a hard life, Bridget Black remained a soft, gentle woman with a pony tail full of jet-black hair.

"I did bad on a test." His eyes darted off to the side.

"Lerch, you always do bad on tests." She touched his arm. "It's got to be something else. You can tell me anything. Did someone touch you? A teacher? A student?"

"No!"

"Then what is it?" She said, running her fingers through his greasy hair.

Lerch smacked his hand on his bed. "Some guys at school have been picking on me."

"What? Who? Did they hit you?"

"Yes. Every day it's something new." Lerch recounted the story to his mother.

"Who did this to—"

The door slammed open and Lerch's dad burst into the room. "What's all the commotion!" He was wearing filthy coveralls, and his hands were black from working on cars all day.

Lerch quickly wiped his tears, sucked back his sobs.

"Bridget, leave the room." His oil-slicked hand was pointing to the door. "I want a moment alone with my son."

"Yes, sir." She lowered her head and left the room with haste. Void, the cat darted out the door and Bridget followed close behind, softly shutting the door behind her.

Lerch's dad, Randy Black took a menacing step forward. "Get up."

"What?"

Randy grabbed Lerch by the shirt and yanked him up to his feet. "Why the fuck are you crying like a little girl?"

Lerch looked upward into his dad's dark eyes and low brow. "I got beat up at school today," he said. "There must have been five of them. They're gonna do it again, Dad. Can you please help me? I can't go back there."

Randy lifted a single finger to his lips. "Shhh." He took off his belt, held it in his right hand, and let the buckle dangle by his cruddy work boots. "No more excuses. I've heard enough. I'm ashamed of how weak you are. I have no choice but to punish you, boy. Take it like a man... or it will last longer." He lifted his hand high as he encroached on Lerch. The belt flopped and the buckle clacked on itself.

"No!" Lerch backed into the corner of the room and burrowed low on the floor. Curling up in a small ball, his dad's shadow loomed. His heart sank.

Lerch lifted an open hand. A failed attempt to block the incoming blow from the buckle of his dad's thick black leather belt. The impact cut the top of his head. The burning sting, the way his mouth contorted on a cracked scream.

"Shut the fuck up!" Lerch's dad reached back his arm and flogged him again. This time it cut his arm. "I'm gonna make a man out of you yet, boy." He stepped on his face with his nasty boot. Rubbed it in. And then offered a half-ass kick to the jaw.

"Stop!" His little body thrashed with writhing pain.

"Who do you fear more?" His dad kicked him in the belly. "Them... or me?" Frothing at the mouth from pure rage, he spit on Lerch's face. "Them or me?" He smacked him with the palm of his hand. It clapped. Loud. "Who do you fear!"

"You!" Lerch was sobbing. But it wasn't the first time.

His dad hovered over the trembling fifteen-year-old young man. "You're weak and stupid," he said, slipping the belt back through the loops in his pants. "I can handle one or the other." He lit up a cigarette. "But not both. I will not tolerate that. If I can't make you smart, I *will* make you strong. Just like my daddy did me. Only, I ain't as mean as my old man. You never got a chance to meet that asshole."

Randy puffed on his cigarette and watched his son tremble like an abused dog. Shaking his head, he took a long drag and stooped low, blowing toxic smoke in Lerch's face. And then he reached forward with the cig in his fingers, snubbing the hot cherry out on Lerch's forehead.

Lerch let out a howl. Curling up into a tighter ball, he screamed at the top of his lungs. "Stop!"

"You little faggot." His dad punched him in the side. "Aren't ya? What an embarrassment. I was quarterback for varsity in tenth grade. My junior year, I was fucking the Homecoming Queen." He shook his head. "Now look at me. I work my ass off all day to come home to this shit. A loser faggot son. A worthless Homecoming whore. And a dimwitted daughter. You better toughen up, cockroach. Life ain't no field trip. Get ready for a miserable existence. The world is gonna eat you up and shit you out."

When Lerch rolled over to protect his liver, his dad punched him in the ear half-speed. "Stop!"

"I'm gonna keep beating your ass until you defend yourself." He hit him in the jaw. "It's a dark world out there, boy. Sink or swim. Hunt or be hunted. You're about to enter a world where the strong take from the weak. And in my mind, the weak deserve to get took. It's the way of the universe. It always has been. It always will be. There is nothing anyone can do to stop it."

"Please stop, Dad. I love you!" His voice was shaky.

"You ain't talking yourself out of this one, Lerch." He hit him in the nose with the backside of his hand.

Lerch shrieked, turning to jam his head in the corner of the wall. Face down, he cried with each blow to his body.

Randy stood tall, lifted his knee, and then stomped his boot on his son's back.

"Dad!"

"Fight back you useless piece of shit." He kicked Lerch in the side.

"Stop!" His voice cracked. "Mom! Help me!"

A soft female voice from the doorway called out, "Dad." The door was swinging open.

Randy turned around. It was Gretchen, Lerch's 12-year-old sister, standing in the doorway with tears in her eyes.

Lerch's dad rushed to the little girl with short cropped black hair, grabbing her by the shirt and jerking her outside of the room. He shoved her out the door so hard she fell and tumbled and started crying. "Mind your fucking business, you little piss-ant. I'll deal with you later."

Gretchen got up and gave him the middle finger.

From the floor, Lerch looked at the sword on the dresser. Rising to his feet, his adrenaline carried him to there. As he reached for the long sword, the door slammed shut and the thunderous bang shook the house. Fear gave him the strength to grip the sword tight.

Randy Black laughed shortly from behind Lerch.

He turned around slowly. The blade was low, but rising higher and higher until it was above Lerch's head.

Randy spread apart his arms. "You don't have the balls."

"Die!" Lerch cried, charging at his dad with short fast steps.

Randy raised his arms to protect his vitals. "Lerch!"

While swinging the stainless-steel blade, Lerch's dad's arm blocked his one shot at freedom.

Randy screamed and then steamrolled right over Lerch with the stainless-steel blade sticking in the meat of his forearm. They both crashed to the carpet. His dad was on top. Blood was gushing on Lerch's face from his dad's wound. The sword dropped to the floor.

Bouncing back up, Randy's left hand shot to hold the dripping gash in his arm. He gripped it tight, eyes exploding with panic.

Lerch was sitting on his backside looking up at his dad. With his eyes shifting to the blood-stained sword that was between them, his lower lip quivered.

"That's better, Lerch." His dad nodded with super heavy fast breaths. "Don't ever let someone push you around again." He turned for the door. "Bridget. Get me the first aid kit and the whiskey bottle! Now!" Randy shuffled out the bedroom door holding his arm.

Lerch licked the blood from his fingertips and clicked his tongue. "That's what victory tastes like." Rising to his feet, his underbite smile shined for an audience of one: Void, the cat.

20

Duluth, Minnesota
April 6, 2026

Bob Sturgis poured a nip of whiskey into a short glass. "I see a pattern unfolding," he said, handing Tarik Brownridge the drink. "And we're the only available targets left." The darkened living room was made even darker by the polished hardwood floors and mahogany décor.

"We should prepare for an attack," Tarik said, taking a big sip of whiskey. "I don't want to end up like Blake or Lee." He winced from the bite of hard liquor.

"I got extra guns and ammo if you need," Bob said, pouring himself a drink.

"Not just with guns, bro," Tarik said. "We should set some booby traps."

"That sounds great," Bob said. "But what if the mailman steps in it? Or... one of my bitches?"

"No, I mean... like video cameras." Tarik gestured toward the door to the outside. "Maybe a pitbull. Alarms. You know what I'm sayin'?"

Bob nodded slowly with the corner of his mouth hitching upward.

"If he gets past all that, then you blow his brains out." Tarik raised his eyebrows.

Bob smiled. "I like how you think, my brother with a different color. Let's trap this guy."

"I just want to stay alive." Tarik took another swig. "This punk is plucking us off one by one."

"Let's get some cameras set up at your house first. Then we'll do mine." Bob sipped his drink slowly.

Tarik nodded his head, cup rising to his lips. "I'm down with that."

"Let me show you my guns while you're here." Bob gulped a good portion of whiskey. "I want you to be able to defend yourself." Bob set the cup on the coaster and flew up the stairs to the spare bedroom.

Tarik followed behind him and stopped in the doorway. "Damn, man," he said, taking in the array of guns laid out on the bed of an otherwise sparsely decorated room. "You ready for whatever."

Bob picked up the shotgun. "That's how I roll." He lifted his chin. "Take one with you." He nodded. "I got so many guns. My grampa was a survivalist. He left me everything."

Tarik grabbed the AK-47 with the banana clip and smiled.

"Be careful. It's loaded."

Tarik nodded his head with his lower lip puffed out. "I like this, right here."

"It's yours." Bob shrugged. "Never thought I'd need to use 'em. Not like this."

"Me neither. Let's just hope it's enough."

"There's safety in numbers. Take a handgun, too."

"Thanks."

"Safety in numbers..." Bob shook his head. "Actually, I think I got a better idea..."

"What's that?"

"Maybe you should just stay here till shit clears over. I know I'd sleep better knowing someone else is here with a loaded gun."

"I'll take you up on that offer," Tarik said, nodding. "We'll watch my house from here. Maybe he'll show his face on camera."

"That's a great ide—" Bob got cut off by the sudden buzzing of the doorbell.

"Who the fuck is that?" Tarik asked, his eyes large.

"I'm not expecting anyone," Bob said, reclaiming the shotgun. "Let's find out."

Tarik grabbed the rifle. "After you."

Bob crept out the door and down the stairs. The doorbell rang again. He stuck out the palm of his hand for Tarik to stop. Cautiously approaching the door, Bob looked out the peephole and saw a heavy man in a trench coat and tie. "Who is it?"

"Detective Reid."

"Hold on a second." Bob gave the shotgun to Tarik and softly told him to hide them in the bedroom and come back. When Tarik was out of sight, Bob unlocked the door and swung it open. "How can I help you, Detective?"

"We haven't spoken since you found the box on your steps," Reid said. "There's been some developments. Do you mind if I come in?"

"All right, but me and Tarik already heard about Lee," Bob said. "It was all over the news."

"I have information you won't hear on the news."

"Okay." Bob opened the door wider and closed it when Reid was fully inside. "I'm listening." Bob made a face at Tarik and gave a half-shrug.

"Pay attention. This is serious."

Bob nodded. "What's going on?"

"Mr. Sturgis, Caleb Hunt's DNA was found on Lee Wallis. Since Caleb's alibi is jail, it can't be him. So, we dropped all charges. He's in protective custody. The real killer has at least one accomplice, and we think they're professional. They cut Mr. Wallis up in pieces and shoved him in a suitcase."

"I thought it was Caleb for sure." Bob was shrugging.

"Definitely not Caleb." Reid shook his head.

Tarik chimed in. "Why didn't the news say anything about the suitcase?"

"Law enforcement withholds information from the general public that they don't need to know. You two have a right to know what you're up against. Two pathological killers have eluded justice. They are *barbaric* in nature. And we think you could be next." Detective Reid paused to glance at both men. "I need to bring you both somewhere safe."

"Thanks, Detective." Bob spread apart his hands. "But we have guns here. And I got combat experience in Iraq. I think we got it under control."

"I don't think you understand." Reid shook his head. "The killer doesn't plan on having a shoot-out in your living room. They stalk their prey and take them when they least expect it. Come with me. We'll keep you alive."

"Thanks, but no thanks." Bob extended his hand like a gentleman.

Reid shook it extra firmly. "You're making a big mistake, Bob."

*****

Pushing a cart in the grocery store, Mars Sundean looked bedraggled, her red hair in a greasy unwashed mess. Yoga pants and a wrinkled T-shirt type of day. She stopped in front of the ice-cream sandwiches, her lips twitched into something nearing a smile. As she reached for the chrome freezer handle, the sound of a sharp voice cursing gave her shoulders a jolt.

Snapping her head over her shoulder, Mars felt a hot flash rush through her body. "Shit," she said under her breath. Blake Connor's girlfriend was parked ten feet behind her with hands on her hips. Sassy dyed blonde hair. Cropped short and stick straight. A full cart in front of her.

"I knew I'd see you sooner or later," Nicole Lorcani said. "I should crack this can of beans over your head, bitch." Her finger pointed at the camera. "But I'm smarter than that." She tapped the side of her head with her finger.

"I didn't do anything to you," Mars said, shrugging with a scrunched-up defensive face.

"I know you had something to do with it." Nicole's shaking finger was pointing at Mars. "How dare you show your face around here."

"Nicole." Mars' right hand clenched at her side. "Come on, you honestly believe what they're saying? You're a fool. At least Caleb's lucky enough to have a girlfriend who can put two and two together."

"Well, they didn't let him out, did they?" Nicole spread her arms apart. "He's guilty. And so are you." She paused to meet her eyes. "Catch you outside. How 'bout dat?"

"You're nuts," Mars said, fighting the urge to knock her lights out. "Now get out of my way, a killer's still on the loose. I need to go get myself a gun. I suggest you do the same." She turned and pushed her cart in the opposite direction.

"Watch your back, bitch!" Nicole tossed an apple at Mars.

When the apple hit her in the back, she flinched, ducked her shoulders, and then turned around slowly. Breathing heavily, Mars' voice box rumbled before she barked. "Put your hands up." Her face was darkening. Fists in front of her jaw.

"Bring it."

Mars charged forward like an alpha female prizefighter, swinging her fists and snarling. Customers shrieked and scattered out of the way as the two women scratched it out in the donut area. Mars was landing punches but her childhood friend had a fistful of hair.

Mars was on top, her fists connecting blow after blow against Nicole's face. Her knuckles were split, and blood splattered the sides of Nicole's hairline but neither woman seemed to notice or care.

Nicole tugged hard on a gripful of Mars' hair, jerking that woman's head back. "Bitch!"

Neither woman heard the sound of rubber-soled shoes careering around the corner of the aisle, nor did they notice the heavyset young man barreling toward them with a vest that identified him as a loss prevention officer.

"Break it up!" He barked out to no avail.

*****

Bob gently set the shotgun on the floor of his living room. Plopping down on the leather sofa next to Tarik, he reached for the bowl of popcorn on the granite coffee table. "We'll sit here and watch your house all night long," he said. "We don't need no witness protection." He popped a handful of buttery kernels in his mouth.

Tarik cracked a beer. "Nah, man." He laughed shortly, but behind that chuckle was a forced sense of casualness. "I think we got this handled. You got military experience, and I got experience on the street. I will not hesitate to pull that trigger." His eyes fell on the AK-47 on the table, and then bounced to the large TV. The screen was split into eight sections. The top four playing live footage of Tarik's house, and the bottom four set up at Bob's. Inside and out.

"I don't trust the pigs," Bod said, "but detective Reid…you know, he's not so bad."

"Still seems drastic to me, that he wanted us to go into witness protection," Tarik said, chugging his beer.

"I know."

Tarik sighed. "I'm not a runner, though."

"Definitely not."

"So, who do you think the killer is anyways?"

Bob took a swig of beer. "Killers. Plural." He glanced down at his feet, grumbling out his confession: "I really thought it was Caleb, but I'm starting to think you guys were right. That dude got set up."

Tarik leaned back in his chair and said: "Yeah, I wondered when you were finally gonna admit you were wrong," he said. "Caleb ain't no killer."

Bob nodded.

"He ain't gay either. Right there, that tells you, we're dealing with a sick asshole who steals pubic hairs and plants them on the body. That means he enters the homes before he kills."

"But who?" Bob shrugged.

"Who hates all five of us?" Tarik pounded his beer. "Who would want to make us look gay? I ain't going out like that. Hell 'naa."

"Me neither." Bob shook his head. "He probably wants to put my DNA on your chin." Holding his belly, he laughed hard and then downed half his bottle of beer.

"Fuck that. I'm gonna put a few holes in his chest." Tarik lifted an eyebrow.

"But who the fuck is it?"

Tarik set his empty beer on the table and cracked another. "If it was just Caleb and Blake, I'd think it was Derek Bane. But what happened to Lee? The target on his back? Nah. Bane ain't never had no problem with him."

Bob tilted his beer to his lips until it was gone, and then he set the empty bottle on a coaster. "Maybe not." He let out a belch. "But I know Blake owed Bane some money." He paused with a sigh. "At least a few thousand from sports bets. Poker. That's a motive in my book."

"Yeah, but why would Bane want *us* dead?" Tarik asked. "I don't owe him no money. Do you?"

Bob shook his head. "Hell no. Me and Lee went to the Army after Caleb went to prison. I only see Bane a few times a year. Usually at the pool hall."

"I cut ties with Bane after Caleb got out. I think he's a piece of shit. No morals."

"We need to think outside the box. What if it's those Asian punks from high school? The ones who stabbed Caleb back in the day."

Tarik's eyebrows raised a notch. "I never thought about that," he said. "So long ago. I remember Caleb, Blake, and Bane firebombed their house in the projects. Caleb took the heat and went to prison."

"And the Asians might think we were part of it. Looking for revenge."

"Yup, that's gotta be it. They want to take out our old crew."

"They're the only people who would want all five of us dead." Bob met Tarik's dark eyes. "Keep thinking, though. We could be wrong. I've learned to never be too sure of anything."

Tarik rubbed his chin. "What about that Lerch punk?"

"Lerch Black?" Bob pinched his face. "I never thought I'd hear that name again. Wow, we tormented that nerd."

"I bet he still hates us." Tarik squirmed in his seat.

"Yeah, but that little twirp couldn't hurt a fly."

*****

On the outskirts of town, Rick Gayton parked his rusty Ford truck two blocks away from Bob Sturgis' house. Glancing at the clock on the dash board, he muttered to himself: "3:47 a.m. A little ahead of schedule." He shook it off and then grabbed his backpack.

Pushing the door to his truck open, he got out and shut it with great caution and finesse. The neighborhood was dark and quiet. Lots of trees. His movements were fast. He glanced from house to house before reaching the dead-end loop.

"He better be right," Gaytan mumbled in the shadows of the gigantic maple trees. "If the cops are watching, I'm fucked."

Gaytan's head snapped at the sound of footsteps behind him. The sight of a thin woman jogging in the street tensed his shoulders. Jerking his face in the other direction, he tried to hide his identity. A line of parked cars separated them, but the woman's head angled toward him as she crossed his path.

"Good morning!" she said and kept running.

Rick said nothing to her, but he cursed under his breath. Clenching his fist with sweat rolling down his side, he veered up the driveway, his jacket getting scratched by the low-hanging branches at the edge of the pavement.

A blue Chevy Suburban was parked in the driveway.

Gaytan crept around to the back door. The motion light flashed on and a jolt of adrenalin shot through his body. He pressed his back against the wall and scanned the now-lit yard. *Just a light,* he thought, and then unzipped the bag, pulling out the lock-picking device. Reaching for the knob, he shoved the needle inside the lock hole.

Click.

The door creaked open. Gaytan stuck his meaty head inside, his eyes shifting around the darkened space. *Nothing,* he thought with a series of short breaths to follow. With his adrenaline rising, he stepped inside and quietly closed the door. He slipped out of his backpack and set it on the kitchen countertop. Unzipping the bag, he pulled out a small vial of Succinylcholine. Upon opening the refrigerator door, he poured it in the orange juice.

His next steps were in the direction of the dark living room and the sound of snoring.

*****

Early that morning, Tarik jerked upright when he glanced at the TV screen. "What the… Bob!" Tarik shook his friend's leg. His voice got louder. "Wake up!"

Bob rolled over on the large leather couch. "What?"

"There's a red exclamation point on the corner of the screen," Tarik said with a heightened voice of alarm.

Bob spun, popping to his feet and reaching for his laptop. "That means there was some movement!"

"What?" Tarik rose, staring intently into the big screen.

"Hold on. I'll be there in two seconds." Bob clicked the mouse. "There. Holy shit." He pointed at a large grizzly man who was crouching in his kitchen. "That's my fucking house!" His head cocked to the kitchen with elevated breaths.

Their eyes were zipping around the four walls. Bob grabbed the shotgun and marched into every room in the house with a pounding heart. When he got back, Tarik was looking out the window with the AK across his chest.

"That asshole was in here," Tarik said with a blank look on his face. "He could have fucking killed us."

"How the hell did neither of us wake up?" Bob was huffing and puffing.

Tarik pointed at the screen. "What the fuck is he doing?"

"We're gonna find out," Bob said, dropping his jaw as the man began tampering with items in the refrigerator.

"He's putting shit in your orange juice!"

"We're supposed to be dead man," Bob said. "Good thing we put up cameras."

Tarik was breathing heavily. "We should call the cops, man."

"Just watch the video. We got to see what he did."

"No, we gotta call the cops, right now." Tarik pulled out his phone. "We have him on camera. They might know who he is. Where he lives."

"Just hold on a minute. I'll call. It's my house."

"Just hit pause."

"Wait!" Bob pointed. "Look, he's putting cameras in my house."

"This must be what they do? He watches his victims before he takes them."

"It's too dark. I can't make out who he is."

"He's definitely white. Not Asian. Not Bane. Not Lerch."

Bob cleared his throat. "Wait. They're watching us right fucking now." His eyes zeroed in on the man's movements on the TV screen. He was now behind them as they slept. A knife in his hands as he lowered it to Bob's neck.

Bob slowly swiveled around until he was looking dead-on at the cleverly hidden camera in the corner bookshelf. "Fuck!" he blurted out even as he walked up to it, his hand grabbing for the device, tugging it free.

"Dude, we should call the cops. They could search the house for more cameras."

"Fine. I'll call Detective Reid."

21

Duluth, Minnesota
February 27, 2004

Mars Sundean was watching a hockey game with her friend Nicole Lorcani at the Duluth Entertainment Center. The puck was buried in the back of the net. "Go big red!" they cheered from behind the plexiglass in the corner of the rink.

Caleb had just scored a goal. His teammates were gathering around him with their sticks held high in the air. They were yelling in celebration. On the opposite side of the glass, the girls were jumping up and down with their hands stretched out above their heads, shrieking with more school spirit than the rest of the high school kids.

When the players broke off, Mars was still pounding on the glass, hooting and hollering like a cheerleader without pompoms. Number twenty-seven turned around and smiled from behind his caged facemask. Effortlessly gliding away.

"Caleb Hunt," Mars said, beaming into his dark eyes. Her jubilance came to a halt as Caleb skated away. "What a heartthrob."

Nicole shoved Mars. "Don't make it so obvious," she said. "Make him wait. Torture him until he's about to die. Then save him with a wet kiss." She barked out a cackle.

Mars shot her a look. "He's too shy to talk to me."

"Give him a hint." Nicole flashed a crooked smile. "Some boys are scared of pretty girls. You might have to initiate a conversation. Maybe touch his arm muscles. Works every time."

Mars watched Celeb take his place in the center of the ice. When the ref dropped the puck, Caleb poked it forward between the other player's skates. Sidestepping the kid, Caleb grabbed the puck with his stick and exploded with a burst of speed right between the pair of defensemen who were twice his size. Caleb was in the clear, striding forward on a breakaway. Just him and the goalie, and Mars watching on his right side.

She held her breath as Celeb deked left, stalling with the puck as the goalie flopped on the ice. Her eyes were following his every movement as he finally hoisted the puck over the goalie's pads and then it chimed off the crossbar, deflecting into the top shelf of the net. Caleb lifted his stick in the air like the Statue of Liberty and his team circled around him for the second time in less than one minute. Mars cheered louder than her friend. As the boy skated closer, she pounded on the glass.

Mars' little heart skipped a beat or three as Caleb skated past her with his head cocked, staring into her eyes, penetrating her soul. He even pointed at her with his free hand. "Do you think he has a girlfriend?"

"Nah." Nicole giggled. "But I can find out. "His best friend has a thing for me."

Caleb straightened his head before he made it to the other side of the net. Skating too close to the goalie got him hacked in the ankle with the goalie's big stick. Caleb went down but shot right back up. Dropping his stick and gloves, he popped off his helmet and slammed it on the ice.

Caleb did not hesitate. He charged the goalie. Reaching with his left hand, he grabbed a fist full of black jersey, yanked and jerked, and then began peeling the goalie's helmet off. And then he threw wild punches at the goalie's head. Three powerful right blows dropped the goalie backward inside the crease of the net. Caleb was still on top. Pounding. And just then a player on the other team tackled him. Three more players jumped on Caleb. All punching.

Caleb's teammates rushed in. The referees were blowing their whistles and screaming to break it up. The fists kept flying.

Mars kept pounding on the thick plexiglass wall. "Get off him!"

*****

After the game, Caleb burst through the glass doors of the arena and felt the cold icy wind scratch at his neck. His bag of equipment was strapped to his back and his stick was in his hand. Cuts on his face. Victory on his mind.

"Caleb!" a young female voice called out to him.

He picked his head up and saw Mars Sundean trotting toward him. His eyes widened with nervousness. Licking his lips, he glanced down at his feet. "Hey, Mars. I didn't know you liked hockey?"

"That was an awesome game!" Mars said, raising her hand high. "I love hockey. It's my favorite sport."

Caleb set his bag down and smacked her hand. "Thanks!" His heart was buzzing. "I hope you didn't see me get my ass kicked?"

"You're a killer. You dominated the entire game. How many goals did you score?"

"Three. Two assists."

"Hat trick." She was beaming. "Awesome. Well, I just wanted tell you, I thought you had a good game." She reached out and squeezed his muscular upper arm then let go.

He looked down at the wanted intrusion of his bubble. "Thanks," Caleb smiled. "I'm usually not that good. I think I stepped my game up after I saw you."

Mars couldn't hold back her smile and blush. Slight bounce on her heels. "Then I'll be sure to be at the next game." She met his eyes, and then spun away, sprinting to the honking car in the parking lot.

*****

A few days later, Caleb opened the door of his mom's house and flung his back-pack on the ratty sofa. He climbed a few steps and hollered up-stairs. "Mom," he said, holding onto the dark oak railing. "Did anyone call?"

He heard something, but he couldn't tell what it was so he climbed the steps and opened his mom's door. She was lying in bed with her fingers pressing on her chest.

"Mom, are you okay?"

"No," she said, shaking her head full of dark brown hair. "I'm having chest pains again. The doctor said it's just indigestion. I'll be okay. Just leave me alone."

"I'm sorry. What can I do to help?"

"Nothing. I just need to rest. It will be better tomorrow."

"Did anyone call?"

"Some Mars girl." She let out a heavy breath. "You better watch out for girls who call boys. She sounds like trouble. Who names their kid Mars, anyways?"

Devoid of Light | 123

Caleb's face tightened. "Leave her alone, Mom," he said with an elevated voice. "She's a good kid. A straight-A student. And I think she likes me."

"Just be careful. The world doesn't need any little Calebs roaming the streets."

"We're just friends, Mom. Please be nice to her if she calls again."

"Leave me alone. I just got a sharp pain."

Caleb let out a breath. "I hope you feel better. I'll come check on you before I go to bed." He grabbed the phone, closed the door, and then raced down the stairs. Thumbing the Caller ID on the screen, he found Mars' number and hit the call button. As it rang, he nervously paced through the house with the portable phone pressed against his ear. He found himself in the cluttered kitchen when she said hello.

"Is this Mars?" Caleb sat down at the kitchen table.

"It sure is," she said with an excited voice.

"Hey, sorry I missed your call," Caleb said, bouncing his knee at the speed of his heart. "What's up?"

"Oh, you know, stupid parents, stupid teachers, stupid friends."

Caleb gazed out the window and saw a pine tree bending in the wind. "I know the feeling."

"My dad's planning my life for me."

"What do you mean?" Caleb listened intently.

She breathed into the phone. "I hate him." She let out a heavy sigh. "He says I'm going to military college. And I don't have a choice."

"What? How do you not have a choice?"

"It's hard to explain. You don't want to hear about my problems."

"Mars, I'm here to listen. You can tell me anything. I got all the time in the world."

"Thanks. Really, he just says everyone in his family served in the military. He thinks it's a good foundation for the rest of my life. He says if I don't go in the military, I'll end up a deadbeat drunk like every other kid in this town."

"What do you want in life?"

"That's the thing. I don't know. I'm fifteen years old. I just want to watch you punch a goalie in the head again." She laughed shortly. "What do you want in life?"

"I just wanna talk to you."

22

Duluth, Minnesota
April 10, 2026

In the middle of their queen-size bed, Caleb rolled off Mars and let out a breath. "Holy shit," he said, panting, dropping his arm around her naked back as she snuggled closer to him. "I missed you so much when I was in jail." He squeezed her tight. Pulled her close.

"I can tell," Mars said amusingly, closing her eyes and smiling against his chest as she listened to the rising and falling of his breath. That was the best part. His heartbeat.

"Sorry. I think I need some practice," Caleb said, his heart still thudding erratically. "After five weeks in jail. I couldn't even last five minutes. How embarrassing."

"Don't worry, Luv." Mars purred softly. "You had to get that out of you." She patted his chest a few times. "I'm just happy you're home. And safe." Her voice softened to a whisper. "With me."

"Me too," he said. "They actually apologized before they set me free."

"You deserve more than an apology." She gusted out a breath of hot air.

"I could probably sue, but they offered me round-the-clock protection till they get the guy."

"How does that work?"

"Well." He paused to swallow. "They think he plans to kill me next. So, they rented out the basement of the neighbor's house. And they set up alarms on my property. They get alerted to any movement outside. I just live my life as before... and when he tries to get me, they'll catch him."

"Wait, what?" Mars crawled out of bed, cursing as she slipped into a sports bra. "What, are they using us for bait?" She pulled up a pair of yoga pants.

"I wouldn't use that word." He got out of bed and stepped into a pair of boxer briefs.

"And you didn't think to ask me about that?" Mars was fully dressed with palms tilted upward in a shrug. When she saw his blank face, she turned and shook her head.

"I'm sorry, babe," he said, jumping into sweatpants as she walked out the bedroom door. "Wait! I just found out about this. How could I say no?"

Mars stopped and turned to face him.

Caleb opened his bare arms. "What, do you want me to call off the twenty-four hour a day surveillance?"

"I just don't want to be part of it." Her dark eyebrows were forming a V.

"What, did you think...the killer was going to stop trying to kill people?"

She shook her head. "No. I just didn't plan on being bait."

"It's not like that, Mars." Caleb took a couple steps in her direction.

"What am I then? Collateral damage?" Mars tilted her head slightly. "I don't think I can do this. I'm not safe here."

"Mars, stop!" He tried to wrap her up in his arms but she batted them away. "I just got out of jail. Please. I need you now more than ever." He overpowered her and wrapped her up in a bear hug. "You're safe here, with me."

She broke loose and hit his muscular chest. "Stop? That's how you talk to me?" Her arms flung outward. "What? Am I a dog or something?"

"No, stop and think." His hands rose to the sides of his head and shook violently. "I just wanted protection, so I know you're safe." The volume of his voice increased. "What's wrong with that?"

Mars blew out a heavy sigh. "Look, Caleb." She paused to look directly into his wide eyes. "I can't live like this. I do care about you. I'm happy you're free, but I'm going to have to take a step back. This situation is forcing my hand."

*****

Sitting in the computer room on the second floor of his house, Dr. Beaumont was staring at the laptop screen where Caleb and Mars were arguing. "You're right," Beaumont said, pausing the video. "We can't go near their houses any more. Tarik is bunkered up with Bob, and Caleb is working with the cops."

Gaytan laughed shortly. "Funny the cops have no idea we bugged Caleb's house six months ago. Now this idiot just told us the cops' plan."

"We'll have to adapt." Beaumont nodded.

"What should we do?"

"I have a plan for Caleb, but that can wait." Beaumont rubbed his freshly shaved chin. "Time is on our side. In the meantime, we could muddy the waters."

Gaytan was tugging on his untamed beard. "How is that?"

"Rick, how many times do I have to tell you? Do not ask questions."

*****

Detective Reid turned on three computer screens. The glare of the bluish-white light highlighted the dank, musky basement he was currently holed-up in.

"Never thought I'd be happy to rent out a basement," he muttered as he took in the squatty room the police had rented — which just so happened to be next door to Caleb. He looked at his partner, Detective Ford. "Three shifts of two officers work from here every day. Same thing next to Bob's house. We'll catch this fuck."

"I'm glad Bob finally agreed to let us protect him," Detective Ford said. "He's lucky the intruder didn't kill him and Tarik when they were sleeping."

"That's not his M.O.," Reid said. "He tends to drug his victim and relocate them to somewhere he feels safe torturing them."

"If he knows we're watching, he'll probably try a distraction. A fire down the block or something."

"I want you to take every single person seriously who goes near that house." Reid touched one finger with another. "That means the mailman, UPS, the kid selling Girl Scout cookies. The pizza man. Everyone!"

"Don't worry, boss," Detective Ford said. "When he makes a move, we'll be ready."

Detective Reid nodded. "Hopefully he takes the bait."

"I'd like to put a bullet in belly." Ford clenched his fist. "Watch him bleed out."

"Don't talk like that." Reid shook his head. "It's bad form. But trust me, if he flinches, I *will* put him down."

"Maybe Caleb kills him." Ford offered a shrug. "The killer put him through a lot of grief."

"I'd congratulate him. He's got to be the only one who wants him dead more than us. Imagine the feeling of being framed, shammed, and then hunted."

"Hunt is being hunted," Ford said with a smirk.

Detective Reid snorted. "Sounds like the name of a book." He nodded. "But in all seriousness, it's up to us, to protect him. Maybe jail kept him alive."

"Maybe it was all just a distraction."

23

Derek Bane unscrewed his pool stick and shoved both pieces in a long black case. "I'm out, bro," he said, and then clasped hands with his partner in crime.

"What, you got some bitches waitin' for ya?" Sam Lugo asked, beer in hand.

"That's right, Sun." Bane smiled with a wink to follow.

Sam's lips stretched upward to show his teeth. "You ain't my daddy."

"That's not what yo mamma said." Bane laughed. "Nah, just kiddin', brother. I call you Sun... cuz you shine like one. Ain't nobody more loyal than you, dawg." They clasped hands and embraced each other briefly.

"I always thought you were bustin' balls."

"Nah, man. I bust other motha fuckers balls. You the only mother fucker I trust with my life."

"Right back at ya, brah. I got yo back one hundred percent."

"Hit me up tomorrow afternoon. I got some boulders of that blue meth comin' around the way. I need you to help me make some drops."

"For sho'."

Derek Bane strutted out the back door. "I'm gonna get some *pussy*," he sang to himself, pressing the unlock button on his key fob. The midnight blue BMW chirped, and the lights flashed twice. Marching across the parking lot, Derek was momentarily pulled out of his thoughts when he saw headlights splash over the dark alley.

Frowning, he glanced over his shoulder. A half-deserted, pot-hole-riddled side street, it was hardly ever used. A dark SUV was slowly rolling toward him. He turned back to his car.

Just as Bane reached for his door handle, an explosion of rapid gunfire dropped him to the ground, ducking for immediate cover. Laying prone between two cars, his jackhammering heart rose to his throat. Ear-piercing gunshots kept coming. Thud sounds of bullets shredding through metal proved close. Glass from his rear windows shattered and spilled shards on his clothes and neck.

His eyes were buzzing left and right, trying to find the best route to make it out alive.

When the gunfire stopped, he heard the roar of the engine taking off. He peeked over the hood of a vehicle and saw a Chevy Tahoe or Suburban peeling off down the alley. "You're fuckin dead, motha fucka!" His hands clenched as the red taillight streaks disappeared past the shadow of the next building. Jumping in the BMW, he ignited the M3 inline six-cylinder engine to a low hum.

Bane pulled a black handgun from the center console, racking the slide back before stuffing it in between his legs. His feet were on the clutch and brake. Popping his left foot, he mashed on the gas pedal. The fat rear-end tires spun and smoked on the damp pavement as the car whipped around in a half-circle. Stomping on the clutch, he slammed the shifter in second gear and pressed down on the gas as the car raced forward and half-sideways down the alley. A trail of dust and exhaust fumes was left behind.

"These mutt motha fuckas can't out run me," Bane barked. "I got the motha' fuckin' BM. They can't see me. I dodge bullets."

The BMW flew down the ally and stopped at the next intersection. Swiveling his head, Bane saw the SUV in the distance to his right. Zero to sixty in five engine screaming seconds brought his car to within fifty yards of the vehicle in question. Letting off the gas he tailed behind the only car between them.

"I'm gonna bust a cap in yo ass, bitch." Bane hopped in the right lane and drove through a green light, passed a gas station, and entered the roundabout that led to the huge bridge that connected Wisconsin and Minnesota over the bay of Lake Superior. "I'll wait till the middle of the bridge. Watch yo ass drive into the big lake." He laughed shortly, glancing at the short guard rail and the black void over the edge.

Bane took in a deep breath as his car cruised on the massive bridge at sixty miles per hour. The SUV was in the fast lane. No other cars around. Downshifting to third gear, the engine chirped and the car rolled parallel to the passenger side of the SUV. Two men were inside. The shaggy, bearded man in the passenger seat was cocking his head toward him with a low brow and tight lip. The driver was a silhouette in a ball cap.

Rolling the window down, Bane lifted the gun, his gaze jumping between the car beside him and the road. His finger pressing down on the trigger and then—

BAM! At that moment, Bane's body jerked in response to the SUV angling toward him in a full-on sideswipe. The crash sound of metal colliding made him flinch as the big SUV redirected his small car.

Slamming on the brakes, Bane sucked in air as the car hit the guardrail too fast. Wrong angle. His eyes bulge as momentum lifted up the car. "Oh, fuck! No, no..." He desperately tried to right the car, turn the wheel...but it was too late.

"FUCK!" Bane screamed at the top of his lungs, and the BMW tumbled one hundred twenty feet, splashing into a cold black Lake Superior.

*****

The gun store was dead that morning. Mars Sundean was the only customer in the establishment. Dressed in just a maroon V-neck t-shirt and dark gray yoga pants, she strode up to the display case and spotted a small black handgun. Leaning her forearm on the glass display case, she peered inside. Though she knew it'd put her cleavage on full view, Mars also knew sometimes that worked to her advantage.

A tall and muscular clerk sidled up to her as she leaned over the glass case. "Glock nine-millimeter," he said, offering a friendly smile.

Mars slowly stood upright, meeting eyes with the handsome man standing behind the counter with his dress shirt tucked into dark slacks. "Hi," she said, offering a slight smile. "How much?"

"Four fifty," he said in low baritone. "But I would suggest you take a look at this." He gently rested a different pistol on the glass case. "Glock 30. Same kick, more damage."

"Can I hold it?"

"Absolutely." His short brown buzz cut made him look like he was still in the military.

She gripped it with her fingers and then supported it with her left hand. Lowering the gun so it was aimed at the floor, she extended her arms then eased up, setting it on the glass. "Not bad."

"You still in the military?"

Mars regarded him. "No. Retired Air Force. How'd you know?"

"For one, that tattoo on your finger," he said. "I got the same one." He patted his beefy shoulder. "I'd show ya, but...." He offered her a crooked smile. "And two, I sell guns to ladies all day. None of them hold a gun like that. I can tell you had military training."

Mars returned the smile. "You're quite perceptive. Five seconds and you know my life story."

"Someday," he said. "But for now, I just want to help you find the right gun."

"Perfect. What else you got?"

"What exactly do you need it for?"

She looked away. "Home protection."

"I figured that. But, are you preparing for the worst, or do you have a specific threat?"

"Well, um, I'm kinda involved," she said, noticing a slight frown forming on his face, "with one of the guys who got a box in the mail. You know, from the serial killer?"

"Damn, yeah, I heard about that." He nodded. "Saw it on the news. That's horrible."

"Yeah, kinda scary. I was there when he found the box."

"What's his name?"

"I'd rather not say. It didn't work out. Had to cut ties. I didn't feel safe around him. Like I was waiting to die."

The sales person's eyebrows hitched upward. "Scary times. I hope you stay safe."

"Uh, yeah. I-I think I'll be all right. I have twenty years of military experience. And I'm about to get a badass gun, right?"

"The gun will help," he said, sliding forward a business card. "But if you *ever* feel like you're in trouble, don't be afraid to shout. I was in the Air Force, too. I want to help, in any way." He looked up and met her light green eyes. He saw a woman with a hint of a smile.

The intimacy of their shared look was broken by the chime of the door opening. A big grizzly man with a ponytail walked in and looked around. Little did they know it was a dangerous man by the name of Richard Gaytan.

"I'll be with ya in a minute, sir." The clerk gave a wave to the rather large customer and then snapped his head directly back to Mars.

Mars nodded. "That's awfully nice of you." She picked up the card and gave it a glance. "Thanks, Andy. I appreciate it."

"No prob." He smiled. "Ya know, I'm not a perv or anything, but I think you're super cute." He flashed a quick smile. "I welcome a conversation... if you ever want to chat."

"I'll just take the Glock 30 and some ammo," she said. "But um, I might consider the chat in the future. My heart is somewhere else right now."

*****

Detective Ford glanced at his watch at the same moment he heard the basement door open. Looking up he found Detective Reid at the door. "Just in time for the switch."

"Seven a.m. tomorrow," Reid said, eyes glued to the row of computer screens that displayed cameras at the homes belonging to Caleb, Bob, and Tarik.

"Sounds good." Ford smiled. "I'll bring some Hardee's bacon egg and cheese biscuits."

Reid nodded in agreement. "That works for me."

"Perfect."

"I don't think you'll get any complaint from the new guy either."

"Where is he? Is he late?"

"No, he's upstairs taking a leak."

Ford nodded. "All right, well, I better hit the road."

Reid shook his hand firmly. "Don't hit it too hard." He flashed a smile.

Ford turned and walked up the basement steps, which led him to the kitchen. Once there, he used the back door and headed out into the chilly night air. The shift was over. Now he could go home and spend some quality time with his wife. By the time he got there, his kids would be sleeping and dreaming about school, and he could have some alone, adult time with his wife. She'll be wearing that black silk nighty she only wore one time every year: their anniversary.

Fumbling with his keys, Detective Ford paused on the fantasy of his wife in bed to surveil the dark driveway and street. Nothing but blackness and parked cars and trees. Wind whistling in his ears. Fast steps. Right hand thumbing his key fob. The locks on the car clunked. Its lights flashed. His hand was on the door handle.

The sound of an engine cranking over made him flinch. Looking up, he didn't see any lights, so he turned toward the idling vehicle up the street. The rusty Ford pick-up truck crept out from its parking spot and flashed its lights on, creating a sudden spark of adrenaline in his chest. Instinctively, he blocked out the bright high-beam lights with the palm of his hand. He could hear tires on the gravel slowly rolling toward him. Then the truck brakes squeaked to a stop.

"What the...." Detective Ford muttered, and then the truck suddenly shot forward, the action creating an explosion of torque and exhaust fumes.

Reaching for his gun was a sudden reflex to a truck barreling toward him. Panic set in Detective Ford's eyes as the truck boomed forward. He squeezed off two shots that shattered the windshield. Sucking in a sharp breath of fear, he felt the full impact of the four-thousand-pound hunk of metal, crushing his flesh and bone, pinning it against the car.

The sound of metal scaping against metal and squealing tires left a pulp of a man on the tarmac. Smoke was rising from the smashed-up car. Steam was rising from the decorated officer of the law. The truck was gone with the chilled wind.

Detective Ford could hear the screams of his men getting closer. It gave him hope that they could get him to a hospital fast enough because he was definitely alive. No pain. No sight. No feeling. No ability to move or speak. But he could hear his fellow officers coming to help him. To be there for him.

*****

Mars stepped out of the shower and reached for her towel. She frowned as she looked at herself in the mirror, thinking of that card Andy gave her.

"He was cute, too. But it doesn't matter. Because Caleb is the one I want. Stupid, stupid Caleb," she muttered as she wrapped the towel around her chest, tucking one corner into the side.

Head down, Mars moped into her bedroom, heartsick and hurting. She finished drying off, and then dropped the towel on the carpet next to the bed, her eyes falling on a pair of white lace panties resting on her comforter. Snatching up the underwear, she stepped into them nicely before putting on a sports bra. Out of the corner of her eye, she saw the black handle of her new Glock 30 handgun resting beneath her pillow for home protection. Just in case.

It was loaded. Ready. All she had to do was press the safety button and pull the trigger. "Stop," Mars said to herself, pushing the negative thoughts out of her head. "You're safer here than—"

She turned at a sound coming from the closet. Taking a tentative step toward it, she glanced back at the Glock under her pillow. When she turned back, she found a large bearded man standing there. Bat in hand.

Her eyes widened as she stumbled backward—but she was too late. In two fast steps, he lunged at her, the bat raised and already swinging in his hand.

She cried, her heart riveting against her ribcage as she tried to duck, to swerve out of his way. "No!" She screamed as the man brought it down against her knee.

Mars went down with groan. Covering her head with both hands from the incoming blow. It worked. Her forearm took the brunt of it and she shrieked in response.

"Shut the fuck up, bitch!" The man was hovering over her. "I'll crack your fucking skull."

"Okay. Okay," Mars said, in a high-pitched desperate squeal. The sharp pain of fear and adrenaline was making her body quake. Fast breaths in and out. Teeth clattering on teeth.

"Get some fucking clothes on," he belted out. "Stupid slut. You're coming with me."

She winced in pain. Rolled on her butt. "I-I can't get up. You fucked up my knee." Her breasts were quite exposed in just a flesh-colored sports bra.

The big man gripped his gloved hand underneath her bare armpit and lifted her to her feet. "Get dressed." His voice was a low growl. An ominous order. "You have one minute."

Limping to her dresser, she stepped into a pair of black yoga pants and slipped into a white V-neck t-shirt. "Y-you're the serial killer... right?" She threw on a gray hooded sweatshirt with a pounding heart underneath. "W-what did I do to you?" The longer she kept him talking, the greater chance she might have to grab the gun.

"No more questions." The man leaned on the bat like it was a cane. "You're gonna drive Blake's car. You try anything, I'll beat you to a pulp."

"What the fuck is that?" She squeaked, her hand pointing to the empty doorway behind Gaytan. "It's Caleb!"

He instinctively looked over his shoulder.

Mars dove on the bed and grabbed her Glock 30 handgun. But before she could press the safety button and aim, Gaytan was on her like a wild bear in the wilderness. No one could hear her screams when he raised his fist high above her face, swinging down.

*****

In the ICU the next morning, Detective Reid was holding onto his friend's hand tightly. The rest of Detective Jerome Ford's body and head was bandaged. Tubes were protruding from his mouth. The sustained beeping Reid heard was the only proof of life. Because of Ford's vegetative state, the family had decided to pull the plug.

"Goodbye, Detective Ford," Reid said, choking back tears, his hand wiping under his eye impatiently as he tried to steady his voice. "It was an honor to watch you rise in the police department. You became a great detective. Five years by my side. I couldn't ask for a better partner." The dam burst and the tears flowed. He stood up, grabbing a tissue to dry his eyes. "Fuck. I'm gonna get this guy. Just like you wanted to do. A bullet in the belly. Maybe two. I owe you that, Ford."

Detective Reid stood looking down on Ford's sleeping body, thinking about the stubborn decisions he made leading up to the truck attack. "It's all my fault. I've never been so sure about a suspect. I've never been so wrong."

*****

Later in the afternoon, Detective Reid was answering questions in Derek Bane's gray-haired mother's kitchen. "No, the plates came back as stolen," he said, a large yellow envelope clamped in his hand. "I'm sorry. No leads on the suspects either."

"My only son got murdered three days ago," Dana Bane said coldly. "You told me you'd have answers. And you don't have shit."

"Ma'am, we've been preoccupied," Reid said sternly. "There was an attack on one of my men last night. My partner died as a result of the injuries." He let out a heavy breath. "On top of that, there was another homicide at a gun store parking lot. This town is going to hell."

"Well, excuse me." Dana shook her head. "I didn't know. I'm sorry. Just trying to find out who killed my Derek." Her voice cracked. "I just don't understand, why are people so wicked?"

"People been asking that question since the beginning of time." Reid handed her a large envelope. "Here's some surveillance pictures from the pool hall and the bridge. It shows the suspects in a Chevy Suburban just before the attack on your son. I don't think this was random. You might be able to ID the suspects. One has a beard." He withheld the fact that one of the men resembled the perpetrator on Bob Sturgis' grainy surveillance video.

Dana pulled the pictures out of the packet and held them in her shaky fingers for a long moment. "I don't recognize them. It's too blurry." She dropped the photos on the table, her dark eyes bursting with tears, the mascara streaking down her cheeks.

Detective Reid nodded. "What about his friends," he said. "Can I have a list? They might be the key to identifying the killers."

"Call Sam Lugo." She wiped her tears with her fingers. "He's Derek's only true friend."

"Thank you, Ms. Bane," he said. "I know this is hard. Trust me. I'm determined to find his killer before he hurts anyone else."

"Please, Detective," she said, her bottom lip trembling over the word. "Find the person who did this to my son." Her hands clenched as she stared at the detective standing in front of her. "I can't...I won't sleep until you do." She sniffled, her hand lifting to cover her face.

"I give you my word." Detective Reid lowered his tone. "I *will* bring your son's killers to justice." Reaching out his arm, he gently touched her shoulder before turning to the door.

24

Amnicon River, Wisconsin
June 17, 2004

Caleb and Mars hiked up a wooded trail under a low red sun. He was following her lead. She walked at a fast pace. Ungluing his eyes from Mars' soccer shorts, he shifted his head to the right where a narrow point in the river was calm and shallow. Boulders of all shapes and sizes were scattered about the rusty waterway.

Mars stopped and turned to face him in a white peace symbol T-shirt. "So, why do you hang out with all the bad boys?"

"Why do you hang out with Nicole and the bad girl club?" Caleb shrugged.

Mars smirked. "Nicole is not bad," she said, her eyebrows pinching together. "She's not a gangster like Derek Bane. I'm serious. I'm not judging you. I just want to know who you are. Are you a gangster? Or are you Mr. Nice Guy?"

"Nicole's not a gangster, but she ain't that innocent."

"You avoided my question."

"Nicole is into a lot worse shit than I'm up to. She makes me look like a choir boy."

"What do you mean by that?"

"I just hear she gets around." He pursed his lips. "And she did coke a few times. Other things."

Mars' eyes narrowed. "What?" She cried. "Who told you that?"

"It's not my place to say. I'm sorry, I shouldn't have said that."

"She's been with Lee since ninth grade. And he thinks he's a little gangster, too. Just like you and Bane and that Tarik kid."

"Let's get this straight," Caleb said, shaking his head. "I am not a gangster. I don't want to be a gangster. I don't approve of the stuff that those guys do." His hands spread apart. "I'm just a mean hockey player with some wild friends. So what?" His eyebrows lifted into an arch. "We've all been friends for years. It's called loyalty. We feel stronger as a team, you know what I'm saying? We trust each other. There's a lot of trouble makers in school, and no one messes with us cuz...."

"Cuz what? What are you going to do?"

"Mars, come on, we just got each other's back. You know?"

"What about that Lerch kid? I saw you and your *team* kicking him down the hall. Dropping his books and shit. That wasn't very nice."

"Correction, you saw my friends kicking him down the hall."

"What's the difference? I saw you there just the same."

"I've never touched the kid. That's the difference. That's what I'm telling you, Mars. I'm not like those guys. I'm different."

Mars cracked a smile. "Lerch was in my choir class," she said. "The kid is weird, but no one should get tormented like that. It's childish."

"Whatever."

Mars shoved him. "Leave the kid alone." Playfully, she pushed him harder. "How would you like it if someone bigger came and pushed you down the ledge?"

"Shit, you're coming with me," Caleb said, grabbing her arm, pulling her down a path that led to the river.

"Where are you taking me?" Mars asked. "There's nothing down there."

"Paradise." Caleb's lips stretched across his face, and then he wrapped his arm around her shoulder, pointing to the rocky river bed. It was a low part of the river. Only a few feet of water but the current was fast enough to take a small child.

"Where?" Mars twisted her head.

"Don't you see what I see?" Caleb gazed off to the center of the stream where a large flat boulder parted the water.

"What, the tiny island?"

"The Island of Mars," Caleb said. "Let's conquer it! You could be the queen. I'll be your loyal subject."

Mars flashed a smile. "How are we going to get over there?"

Pointing to the satellites of the big rock, he helped her to open her eyes and see what she couldn't see before. "You don't see the three rocks? It's a hop, skip, and a jump."

"Like a frog?"

"Exactly! Let's go. It will be fun."

"Okay, you lead the way."

Caleb leaped to the first boulder and turned back. "Come on."

She bent her knees but held back. "That's too far. I can't do it."

"Never say can't."

Mars crept up to the water's edge. Bent her knees further. "I can't"

"Fine. The island just got renamed." He smiled. "Hunt Royal." He laughed, and then hopped to the next rock.

Mars shook her head. "Wait!" She took two big steps and then jumped onto the small boulder. Staggered. Arms out.

When she regained her balance, she giggled and met eyes with Caleb who had his arm extended. Handsome smile.

She leaped to boulder number two and stumbled into Caleb's arms. She giggled and he joined her. Together, they stretched out in the air and landed on her tiny island in the center of the muddy waters.

"You made it!"

"I wasn't going to let you conquer my island without a fight."

Caleb's arms were wrapped around her waist. Eyes locked with hers. "The island is yours, but you... are mine." The space between them closed and their lips were one. Caleb's body was buzzing with adrenaline as he tightened his grip.

With water flowing around them, they molded together with their eyes closed, passionately kissing each other with no reason to stop.

Mars broke her lips free and released a soft gasp. Caleb kissed her neck softly and relocated his hands.

"Woah," Mars said, removing his hand from underneath her shirt. "That's a little too fast for my liking."

Caleb showed her the palms of his hands. "I'm sorry." His head was shaking slowly. "I-I thought we were having a moment."

"We were." She smiled and moved in for a peck on the lips. "You ruined it." She giggled. "Just kidding. But gosh, someone could be watching us."

His head swiveled both ways. "So, I'm not in trouble?"

"Caleb, this is the most beautiful moment of my life. Just shut up and kiss me."

25

Two Harbors, Minnesota
May 24, 2026

In a cold cinder block basement, Mars Sundean was trembling on an ancient workbench. She was fully restrained with a small man in a white lab coat hovering above her. A large bearded man was lurking behind him.

"Do you remember me, Mars?" The man was standing next to the bench, peering down on her scrunched-up little face and bruised puffy eyes.

Mars' jaw was quivering. "I-I met you at the reunion." The tears were streaming down each side of her face. "Y-you're Dr. Beaumont, right?"

"That's not where you met me, Mars," he said slowly. "You met me in seventh grade. We were in the same choir class. You were nice to me that year. I thought we were friends. But after that year, I became chopped liver."

"I don't remember." Her head shook. "I'm sorry."

"Your boyfriend's crew picked on me." Dr. Beaumont's upper lip curled enough to reveal his pearly white false teeth. "You don't remember how they tormented me every day?" He stomped his foot.

With fast breaths, Mars studied the man above her. Squinting, she pictured this clean-cut man with dirty clothes, yellow teeth, zits on his face, and a greasy black mullet. The memories flooded into her mind. She could see everyone pointing. She could hear everyone laughing. "Lerch?"

"Bingo."

She was breathing raggedly. "It's not fair. What they did to you. No one should ever have to go through that."

"Then why didn't you stop it?"

"I tried." As she shook her head, the canvas strap scratched on her neck like coarse sand paper. "But I was young, scared. Just trying to fit in. I didn't want to be a snitch. It's human instinct."

Dr. Beaumont turned for the nearest wall where another work bench rested with tools and potential weapons. Up against the wall was his three-tier samurai sword rack. Reaching for the smallest sword on the top, he gripped it tight in his hands. He had a few memories with the long sword. Only dreams with the short dagger.

Spinning back to face Mars, Beaumont strutted toward her. He could feel her eyes burning a hole in his skull. "Wrong answer, Mars. Just the wrong words. Human instinct... should be to help. To stop it. To tell a teacher."

"W-why didn't you tell someone?" Her eyes were on the foot-long sword.

"I did tell someone. And guess what that got me?"

"What?" she asked with a soft raspy tone. Talking was good. She needed time.

Dr. Beaumont pursed his lips. "It got me a real thumping." He let out a loud sigh and looked down on her. "My dad told me I was weak and stupid. And I didn't like that very much."

"But you're not stupid, you're a doctor." She looked him in the eye. "You're not weak, you killed two men."

"Correction. I killed five men recently." Beaumont barked out a short laugh. "I forgot to tell you... I just shot your new friend from the gun store. What's his name? Andy? Was it? I forgot."

"What?" she cried. "No! Why?"

"To soften you up for what's coming."

"What do you mean?" Mars' eyes were wide and panicky.

"First things first." Beaumont dropped his hand on her wrist and gripped it tight. "Let me tell you something you don't know about me. I've been killing for a long time." His eyes looked up. Widened. A brief smile appeared on his blushing face.

"I remember when you disappeared," Mars said. "Everyone thought you switched schools." Her mind was cranking. Twisting. Searching for a way out. A pardon. A moment of weakness. Sympathy.

"I completed high school at an asylum for the criminally ill." Beaumont offered a short smile then continued. "They pumped me with a lot of drugs, but I still got my diploma. And then, I was exonerated for the murder of my father. I won a settlement for false incarceration. So, I went to college. I joined the National Guard. I went to war in Afghanistan. And then I died." He lifted two air quotes with his fingers before he continued. "In a horrible attack on my unit." He winked at her. "I'm dead, Mars. And you're gonna be dead, too. But first, I need to lure your boyfriend to the slaughter."

"I'll never do it. Just kill me."

"Oh, Mars, I will in time." He twitched his finger and clicked his tongue several times. "Trust me, your screams will soon belong to me. But first, you *will* lure him." He smiled. "With your pinky finger." His gaze lowered to her clenched hand. "The one with the tattoo."

Mars' eyes exploded. "No! Please." She was blinking rapidly, eyes shifting back and forth.

The big man came forward. "Don't fight it."

Her jaw began to quiver. "Please, don't do it."

Gaytan held her left hand still on the work bench. He pried open her fingers and pinned her hand flat on the wood desk. "Do it."

"NO!" Mars was bucking her restraints, making amputation impossible no matter how strong Gaytan was.

Lerch poked her in the neck with the dagger. "Finger or throat? You have three seconds to decide."

"Fuck you! You need me!"

"Mars, I could slit your throat and still send Caleb your pinky. He's so gullible, he'll do anything to get next to you."

"Please. Stop."

"Two."

"NO!"

"Three." Lerch increased the pressure on her neck.

"Fine!" Mars shrieked with spittle shooting from her mouth. "Take my fucking finger you piece of fucking shit!" Her fist was still clenched.

"Now, now," Dr. Beaumont said, bringing a hand up to her cheek. "Just the pinky. Come on now, stick it out," he said, his hand patting her cheek. Once. Twice.

The third time, he slapped her hard.

She complied, but her finger had a slight tremor.

Bringing the dagger above the table, Beaumont slowly pressed the blade on the finger in question. Mars spit in his face.

"Bad move, bitch." Beaumont wiped off the spit with his hand. Rubbed it off on his black pants. Glancing at Gayton, he saw a smirk on his subordinate's bearded face. "Okay, that's it. Go get the Succinylcholine."

"What the fuck is that?" Mars barked aggressively.

"Let's just say, when you wake up, you won't know what day it is."

26

In the back row of history class, Blake handed Caleb a small squirt gun under the desk.

"What?" Caleb whispered. Everyone else in the class had their head buried in a textbook, reading the assigned chapter as dictated by the gray-haired teacher. She was busy at her desk correcting the weekly pop quizzes.

Blake pointed at Lerch Black who was sitting directly in front of Caleb. "Do it," he said with a hushed voice. "Right in the neck."

Caleb shook his head. "I'm straight."

"Quit being a little pussy. Blast that dirtball."

"What do I gain from—"

"Caleb!" Ms. Sanger snipped. "Did you already finish reading?"

"Uh... yeah. I'm done."

The hefty teacher stood up in a tent dress. "So, you won't have a problem explaining to the class... your opinion of the League of Nations?"

"Uh, no, ma'am." Caleb took a breath. "The League of Nations was a failed attempt at a one- world government."

"That's an interesting way to sum it up." Her voice lowered. "I think you should quit talking with Blake and read it again."

Caleb tucked his chin. Eyes now on the pages.

The teacher sat down at her desk and picked up her pen.

Blake was snickering. "Do it." His words were softer than a whisper.

Caleb lowered his hand below the desk top. He gave him the middle finger.

Blake hit his arm. "Fine, give it back."

Caleb handed him the squirt gun under the table.

Blake opened his mouth and squirted some water inside. He then turned it on Lerch Black. With the squirt gun tilted sideways like a gangster, his eyebrows lowered. Squeezing the trigger, a line of cold water blasted Lerch in the back of his flinching mullet and shoulders. Blake squeezed the trigger a few more times and then hid the gun under his oversized hooded sweatshirt.

Lerch's shoulders jerked upward, his head craning to face Caleb. "Stop it," he said softly but angrily. He was sporting a peach fuzz mustache and a gnarly outbreak of acne all over his face.

Caleb's brow lowered, his head shifting to glare at Blake.

When Lerch straightened himself back in his seat, Blake hit him with another stream of water. Immediately, Blake hid his face in his folded arms on the desk and tried to contain his laughter.

"I said stop!" Lerch popped out of his desk and screamed. "Leave me alone!" He tipped over his desk and raised two fists in the air. A psychotic roar emanated from his lips.

The room full of kids whooshed to a standstill. All eyes were glancing up, their bodies stiffening in shocked reaction. Every single kid in class was staring at Lerch Black and his beet- red face. Caleb was frozen with wide eyes. Blake was choking down his uncontainable laughter.

As Lerch approached Caleb with clenched fists, the Ms. Sanger hollered. "Lerch, settle down." She grabbed him by the back of the neck and escorted him to the principal's office. He did not resist her but he did twist his neck to stare down Caleb.

"He thought it was you, dawgy." Blake playfully hit Caleb in the shoulder.

"That dude's gonna snap someday."
*****
Lerch got sent home early that afternoon. He was now sitting on a chair in his bedroom, sharpening his samurai sword, thinking of how he could get away with murder. His cat jumped up on his lap. Tried to knead his arm. "Get away from me, Void!" He threw the cat across the room but it landed on its feet, pranced right back, and looked up at him.

"Meow."

"I'm busy. I'll play with you later."

"Meow. Meow."

"Shut up! Or else."

Void tried to jump on his lap, clawing into his leg. "Meow."

"That's it, you stupid cat." Lerch rose to his feet, looking downward. "I warned you. I had a really bad day." He grabbed the purring little cat and stuffed him in the bag-lined trash can. Twisting the bag, he poked an air hole so he could think of his next three steps. With a blank, almost hypnotic stare, a few moments passed before his eyes landed on his closet. It was filled with tacky colorful clothes his mom got from the thrift store. He didn't like any color. That's why he always wore black.

The cat cried and even hissed from inside the bag. It's nails were poking through the plastic as it swayed like pendulum in the troubled youth's hands.

Letting out a breath, Lerch strode over to the closet. "This will do," he said, grabbing an ugly orange sweater that his mom had been harping on him to wear. With the lump of cat in the bag crying, he wrapped it up in the sweater to muffle the sound from his mom. He then cradled it in his arms.

Breathing heavily, he felt sharp claws digging into his skin. He squeezed the sweater fiercely. "You want to cut me?"

The cat was screeching and thrashing. Her voice was muffled. Silenced but not silent. "Hmm," He stormed out the bedroom door, through the dining room, and made it to the kitchen when his mom questioned him from the sink with the hot water running as she did the dishes barefoot and a little bit pregnant.

"Lerch!" she snipped with her neck craning to face him. "Where do you think you're going?"

He nervously twisted back with the sweatshirt in his arms. The look on her face told him she knew what he was about to do. He had to make up a story. "I'm heading over to my friend's house," he said, eyes shifting to the left. "I need help studying for my history test tomorrow."

"Dinner's ready in an hour," she said. "Hot dogs and crawfish."

"I'll just eat over there." The cat's hooked claws were digging into his arms. As the muffled hiss turned into a low growl, Lerch turned to the door with a racing heart and the frantic urge to flee before he got caught.

"Lerch!" She cried. "Don't you turn your back on me, boy."

With fear of her telling his dad, he glanced back to look at his mom.

"You know what dad will do if you're not here for dinner."

"Fine, I'll be back." He opened the back door and slammed it shut while his mom was still speaking. From his back stoop, he marched to the pot-hole-riddled alley. Turning up the sidewalk, he climbed the avenue all the way to the twelfth street bridge in the middle of the city. A monstrosity of concrete arching over the jagged chasm in the earth.

Following the sidewalk on the bridge, he watched cars speed past him. Toward the center of the bridge, he slowed down and came to a stop. Turning to look over the black iron barrier, he saw the rocky creek flowing one hundred feet beneath him. The friction of the warm air pressing his shirt against his body, made him feel alive. Not as much as the sharp nails gouging his skin.

He looked at the resistance as a warning not to do it. The strained cry from his cat. The nails, the wind. His mom. The steep hill.

"Ooouch!" Lerch cried. Gripping a handful of the sweater, he shook it violently. "You cut the shit out of me. Now I have to go to school with bruises *and* scratches. Give 'em one more thing to tease me about."

Lerch looked over the ledge and his heart sped up. Peering down, he saw rocks and white rapids. Endless evergreen trees. Two people walking dogs on the trail. Graffiti.

Maybe I should just jump.

*****

Saturday night, Caleb Hunt was looking in the mirror, the muffled music of the school dance just breaking through the bathroom walls. He saw himself in his best form: A rented black-on-black tuxedo and short cropped gel-parted hair. "Go out there," he whispered to himself. "Take her hand, give her the last dance. And then she's yours." He grabbed a few paper towels, dried his hands, and then tossed them in the trash can before swinging open the door.

Exiting the bathroom, he winced; the pop music blasted in his ears as he stepped into the ballroom. Scores of classmates were on the dance floor. After a quick scan, he found Mars like a beacon in the dark. Her dark auburn hair signaled him from across the way. Her tight red dress and a plunging neckline reeled him in. She was all he saw. Smiling at the beauty that would soon belong to him, he slowed down to a halt as his vision expanded. "What the...."

Caleb's steps faltered at the sight of Mars standing in the shadow of the quarterback on the football team. *They're just talking*, he thought, trying to gauge her reaction as she smiled up at the tall athlete. The song switched and Caleb's heart sank at the same time.

U2 - *I can't live, with or without you* began playing.

Caleb took a few steps toward Mars, only to stop again when the muscular football player took her by the hand and led her to the dance floor. *What the fuck?*

His right fist clenched in his pocket. He walked closer and observed from twenty feet. They were dancing close. Rocking back and forth. The quarterback's hands were low on her hips. Too low. When the hands groped lower, Caleb shook his head and stormed out of the ballroom. He drove home in his mom's rusty Jeep Cherokee. Lead foot all the way across town.

*****

When Mars got home from the dance, the first thing she did was call Caleb. The line rang five times, and then she hung up. Sniffled. Looked in the mirror at her messed-up make-up from the teary ride home from the dance.

The sudden ringing of the phone caused her heart to speed up. She looked at the Caller ID and breathed out a sigh of relief as her thumb poked the talked button. "Caleb, why the hell did you leave me stranded at the dance?" She sniffled. "My dad had to come get me. He was not impressed."

"I left when I saw Mr. Football grabbing your ass," Caleb said. "Thanks. It felt like a dagger in my back."

Mars felt a sharp sting in her chest. "You actually think I let him?" she said, her voice cracking. "Caleb, that dude is an asshole. I didn't want that. You must have left before I smacked him in the face. Cussed him out in front of everyone."

"Yeah, right," Caleb said. "Why were you dancing with him in the first place?"

"Um, because my date was nowhere to be found." Her hand was on her hip. "And because he asked me. I thought he was a friend. Just a quick dance. Now I know how much of a perv he is."

"So, you turn it on me? It's my fault?"

"No, just saying, you seem to be my best friend on the phone and when it's just me and you. But you clam up in public. You act like you barely even know me. You're my date and—"

"I'm sorry," Caleb said. "I don't know what's wrong with me. I'm shy. I have anxiety in public. It's nothing about you. I'm crazy about you, Mars. That's what matters."

"Well, that's good to know," she said. "But you're too late."

"What do you mean? Is there someone else?"

"No, dummy. My dad got a promotion in the Air Force. We're moving to Germany. Monday."

"What? No way. When did you know about this?"

Mars let out a heavy sigh. "Two weeks ago."

"Two weeks!" Caleb's tone sharpened to a high pitch. "Holy shit. Why am I just hearing about this now?"

"I couldn't bring myself to tell you." Mars wiped her nose. "I really do care about you, Caleb. My heart is breaking right now. That's why I called. I need to see you again." She sniffled.

"This is a lot to take in, right now," Caleb said, pausing to clear his scratchy throat. When he continued, he did so with a strained voice. "You're moving to Germany? How long?"

"Years. He's forcing me into military college. And then probably the Air Force so I can be under his thumb."

"Why don't you just say no?"

"I did. What, do you want me to run away?"

"No, but when you turn eighteen you can do what you want. Come back home. To me."

"It's not that easy. My parents said they'd disown me. Cut me off."

"Money? That's what this is all about?"

Mars let out a breathy short laugh. "Yeah. How am I going to survive?"

"I have no money. How am I gonna survive?"

"That's different." Mars stomped her foot. "I'm not as independent as you. Look, do you want to see me on Monday? Or not?"

"Why not tomorrow? All day."

"Tomorrow, I have to help my parents pack the house in a shipping container. I just don't think they'll let me go anywhere."

"Okay. Monday. I'll skip school. Just tell me where to be and I'll be there."

Mars smiled. "Lunch break," she said. "I'll pick you up in front. I'll have my mom's Lexus.

"I'll have my bells on."

On Monday morning before third-hour class, Caleb strutted past Denzel the security guard in the empty hallway. His hat was in his hand. His full backpack was slipping off his shoulder as he nodded to the bouncer. "What's up, Denzel?"

"You." Denzel folded his arms across his bulky chest. "You up fo' detention. You late. Third time this week." He shook his head.

Caleb stopped with a shrug. "Sorry, I still got to stop in the men's room. I am going to class though. Getting good grades."

"You better hurry up, boy. I don't wanna write you up. I will though. One more time. That's it. Last warning."

"Thanks. It won't happen again." Caleb kept walking toward the bathroom. When he opened the door, he heard boys speaking a different language. Upon entering, he saw three short Asian kids with baggy clothes and slicked black hair. Hard, stone-like faces.

"Hey, guys," Caleb said with a nod, and then stepped toward the corner urinal. Unzipping his fly, he listened to the young men speak to each other in fast Korean. One of them laughed.

Out of his peripheral vision, Caleb saw the biggest one looking right at him as he spoke. In response, the other kids flicked a glance his way before responding in laughter. Caleb didn't understand a word, but the laughter bothered him until he zipped up his pants. Turning on his heel, he made a line to the sink.

The laughing continued with sharp words that seemed to be aimed at him. Listening closely, his eyes narrowed with frustration. With a rumble in his throat, his head rolled toward them. "What's so funny?" Caleb asked as he rinsed off his soapy hands in the lukewarm water.

"You white boys think you *so* tough," The shortest of the Asian kids said in broken English. "You have no idea... what we capable of."

"I ain't got no beef with you, Kong," Caleb said with a half shrug while staring directly into Kong Zang's dark eyes. "We were always cool in gym class, right?"

"Yeah, we coo." Kong nodded a few times. "But we ain't coo with Blake or Bane. Any of them punks."

"Anything ever happens to Blake, you'll have to answer to me." Caleb tapped his chest.

Kong laughed. "Ya'll niggaz don't spit bullets like we do."

"Is that a threat?" Caleb took a step forward.

"Na, nigga, dat's a fact." He lifted his shirt, reveling the handle of a black pistol in his waistline. "You better watch yo back, sucka."

"Fuck you, Kong." Caleb spread apart his arms, nervously shifting his eyes to the other two potential threats in the room. "You ain't gonna do shit. I've known you since seventh grade when you barely spoke any English. I was the one dude who treated you with respect. You forget about that?"

Kong pulled the gun out and cocked it. Let it hang at his side. "That was then." He lifted his chin proudly. "This is now. Nobody talks to me like that." He gestured with his head. "Show dis white boy how we get down."

Caleb watched Kong's sidekick whip out a switchblade. Adrenaline shot threw his veins. Before he could react, the kid lunged forward and Caleb sidestepped the blade. With his right hand, Caleb thew a hard punch at the kid's jaw, dropping him to the nasty floor.

Caleb descended on him, pounding the side of his face and ear repetitively. Pulling his arm back for the knockout blow, he winced from a penetrating sting of something hitting his flesh. His back stiffened before jerking around with a gurgling scream that ripped across the air as he turned on instinct. Charging forward, he tackled the second attacker.

"Mother fucker!" Caleb climbed on top in a full-on mount, exploding his nose with a right blow. Before he could hit him again, a thunderous gunshot exploded from behind him, the concussion of the bullet tearing through his back and propelling him to the floor. Blood was spilling from his wound. He couldn't move. There was ringing in his ears. His vision fading to black.

Kong angled the smoking Glock 9mm handgun downward. "You fucked up, Caleb."

The bathroom door swung open, and Denzel stepped inside. "Drop the gun!"

Kong Zang was hovering over Caleb with the snub-nose pistol two feet from his face. His head shifted to face Denzel.

"Don't shoot!" Denzel barked. "Aim the gun at me. Kong? It's okay. It's over."

Kong turned the gun on Denzel. "Okay," he said under his breath. His lip curled up just a little bit. "I ain't going to jail. Step aside."

"Everything's gonna be okay, Kong. Drop the gun. Don't make it any worse."

Kong's arm was extended, the gun tilted sideways and shaking. "Step aside or die."

"Just put the gun on the floor." Denzel took a slow step forward.

Three loud clacks from the gun dropped Denzel. Looking down, Kong saw his two cousins laying still next to Caleb. "Get up!" he said but they didn't budge. "Fuck. *Fuck!*" He screamed something in Korean, and then he ran out the door.

Two liaison officers were standing in the hallway. Guns drawn. "Drop the fucking gun!"

*****

At noon, Mars pulled into the Lincoln High school parking lot and saw countless cop cars and clusters of officers congregating in front of the school. Her wide, panicked eyes overlooked the female officer flagging her away. Bringing the car to a stop, she rolled the window down with an elevated heartbeat. "Hey, what's going on here?"

"There was a shooting," the officer said. "The school has been evacuated. Turn around and wait for instructions from the school."

"Who was it?"

"Three critically injured." She swiped her hand. "We don't have any further information. Keep it moving."

Mars nodded and turned to exit, slamming her hand on the steering wheel repetitively. "My God. Who could it be? I hope they're okay."

She drove down the S-curved road and merged with traffic on the busiest street in town. Hands tightened on the wheel, Mars drove blindly forward. With no destination in mind, she let her thoughts churn: what the hell had happened at school? Was Caleb safe? Nicole?

Tears burned in her eyes. Something bad had happened. She could taste it.

Mars drove around the area of the school a few times just in case Caleb might be walking. "It couldn't be him." Mars kept driving up and down every road near the school. With no results, she pulled into a gas station and parked. She sucked in a heavy breath and let it out.

Pulling out her cellphone, she scrolled through the call log until she found Caleb. Just as she was about to hit the call button, the phone vibrated and rang. A jolt of adrenaline shook her as she read the screen. It said: Mom, but she was hoping it said Caleb.

Upon answering it, her voice whimpered. "Hello."

"Mars," her mom said. "The plane leaves in an hour. Get your ass home, right now."

"But—"

"No buts." Mom's voice raised. "Just get home."

The phone clicked.

*****

Two days later, Caleb was sitting in an elevated hospital bed with his eyes closed. Blake Connor walked in the door with a box of pastries. Derek Bane followed and he quietly shut the door behind them. The noise snapped Caleb's eyes open.

"Caleb," Blake said with a soft tone and raised eyebrows. "My mom made you some cannoli." Setting the small box of pastries on his food tray, he reached out an arm and squeezed Caleb's shoulder.

"Thanks," Caleb said with a faint, shaky voice. "Tell her I'm gonna be okay." His head nodded confidently.

"You're one tough mother fucker," Bane said. "I heard you beat down five dudes with knives. Then Kong's bitch ass shot you in the back."

"Yeah, I got lucky," Caleb said, turning his head to face Blake. "I heard Denzel got it worse?"

Blake looked down and then picked his head up with a blowing sigh. "Yeah, I guess he's in bad shape, bro. Three shots to the chest. He's still alive though."

Caleb's face scrunched up, the anger boiling inside of him. "Denzel saved my life. I'd be dead if it wasn't for him." Closing his eyes, he tried to bring his thoughts to his happy place: Mars Sundean. The thought added to his anger. *If she gave a shit, she'd at least call.*

"Damn, man." Bane shook his head. "Mark my words. Them punks are done for."

"Don't do nothing till I get out," Caleb said, his face reddening. "I want blood."

Blake chimed in. "You'll have to find him in prison," he said. "Kong tried to shoot it out with the cops. They put him down real quick. Probably recovering in this same hospital."

"Then we'll take out his cousins." Caleb's eyebrows were low. Fist clenched; he pounded the rails of his elevated bed. "They stabbed me in the back."

Blake shook his head. "They'll be in prison, too."

Caleb let out a short growl. As he clenched his fist, his face winced from the pain it took to flex those muscles after surgery.

"Calm down, bro," Bane said. "The pigs would know it was you anyway. We have to wait. We have to be smart. You know what I'm sayin'?"

Blake let out a breath. "You need to rest," he said. "Get better. We'll get these fucks. Time is on our side, brother."

"Kong shot me in the back." Caleb glared at Blake. "I can't let that slide."

27

In the back of Shark's Pool Hall, Detective Reid was sitting in a booth across from Sam Lugo, whose ball cap was so low it partially covered his eyes. Pictures were splayed out on the table between them.

"I don't recognize the SUV *or* the guys inside," Sam said, shaking his head with one corner of his mouth hitching upward.

"You sure?" Detective Reid asked, a coffee cup in his hands. Dark circles around his eyes.

"Sorry, man." Sam puffed out his lower lip. "I wish I could help ya. I hope you get the mother fuckers."

Reid's head ticked back, shocked at the language in front of an authority figure like himself. "Do you know of any reason someone might want to harm your friend?"

"Nope." Sam shook his head.

"Come on, Mr. Lugo," Reid said. "I'm trying to get to the bottom of this. I'm a homicide detective. I'm not on the Drug and Gang Taskforce."

"What's the difference?"

"Look, I'm not your enemy. I'm here to help. I got those pictures... and whatever you give me. Don't you want justice for your friend?"

Sam's eyes shifted. "If I think of something, I'll let you know." He stood up.

"Wait." Reid shot up, reaching out his arm to stop him. "I know you know something."

Sam jerked his shoulder back. "Don't fucking touch me."

"Who was in that picture?"

Sam's eyes skirted. "I have no idea." He started to walk away.

Reid pulled out a business card and offered it to Sam. "Call me. Don't go taking the law into your own hands."

"I won't." Sam took the card and stuffed it in his jeans pocket. "Am I free to go?"

"Go on." The detective shook his head and watched Sam strut out the door.

*****

Late that very night, Sam Lugo parked his car in a dark wooded alley. They were a block down from Bob Sturgis' house with guns on their laps. "Follow my lead," he said to Aiden who was wearing a three-hole ski mask, a long-sleeved shirt, and thin batting gloves. All black.

"I got your back, brother," Aiden said, cocking his handgun. "I'm ready for whateva'."

Sam's head shifted toward the passenger seat. "Bob fucked with the wrong mother fucker," he said. "I know it was him. That pig showed me the pictures of his truck on the bridge. I saw his big ugly ass in the passenger seat. You do this for Bane, you earn your stripes. Start making a ton of money."

"I'm ready, dawg," Aiden nodded his head. "Let's do this."

"Be on your top game," Sam said. "This dude is ex-military. Country boy. He's got guns fo' sho'." He opened the door and shut it softly. After making a forward signal with his gloved hand, he started speedwalking down the dark alley lined with rickety old garages.

As the avenue grew near, he slowed down and tucked close to a thick tree trunk. Looking both ways, he saw nothing but darkness so he trotted across the road. Aiden was shadowing behind him. Sam's pace sped up as they entered the alley where Bob lived. His head was on a swivel as he passed each garage. The closer he got to Bob's house, the harder his heart pounded.

Stopping at the garage in question, Sam bent over and took in short fast breaths. He pulled his gun out of his waistline and studied Aiden's fidgety demeanor. As he pressed the safety button, he noticed that his hands were trembling, too. A few deep breaths helped him to cock the gun. "This is for you, Bane." The adrenalized quaking spread to his arms and legs.

Peeking around the corner, Sam pulled back and nodded to his accomplice. "Go," he said softly but firmly. Aiden took off and sprinted past a blue Suburban and toward the two-story house.

Sam followed him up the sidewalk and stopped at the back door. Aiden kicked the door and it flew open. Sam breached the threshold and entered a dark kitchen. The only light came from a digital clock on the refrigerator on the left side of the room. With the gun fully extended, his finger pulsed on the trigger. With each slow step deeper into the house, his heart pounded faster in his chest and ears.

Creeping past the cupboards on the left side of the kitchen, Sam got down low and tucked himself next to the sink base. The entrance to the dining room was directly around the corner. Twisting his head, he watched Aiden take cover next to the fridge. After taking a deep breath, he peeked his head around the corner and caught a brief glimpse of a silhouette of a man standing behind a long gun. And then it exploded in the dark. The sound of shotgun pellets ripping through drywall propelled Sam to the floor. They just missed him.

A second rifle erupted, and a dozen fast pops made Sam's ears ring. Projectiles were rocketing through the wall and air above his head. He was damn near paralyzed with fear.

Aiden fired off four blind shots in the dark. Sam retreated ten feet and hid behind the refrigerator. "Bob!" Sam barked. "You're a fucking dead man!"

The reply was a rope of gunfire that kept Sam and Aiden pinned down behind the fridge.

Aiden's eyes were big. "When he re-loads," he hollered over the endless crackle of gunfire. "I'll lay down some cover fire."

Sam nodded, his breaths fast and heavy. As the loud bangs continued without pause, he could feel sweat dripping under his ski-mask. From his prone position, the back door was reachable, but the buzz of adrenaline and his determination overpowered his fear.

Suddenly, the shooting stopped.

Flashlights could be seen in the windows from outside.

"Come out with your hands up!" A disembodied voice barked from behind the house. "It's the police!"

Aiden bounced up. "Fuck you!" he screamed, his gun bursting rapidly into the living room, his aim sporadic.

"Dammit!" The anguished curse, coming from the living room, gave Sam a feeling of hope. Aiden had hit his target.

"Police!" A loud voice barked. "We're coming in."

Sam pushed forward on his hands and knees. Crawling toward the living room entrance, his eyes sizing up the room, trying to see through the curtain of smoke, trying to detect movement—there! Out of the corner of his eye, he saw Bob crawling away on the carpet.

Swinging his gun low, Sam popped off three rounds into the side of Bob's head. While gazing down in satisfaction, the sound of a gunshot clapped.

Sam could feel the sting, the shocked surprise as hot pain ripped through his neck. Spinning around from the concussion, he crumpled to the floor next to Bob. Wincing in pain, his eyes locked on the black shadow on the staircase. Muzzle flashes looked like fireworks exploding in the dark. As the blood sprayed from his flesh, he bucked his gun four times in desperation. Tiny missiles were crossing paths. And then everything went black.

On the staircase, Tarik Brownridge took one of those blind shots. Clutching his chest, he felt the destruction in his lung. The pain and fear blurred his vision. He dropped the rifle. Coughing up blood, he tumbled down the steps in a slow descent to death.

In the kitchen, Aiden was jamming another magazine into his gun when a flash-bang grenade blew up in the kitchen. The room instantly became white and Aiden was curled up in a ball. "Fuck." When he opened his eyes, the room was thick with smoke and he felt disoriented.

From somewhere in the kitchen, a powerful voice yelled. "Don't fucking move!"

Aiden popped up with his gun stuck out. Three loud bangs shoved him on his back. Snapping his hands to his chest, he let out a horrible groan. As he lay there bleeding out, he could hear the sound of boots on the floor as the cops crowded into the house.

"Help," Aiden cried so softly no one heard. Blood was seeping through the gaps of his limp gloved fingers. "Help me."

*****

Caleb grabbed a cold beer from the fridge and staggered into the living room. Angling toward the coffee table that was loaded with empty beer bottles, his mind obsessed about the unsolved murders and constant threat against his life. Just before he was about to sit down, he stopped, head cocking to the packed bookshelf in the corner of the room. A tall book with a thin red spine was calling out to him. He set the beer down on the cluttered table.

Caleb dropped to his knees, reaching for the yearbook with white letters. He pulled it out, his hand wiping across the hard leather cover even as he blew the dust off it and into the air. Rising to his feet, he turned from the cloud and dropped down on the couch. Flipping through the pages of classmates and signatures, the book magically opened to a page where a folded note was stuffed in the crease. With a rapidly thumping chest, he lifted the faded piece of stationery. It revealed a black-and-white picture of a zit-faced kid with a mullet and cold dark eyes.

"Lerch fucking Black," he slurred his speech, eyes nearly burning a hole in the page. "You killed my friends. And I'm gonna rip out your fucking throat."

The picture of Lerch brought him back to a distant memory of the dirt-poor kid his friends ruthlessly bullied on a regular basis. As he unfolded the note, his mind brought him back to the moment the kid with two black eyes and cuts on his arms turned in history class with something in his hands.

"*What's this?*" Caleb remembered asking softly.

"*My revenge list,*" Lerch had said, winking before spinning back in his seat.

Caleb remembered sitting at his desk with blood boiling in his veins. He was more angry than afraid of the threat against him and his friends. He thought it was just a suicide note, so he folded it up, put it in his pocket, and never showed anyone. At the time, he didn't want to do Lerch a favor, because Blake and Bane would have killed him.

Now, like then, Caleb was prying open the many folds of the old paper. He flattened the creased note on the coffee table. Staring back at him was a numbered list of names written in black ink. "Blake," he said softly, pausing to embrace the sharp pain of grief inside his thudding chest. Picking up the note, he brought it closer to his eyes and continued. "Number two: Lee Wallis," he said louder. Harder. Slower. "Derek Bane... Bob Sturgis... Tarik Brownridge." His voice became a hushed murmur. "And me." His hand shook a little, and the paper floated to the floor. Swallowing a lump of anxiety, the trembling sensation of impending doom took hold and he became sober.

"I better call Mars." Caleb sprung to his feet. *She might not be safe,* he thought.

He flew up the stairs and breached his bedroom. Grabbing his phone on the nightstand next to his bed, he dialed her number. It went straight to voicemail. He pressed the phone close to his mouth. "Mars, call me back." He breathed into the receiver. "I-I know who the killer is. It's Lerch Black from high school. Call me right away."

Caleb hung up. His shaking fingers dialed another number from his call log and pressed the phone to his ear. It rang two times.

"Detective Reid," the man on the other end said in an irritated voice.

"I-I found out who it is!"

"Slow down. What?"

"L-Lerch Black!" Caleb slurred his words. "I-I have evidence. Where you at?"

"I'm at a crime scene. You sound intoxicated."

"Yeah, I've had a few, but I'm bringing you the evidence. What's the address?"

"Hold on." Reid paused with a breath. "I'll come to you if it's important. What do you have?"

"I-I got a r-revenge list from this punk we used to pick on in high school. His name is Lerch Black. The list has all six of us. I'm last."

28

Duluth, Minnesota
May 13, 2005

"Gretchen!" Lerch's dad barked from across the kitchen table in a pair of greasy work overalls. "Quit playing with your food. Eat it." The family chatter hushed, and three hand-shy heads ducked.

"I'm sorry, Dad," Gretchen said. "I-I haven't been feeling good all day. I can't eat. May I please be excused?"

"No. Eat your shit." Randy Black dropped a closed fist on the table and everyone's fork bounced and clanked on their plates. "I worked too damn hard for that meal."

"Leave her alone!" Lerch dropped his fist on the table harder than his pops. All the plates and silverware clinked and clanked. "She's sick, damn it."

"Shut the fuck up, Lerch!" Randy rose from his seat and pointed at Lerch with a finger and hand that was still caked in black sludge from work. "No one was talking to you."

"Just leave her alone." Lerch's chin tilted upward.

"Mind your fucking business," Randy said curtly but then shifted to face Gretchen, speaking with a softer, more gentle tone. "Eat, Gretchen. It will make you feel better."

Lerch's mom leaned forward and whispered. "Sweety, take a sip of milk. And then... try to take a little bite of that hot dog. Dad just doesn't want to waste the food he worked so hard for."

Gretchen did as she was told. A few moments later, she rushed to the bathroom holding her stomach and her mouth. She slammed the door shut and locked it behind her.

"I don't believe her." Randy shot up, looking down at his wide-eyed wife. "I think it's an act." He turned for the bathroom at the end of the hall.

"She's not lying." Lerch raised his voice. "I heard her puking earlier."

Randy turned back, his fingers flexing as he leveled a look at his son. "You've been warned." He took off his belt. Let the buckle dangle at his side. "Test me."

"Randy!" Mom snipped.

"Oh, you want some, twat?" Randy reached back and smacked her with the back of his knuckles.

Lerch stood up, his gaze hopping from his trembling mom on the hardwood floor, to his dad with a raised hand. Without notice, his dad flogged her with the belt buckle. Before he could blink, he hit her again. Lerch clenched his fists.

Lerch's mom cried out with each lashing she took for her son. She dropped lower, reaching for his feet. "Please, Randy. Stop!"

Lerch froze for a moment, and then he darted to his bedroom.

Randy halted the attack on his wife because he won. She was quivering at his feet, begging for mercy. "If I wanted any lip from you, I'd jingle my zipper." He snapped his fingers. "Keep your fucking mouth shut. Bitch."

Bridget kissed his filthy work boots and wrapped her arms around his ankles. Tears were flowing from her eyes as she saw her only son tiptoeing behind Randy in holey black socks. A samurai sword was gripped in his hands. He was holding it tight to his chest. She let go of Randy's legs and slithered backward.

Creeping slowly, Lerch bent his knees, drawing his hands back like a batter in the batter's box. The pulse of hate flowed through his veins and spurred the blade to swing low and fast. The well-sharpened sword slit through his dad's Achilles tendon like a stick of warm butter.

Randy collapsed to the floor with a loud thud. He was writhing in pain, his eyes squeezing tight as he yelled at the top of his lungs. "Fuck!" Reaching for his ankle, he let out a prolonged blood-curdling scream. "HELP!"

"Payback's a bitch." Lerch raised his voice.

Randy stared up at his son with big, panicked eyes. "Please, Lerch," he said with a fast voice. "Call 911."

"No," Lerch said. Gripping the sword tightly, he raised it high and off to one side.

"I'll say it was an accident." Randy stuck his arm out in front of his face. "Please. I need an ambulance."

"No, Lerch." His mom was crying hard with a wet crumpled face. "Don't do it!"

"Shut up, Mom. This piece of shit has been abusing all of us for as long as I can remember." He shook his head. "Not anymore. He has to pay the price."

Randy swallowed hard and then lifted his chin. "You better fucking kill me, Lerch. Cuz if you—"

Randy Black's last words were cut in half by the shiny blade hitting him in the forehead. His body went stiff and fell flat on his face, blood oozing on the floor. One leg twitched for a long moment before his body went limp.

Lerch let go of the sword. It bounced on the floor. He gazed at the mess he made.

With his mom crying by his feet, Lerch hovered over his dad's remains and lifted the corner of his mouth in satisfaction. With a soft chuckle on his lips, he reached low, grabbed his mom's hand, and then lifted her to her feet. Bridget Beaumont Black curled her arm around him.

Gretchen returned from hiding in the bathroom and quietly nudged herself in the middle. She wept with her head buried in her brother's chest. "You saved us, Lerch. Thank you."

29

Two weeks after graduation, Caleb parked his 1992 Jeep Cherokee on a little used dirt road behind the housing projects. His passengers, Blake and Derek Bane were looking out the windows in every direction but saw only trees and darkness. A few streetlights twinkled in the distance.

Behind the Jeep was a heavily wooded road that led to the skyline of the city. From there, they would have multiple means of escape.

"You sure you want to do this?" Blake asked Caleb from the passenger seat.

"Kong's cousins think they're safe," Caleb said in a low conspiratorial voice. "I can't accept that. They need to understand that I'm ready to take shit to the next level."

From the back seat, Bane handed Caleb a Molotov cocktail. "Caleb's right," he said and gave one to Blake, too. "These punks ain't getting away with stabbing our boy. We gots to take the law into our own hands." He tied a black bandana around his face.

"And I want to get to them before Kong's people do," Caleb said. "I'm pretty sure Kong won't forgive them for testifying against him." He opened the door. "They're rats."

"Wait," Blake said from behind a black ski mask. "Where's your mask, bro?"

"Fuck a mask." Caleb stepped out and shut the door. "They can't see me."

Blake and Bane followed suit. They all huddled around the Jeep.

"Let's do this," Bane said softly.

"All right, Me and Bane will smash the two side windows," Caleb said. "Blake, you smash it outside the front door."

Blake nodded with silent reservation, but he didn't say anything because he was the odd man out. It was too late to turn back. Too late to say no. *I created a monster.*

As a team, they marched in the direction of their mission. Each clutching a forty-ounce glass bottle filled with flammable liquid that splashed with each bouncing step. Under a streetlight, they passed the project basketball court and community shack. Just before they entered the dark shadow between two rows of apartments, Caleb and Blake shared a look.

Creeping toward the back corner of the house in question, Caleb stopped and waved in his boys for a pre-game huddle between the two houses. "We all got to do it at the same time." He pulled out a lighter and lit the gasoline-soaked cloth for a wick. It flickered in the pitch-dark shadow of the walls.

Bane and Blake nodded. They both lit their wicks.

"All right, let's do this." There was an urgency to Caleb's voice.

Blake walked toward the front door with the flaming bottle.

Caleb met eyes with Bane. After a brief pause, he reached his arm back and whipped the makeshift bomb at the window. The unmistakable chime of broken glass shattered the midnight silence in the poverty-stricken neighborhood.

Blake and Bane both flung their mini bombs, adding to the chaotic sound of footsteps from inside—a frantic, panicked voice saying something in another language. And then a scream.

Blake was twenty feet behind the gang. Craning his neck, he saw the light of flames expanding in the middle of darkness. More screams of women and children. The shrieks made his heart sink and his legs run faster. "What the fuck did we do?"

30

Duluth, Minnesota
April 25, 2026

Sitting at the edge of his seat, Caleb stared at Detective Reid. "That's impossible."

"I'm sorry," Detective Reid said. "But it's a fact. Lerch Black was killed in Afghanistan in 2012." The detective let out a sigh. "In battle. The man is a fallen hero."

"No way," Caleb said, still shaking his head.

"Look, we have to focus on what we know." Reid glanced down at the dozen empty bottles of beer on the coffee table, and then returned his gaze to the shit-faced man in front of him. "The killer is still out there. And Bob and Tarik last night? My partner. Even Bane. I think the killer had a hand in their deaths, too. Used them to try and distract us." He leaned forward, slowing his voice down. "Caleb, of all the people who received a box, you're the only one left."

"No." Caleb stood up with a darkening face. "Lerch is still alive!" His hands were spread wide. "And yes, he is responsible for Bob and Tarik's death. That ain't no coincidence. Please believe me, sir. Everything that's happening is his design. Don't you see? Look at the list I gave you. It was made more than twenty years ago. Look at the people who received one of Blake's body parts. I'm telling you the facts. Look at the order of deaths. It's all in order!"

Detective Reid rose and then walked around the coffee table, gently setting his hand on his shoulder. "Caleb, calm down. We're going to protect you around the clock." He sat down next to him. "You've experienced more death than is healthy. I'm sorry for that. I will not rest till we get this guy." He shook his head. "But trust me... it's not Lerch Black."

"Then it's someone close to him." Caleb let out a ragged breath. "A brother. Boyfriend. I don't know." He gave a half shrug. "But I'm telling you the truth. That list is real. 2005. He looked me in the eye and promised revenge." The thought riddled him with guilt. He could have stopped this after he found the box on his step. He should have known. He should have remembered, but he didn't. And now everyone's dead. And the detective doesn't believe him.

Reid stood up and adjusted his tie. "You did the right thing to call me. Do it every time you get a lead. I'm here to help. I want this guy as bad as you. He killed my friend, too."

"I barely even sleep," Caleb said. "All I can think about is taking the life from this piece of shit." Shifting his head, his eyes narrowed. "Maybe then, I can live the rest of my life in peace." He looked off into the distance and saw a blur. "But who knows, I'll probably never be the same. Always on edge, looking over my shoulder at every little noise in my own house. Every time a car door shuts. Every—"

Reid held up his hand and cut Caleb off. "Do *not*...be a vigilante." He understood where that line of thinking leads. "You have to control your anger. And you have to stop drinking. I need you sober. Smart."

"Your guys better keep their eyes open. This guy is smarter than all of us. Everything he does has a distraction. He's two steps ahead of all of us all the time. He's unpredictable."

"We got four guys watching you at all times. Trust me, you're safe."

"I do appreciate you and your men." Caleb tilted his right hand in question. "But Bob and Tarik had the same protection. I reserve the right to put him down if he gets past you."

Detective Reid stuck out his hand like he was ending the interview. "Just be careful." The two men shook hands firmly. "Remember, my men will be the first responders. Keep that in mind."

Caleb was staggering slightly as he followed the detective to the door. "You're wrong, Detective," he said. "Six guys on the list. Five dead. Let that sink in."

The detective nodded and walked out the door. Caleb slammed it louder than necessary. Locking the dead bolt, he returned to his beer and then lit up a joint to block the pain out.

*****

The next night after dinner, Caleb was sprawled out on his couch. Lights off. TV on cable news. Third day off from work in a row. He spent most of it sleeping or getting drunk and high at the same time. The table was cluttered with a new round of empty beer bottles. The ashtray full of charred cigarette butts had a half-smoked joint resting on the rim. A quarter bottle of whiskey was standing on the edge of the table and a pizza box was sitting in the center.

The volume on the TV was set low, and President Clacher was on the screen. The headline at the bottom read: Clacher touts post-war takedown of high-level arms dealer in Pakistan. Stockpiles of biological and chemical weapons have been seized in the mountains between Pakistan and Afghanistan.

At the first ring of his cellphone, Caleb's eyes peeled open, groggy as he glanced at the ringing phone. His head hurt; his mouth felt like a bucket of tar just went down his throat.

Jerking forward to his phone on the coffee table, he pressed it to his ear. "Hello?" He didn't recognize the number.

"It's Denzel." The man on the other end let out a heavy breath. "I need to talk to you. In person."

Caleb swung his feet from the couch to the carpet. "Is everything okay?"

"It's been better," Denzel said in a curt tone that he usually only used on the job site. "How 'bout you meet me at the Great Lake Saloon? Tonight."

"Dude, my life is fucked. I'm not in the mood for the club. Why don't you stop over here? We'll chat."

"That's not gonna work. I need to talk…in private. It's important."

"About what?"

Denzel sighed. "I'll tell you there."

"What time?"

"Get ready and meet me there in an hour."

"I'm drunk."

"Take a cold shower and make a cup of coffee."

*****

Dr. Beaumont slowly peeled the brownish gauze from Mars' nub where her pinky finger was missing. "I know. I know," he said, looking up at Mars. "Shhh. We got to clean it."

Mars cried from the work bench. "What's wrong with you?" The straps holding her down were so tight she could barely click her shoes together in defiance.

"Do you want it clean or not?" Beaumont poured some hydrogen peroxide on her wound.

Wincing from the sting, she bucked at her restraints. "You're fucking nuts."

Devoid of Light | 183

"There's nothing wrong with me, Mars." Beaumont paused, dropping the soiled bandage in a trash can. "I'm just motivated. I have a mission, and the ability to achieve that mission. Unfortunately for you, your boyfriend is a big part of my plan. I needed you... to get to him." Grabbing her forearm, he dumped more peroxide on the green and brown puss growing on the opened wound.

Mars closed her eyes tightly, pinching off a swear word at the stinging sensation. "Fuck!"

"Almost done."

"Just kill me."

"Then my mission would be more difficult. You're still useful to me, Mars. Caleb will do anything to save you. I remember how he used to stare at you in high school. Like a lost puppy dog."

"You're sick."

"No, Mars. It is you that's sick. Your wound is green, and your pretty little face is pale. Oh, and you stink. Like a fish. I can smell you from here."

"Fuck you!"

"Oh, I'd like to, my sweet." Dr. Beaumont wrapped her hand with gauze and taped it to the other fingers. "But I don't rape girls. Not like Caleb and the boys. You heard about their wild parties, right? The rape rooms?"

"That never happened."

"Oh. Don't you sound adorable, Mars? So naïve. Poor little Caleb could never do such a thing. He plays such a good act. But under that handsome face is an ugly predator. He's the sick one. He hurt innocent people." He threw out his arms. "Do a criminal background check. You'll see he firebombed a house and burnt a little kid. Traumatized a family full of immigrants.

Now that's sick. What I'm doing here is honorable in some religions."

"No matter what they did, they don't deserve to die. I didn't deserve to get my finger cut off."

"I admit, you don't deserve what happened to you," Beaumont said. "It's not fair. Life isn't fair. That was something I had to teach myself at a young age. Hell, I killed my cat. I had to make sure I understood that fact about life. I loved that cat; Void was probably my only friend." He paused, glancing at Rick Gaytan. "I'm sorry to break it to ya Mars, but Caleb *definitely* deserves exactly what's going to happen to him." Lerch tried to suppress the smile that was starting to grow.

*****

Cruising on the freeway in his Chevy truck, Caleb pulled his ringing phone out of his pocket. "Yep," he said, glancing at the headlights in the rear-view mirror.

"Caleb, you can't leave the house without letting us know," Detective Reid said. "It's not safe out there. Where the hell are you going?"

"I feel like a prisoner in my own home," Caleb said with a touch of irritation. "I'm just going out for a drink or two. Feel free to follow me."

"I'm following you with the tracker," Reid said. "I can't stop you, but I *highly* recommend you turn around and go home."

Caleb exited the freeway. "I need to socialize. I'm going stir crazy."

"Okay." Reid let out a heavy sigh. "Just don't lose that tracking devise."

"I won't. It's in my pocket."

"Good. That's your life line."

"That's why I brought it," Caleb said. "Look, I appreciate your concern. I'll be careful." He hit the blinker and veered right for the exit. "One hour. That's all I need." He hung up and stopped at a red light. In no time at all the light turned green. His foot let off the brake.

Canal Park of Duluth was buzzing with traffic. Caleb had one hand on the wheel. "Nowhere to park," he said. "Oh, there's a spot."

He parallel-parked between a black Chevy Cruze with tinted windows and a shiny new Dodge Challenger. Cutting the engine, he let out a breath, unbuckled his seatbelt, and then hopped out of the truck. At a fast pace, he walked almost two blocks to the club. There was a line forming outside of the building, but it was steadily moving along. Caleb stepped behind a group of young girls in risqué outfits. One had blood red hair, one white, and the other electric blue.

I'm too old for this, he thought, pulling out his I.D. A little man in black was behind him. Far too close for comfort.

"Three bucks," the tall and large door person said with a deep voice and stringy bleached blond shoulder-length hair. Dark make-up around the eyes.

Is that a guy or a girl? Caleb thought, slipping the person a five spot.

"Enjoy," the door person said, stamping his hand with the strong grip of a man on his wrist. When the individual let go, Caleb took a couple of steps forward and glanced back for a double take of the new America. The muscular person in question was now stamping the wrist of the short white guy in a black ball cap and tinted rectangular eyeglasses. Black from head to toe. A nobody in Caleb's mind, so he straightened himself and pressed forward.

Caleb climbed the steps to the main nightclub. Scanning the bar, he saw a wild party full of college kids dancing and drinking. Congregating all around the island bar in the back portion of the club. And there was his friend, Denzel, sitting at a tall circular table, tilting a beer back in the corner by the bathroom sign.

Upon approach, Caleb noticed Denzel's ball cap was low and somewhat covering his face. *Denzel never wears a hat,* he thought as his friend's head snapped in his direction. *Damn, he don't look happy at all.*

Sitting down on the stool next to Denzel, Caleb swiveled to meet his eyes. "What's the big news?"

"I got this in the mail," Denzel said, gesturing toward a small rectangular box under the table. "It had two notes attached to it. One for me and one for you. Mine said to deliver the box to you. ASAP." The club was stuffy, and Denzel looked warm in a bulky dark-gray hooded sweatshirt.

Caleb grabbed the cardboard box and studied it under the table. "The last time I got a box in the mail…"

"I know, this is crazy." Denzel let out a heavy breath. "It's either a cruel hoax or the real deal. The letter said he knows the cops are protecting you. He said if you want to save a life, you have to lose the cops." Denzel leaned closer. "He said to switch clothes with me."

"The cops will be here any minute."

"Go in the bathroom. Read the note."

*****

From inside the bathroom stall, Caleb stood holding the small box and the hand written note. His hands were trembling as he read the neat penmanship of a madman. He read it silently:

Caleb, I look forward to seeing you in person. It's been a long time. It will be fun catching up. I have big plans for you. Open the box. Use the phone to get the next set of instructions. Your Ex-girlfriend's health is depending on that call. You only got one chance to save her. Any cops and...

"What the...?" Caleb shoved the note into his pocket. Ripping the tape from the box, he lifted the cover and a cheap burner phone was wobbling inside.

From the other side of the stall, Denzel knocked on the door. "What is it?"

"A phone," Caleb said and picked up the device. "Oh God," he cried, his voice winded as he stared down at what lay beneath it. "Oh fuck!"

"Caleb, you okay?" Denzel's voice traveled through the metal door.

"No." Caleb scrunched up his face, his eyes bursting with tears. "It's Mars." He whimpered, one hand clutching his chest. A sharp pain had just pierced his heart. But after a moment, the hot surge of adrenaline sparked options in his mind. All the fear and doubt and timidity that plagued him since he was a kid got vaporized after one look at Mars' finger. He immediately chose the only option.

"Caleb? Caleb—what's going on?"

At the pounding on the stall door, Caleb moved on instinct. Shoved the phone in his back pocket before opening the door. Sniffling, he stepped out with a sunken head, glossy red eyes lifting to face Denzel. "He... he got Mars," Caleb said with a trembling lower lip. "He sent you her finger... to lure me in."

"Oh, no, Caleb," Denzel said, raising his hand to cover his open mouth. "What does he want?"

"He wants me." Caleb wiped his eyes dry with the inside of his shirt collar.

"What can I do to help?" Denzel dropped a hand on Caleb's shoulder.

Caleb looked at the hooded sweatshirt Denzel was wearing. "Switch cloths with me." He walked in the left stall.

Denzel stood just outside the open door. "Hold up," he said. "You can't go there. He'll kill both of you."

"I'm going with or without your help." Caleb unbuttoned his guide shirt. "You gonna switch clothes or what?"

Denzel shook his head in protest. "Caleb. Please."

"Sorry." Caleb clubbed the wall with the side of his fist. "This is my fucking fault. I have to save her. I can do it. Trust me."

"Fine." Denzel entered the stall next door to Caleb.

Caleb hung his shirt over the barrier separating the stalls.

"I hope you got a plan," Denzel said, taking the shirt and replacing it with his hooded sweatshirt.

"I got a few ideas." Caleb found a black ball cap inside the sweatshirt. He put them both on and pulled the hood over his head. Opening the stall, he met eyes with his friend. "Thank you. This is the second time you put your life on the line for me. I won't forget it."

Denzel let out a breath. "Caleb, I believe in you." He met eyes with his friend, protégé, and employee. "But I got a bad feeling about this." He handed him his car keys. "Please be safe. I'm parked on the avenue two blocks down."

"Thank you." Caleb gave Denzel a firm hug. A hard few pats.

Denzel smacked Caleb's back then let go. "I have a screwdriver in my center console. Put it in your sock. It might come in handy."

"Thanks." Caleb adjusted the brim of the hat low on his head. "I can't let him kill Mars without a fight. I wouldn't be able to live with myself. Give the box and tracking device to Detective Reid when they come looking for me. Tell him the finger belongs to Mars Sundean. Tell him I'm going to save her."

"Okay, the killer said no cops. Should I tell the detective about the insurance tracker on my car?"

Caleb regarded him with a raised eyebrow. "Yeah, it might help. I'll have a head start. Hopefully the Calvary saves us before it's too late."

Caleb turned and walked out the bathroom with his head sunk. Turning left to the smokers' patio, he milled around the drunk people. A young woman with spiked purple hair pushed the door open, and Caleb followed behind her. The tight area was elbow to elbow with a thick cloud of smoke rising into the mild spring air. Caleb found his way down the back staircase where a buzz-cut man was speaking into a walkie-talkie by the dumpster.

Three other college-age kids were smoking at the bottom of the steps. His heart sank as he walked past one of the street-clothed cops on his protective detail. With his head cocked in the other direction, he slid past without alerting suspicion. As he picked up the pace, he entered the dark alley. The blacktop was wet. Caleb started running. With each galloping step, his mind pictured him and Mars escaping together, trampling over Lerch Black's dead body.

*****

Five minutes earlier, Detective Reid parked his unmarked squad car in the alley and turned to his new partner, Sergeant

Dulles. "Follow my lead," he said, pulling out his radio to give orders to the team. "Mr. Hunt is recalcitrant. We're going in. I want you two on foot. One watching the front door, one watching the back. Be on the lookout for Caleb or anyone big with an untamed beard."

"Copy," the voice of the second team said through the radio.

Reid looked at Dulles who was young and fit with wide eyes. "Let's go babysit our drunk witness."

Sergeant Dulles nodded, his hand reaching for the door handle. By the time he opened the door and got out, Detective Reid was already sprinting across the street.

Detective Reid pulled out his badge and cut through the line. He showed the hulking front door person with long stringy blond hair his free admission pass. "I got one more cop coming."

The person gestured with an open hand. "You're good."

Reid scanned the downstairs bar area. No Caleb Hunt, so he climbed the steps and found himself in the middle of a wild party with loud techno music and a sea of babbling drunk twenty-somethings frolicking about. "You got to be kidding me." He whipped out his phone and tapped the tracking device app. "I'll find you." The red dot was close. Holding the phone in his hand, he cut through the thick crowd, with his nose buried in the screen. People were packed like sardines, in front and behind him as he inched closer to the red dot blinking on his phone.

The current of the crowd stopped and Detective Reid ran into a woman who was bigger than him. He dropped his phone. She spilled her red drink on his shirt. Cursing, she bulldozed her way through the crowd in a tiny dress. Everyone started pushing and swearing.

Reid cursed and dropped to his knees. Legs and shoes and a sticky wet floor are all he saw. *There,* he thought, reaching for his phone. People were stampeding around him. It was just out of reach. Constantly getting stepped on and kicked further along. Crawling on his belly, he stretched out fully, and then he grabbed it, bouncing to his feet. He parted the crowd and scurried to the side of the bar. "Fuck, fuck, fuck." After cleaning the liquid off the screen, he followed the blip on the radar into a white-tile bathroom. "Caleb?"

A stall opened and a familiar muscled black man stepped out. He was holding the tracking device in his hands. "Detective Reid?"

"Where the fuck's Caleb?"

"I couldn't stop him," Denzel said. "He left five minutes ago. The killer has Mars Sundean, and Caleb said he has to save her."

Detective Reid's eyes were big, eyebrows arched. "Where did he go?"

"He said to meet Lerch Black. Make a deal."

"Fuck!" The detective screamed. "What else do you know?"

Denzel reached into his pocket and gave him a small box. "Mars Sundean's finger is in there." He pointed toward the door. "And Caleb took my car. It's a dark gray Dodge Challenger. I got a tracker on my insurance." He handed him his cellphone. "The app is on the home screen."

*****

Parked in a dark alley, Dr. Beaumont pressed his phone harder against his ear. "Yes, she's alive."

"Prove it," Caleb said, huffing and puffing on the other end of the line. "Put her on the phone."

"I can't," Beaumont said. "She's not with me."

"Where is she?"

"Oh, you'll find out very soon, Caleb."

"I'm not going anywhere until you prove she's alive." Caleb dropped a few F-bombs in frustration, his hurried breaths audible in Beaumont's receiver.

"Oh, Caleb. It's been so long since we crossed paths." Beaumont laughed shortly. "You have twenty minutes to get to Brighton Beach, or your pretty little Mars will be missing an eye. And then I'll send you her head in a box. Just like Blake."

"Okay, okay. Fuck."

"Toss your personal phone out the window."

Beaumont heard the sound of a window rolling down.

"Fine. It's gone."

"When you get here, I'm going to scan you and your car." Beaumont cleared his throat. "If you have a tracking device, she dies. If I catch a whiff of a cop, she dies. You understand?"

"I don't have a bug," Caleb said. "I ditched the cops. Took my friend's car."

"I know you did," Lerch said. "I've been watching you since you tipped the transvestite at the bar. Brighton Beach. Twenty minutes." He ended the call with his thumb on the red button.

*****

Caleb was rocketing up the wooded North Shore Road under a dark sky with no stars. The road curved with the edge of the Great Lake and guided him to blackness.

Mars, he thought, and continued thinking about her laugh, the way it spilled out of her mouth so freely, the way it reminded him of his childhood. The natural buzz he felt every time he was close to her.

Caleb's thoughts about Mars sent his foot pressing down harder on the gas pedal. The more fuel he fed the muscle car, the louder the air groaned. A glance at the speedometer read eighty-six and climbing. Both of his hands were tightening on the leather steering wheel. Fire was burning in his eyes. Adrenaline was guiding his body. The car was cruising, but he felt like someone else was in control of the gas and the wheel.

Flying down the road, he tapped the brakes to slow down—his turn was coming up soon. A mile down the highway, Caleb's eyes shifted to the right shoulder of the road where a green sign popped into sight. In a fraction of a second, the words became clear. *Brighton Beach,* he worded, and then pumped the brakes, turning down the wooded passageway that led to the state park and rocky shoreline. The wide tires of the car hummed on the gravel road. After a minute or two of driving, Caleb saw a gap in the trees coming up on the left. Strangling the wheel, he slowed the car down to a crawl, and then turned into a parking spot next to a black Chevy Cruze.

Throwing the shifter in park, his head rolled to the black car next to him. "I'm going to torture him and find out where she is." He opened the center console. A Phillips screwdriver was calling out to him. It was about medium size. Grabbing the crude weapon, he stuffed it inside his pants at the small of his back.

Caleb's new phone started ringing. His shaky hands answered it. "Yep."

"Turn off the car," a fast baritone voice ordered.

"Okay." Caleb was breathing heavily. He killed the engine.

"Step out with your hands up. Slow movements."

Caleb hung up the phone. Letting out the heaviest sigh of his life, he swung open the door. "Game time," he said softly, dropping his feet to the gravel. Caleb rose slowly and closed the door. His head was on a swivel, ears desperate for any movement.

The trunk of the Chevy Cruze clicked and popped open. Caleb flinched. What the....

"Caleb," a disembodied voice shouted. The darkness hid Beaumont's location. The echo was whipping across the trees and floating over the boulders, making it impossible to gauge the precise location.

Caleb's body was twisting back and forth in every direction. "Where are you?" His body was quaking. His fist was clenched. Every muscle in his body was flexing. Throbbing with blood rushing through his veins.

"Get in the trunk! Don't ask questions."

Caleb spread apart his hands in protest. "I can't fit in there!"

"You have ten seconds!" The man in the shadow barked. "Get in the trunk or the girl dies."

Caleb paced to the car, cursing under his rapid panting breaths. He kicked dirt and felt the scratch of the screwdriver in his ass-crack. The sharpness gave him enough hope to crawl into the tight space of the compact car. Curled up in the fetal position, Caleb ground his teeth with rage. He thought about Mars and the consequences of acting too soon. *Maybe I should wait.*

*****

Dr. Beaumont stepped out from behind a fat maple tree. A black pistol was at his side. With long purposeful strides, he marched to the car, glowering at Caleb as he got closer. Clad in black, he aimed the gun in the trunk, peering down on Caleb's low brow. "Don't look so happy to see me."

"Fuck you, Lerch."

"If I were you, I'd check my tone, Caleb," Dr. Beaumont said the last word with contempt, pulling a small black device out of his jacket pocket.

"I-I should have known it was you all along," Caleb said with a clattering jaw.

Beaumont bent over and slowly waved the bug scanner from Caleb's head to his toes. "You're lucky you don't have a tracking device." He reached for the trunk with a smug look on his face. "Time to go."

"Wait! I got to take a piss."

The man Caleb only new as Lerch laughed shortly. "Too bad," he said with his hands on the trunk, and then he slammed it downward.

Caleb shot one foot out and stopped the trunk from shutting. His fingers gripped the screwdriver tighter as the trunk bounced off his leather hiking boot. Thrusting forward, he stabbed Beaumont in the groin. He grunted and dropped the gun on the ground. When his hands snapped to the wound, Caleb grabbed his jacket and jerked Beaumont's head toward him, cracking it on the truck of the car.

Beaumont yelped, and the next thing he knew, he was on his back with Caleb kneeling on his chest, pounding on his face until blood spattered. One more punch and then the beating stopped.

"Where is she?" Caleb screamed with his fist raised high and shaking.

Beaumont turned his head and spit blood. "If I don't call in two minutes," he said slowly, "she will die. That is a fact. Do you want to live with that? She gets raped and killed becau...."

Caleb dropped a tight fist on his nose, bursting more blood. "Where is she?"

"I'll give you the address, but she dies if I don't make that call."

"Call him right now." Caleb gripped his hands around Beaumont's neck and gripped tightly. "Tell him everything is fine."

Beaumont made a gagging noise. "I'll call. I'll call." His face was turning red.

"Good." Celeb let go but held a clenched fist over his face.

Beaumont coughed raggedly. "I'll make the call." He coughed once more. "But when I don't use the code word, he'll know something's wrong. And then she's dead. Don't you get it, Caleb? I've thought over every possibility. Every angle. I predicted you might do something like this."

"Fuck!" Caleb dismounted Dr. Beaumont. Swooping up the gun, he aimed at his head. "Get the fuck up." He kicked his legs. Cocked the gun.

Beaumont hopped to his feet. Wiping blood from his nose and mouth, he then rubbed his pants on the area around his crotch. "You missed my nuts by an inch."

"I won't miss again." Caleb lowered the gun to his genitals.

"Tick tock," Beaumont said. "What are you gonna do, Caleb? It's all up to you. I'd hate to damage Mars' pretty little face."

"Shut up!" Caleb barked with the gun pointing in Beaumont's direction. "Get in the car!"

"No." Beaumont shook his head vehemently. "You're going to choose. Right here, right now. Me dead or her alive."

Caleb's trembling finger was itching the trigger. "Fuck!" He lowered the gun and paced back and forth, fighting the overwhelming urge to put a bullet in his head.

"Give me the gun and she lives."

Breathing heavily, Caleb met Beaumont's eyes. "You win, Lerch." He then tossed the gun on the gravel by his feet.

"Get back in the trunk." Beaumont stooped to reclaim his gun.

Caleb's chest was rising and falling with each cursing breath. He had no choice. He looked at the man who was bleeding because of him. And then he looked at the gun. Letting out a heavy sigh, he slowly climbed in the trunk.

"Caleb Hunt," Beaumont said, smiling down at his primary target. "From this moment forward, you belong to me." He slammed the trunk shut.

Caleb's muffled curse words made Beaumont's smile more crooked than it already was.

Opening his back door, Dr. Beaumont grabbed a medical-grade bag of blood. Carrying it to the car Caleb borrowed, he opened the driver-side door and pulled out a pocketknife. After poking the bag and tearing a two-inch hole, he quickly slid the knife in his pocket. With both hands, he then squeezed the bag over the driver's seat, steering wheel, and dashboard until it was almost empty and looking exactly like the scene of a heinous murder.

Leaning inside the cockpit of the Dodge Challenger, he saw the key was still in the ignition. With a snap of the wrist, the engine grumbled to a low idle. Reaching for the shifter, he put it into gear and stepped aside as the car began rolling toward the black choppy lake.

At the distant sound of sirens, he cursed under his breath, his head twisting to the south. "I said no cops," he muttered as he turned toward his waiting vehicle. "A good excuse for me to kill Mars." He dropped into the front seat of his car.

*****

Detective Reid was flying up the north shore of Lake Superior in his unmarked squad car. He took his eyes off the road for three seconds to read the insurance tracker on Denzel's cellphone. The blip on the radar had just stopped moving. It was less than ten miles straight ahead.

Glancing in the rearview mirror, Reid saw blue and red lights as far as the eye could see. He was the leader in the pack. He decided to increase the speed to nearly seventy miles per hour in the residential zone filled with ancient brick mansions and sprawling trees. Lives were on the line. He had to push his limits to the max. After a little more than five miles, he tapped the brakes, zipped across the highway, and slammed on the gas for another mile down the wooded expressway until a small green sign with glinting white letters popped up on his right. Slowing to a crawl, he yanked the wheel and fishtailed on the dark gravel road leading to Brighton Beach. A wall of pine trees lined both sides of the road.

The car in question was close. Reid's head was on a swivel as the tires hummed and spit a trail of dust behind him. Out of the left corner of his eye, he saw a red light beaming through the dark murky woods. "Ooh," he said, pumping the brakes. There was a large gap in the trees and he skidded sideways in the first parking spot on the beach. With a pounding heart, he whipped his head toward the red light and saw a car with taillights just like his—half-sunk in the black lake. "Holy shit!"

Jamming the shifter in park, Reid swung open the door and whipped out his gun. Behind the cover of the squad car, he scanned the area with his arms extended. The boys in blue were right behind him.

"Seal off the area," Reid barked into his radio. Turning to look at his men, he gave two hand signals and then charged the first camp site on the beach. Shuffling forward on the gravel parking spot, he eyed the idling car on the pebble shore, halfway in the lake. "Caleb!" he screamed at the top of his lungs, his eyes canvassing the car all the while running over the unstable ground of the stony terrain.

Breathing heavily, he reached the Dodge Challenger that was stuck on a plateau of large rocks just a few feet in the water. Exhaust was still coming out of the two wide tailpipes and the car was grumbling.

"You in there?" Reid hollered, and the tide slammed against the rocks and the car. Stepping both feet in the cold water, he braced his left hand on the rear fender of the muscle car. A hot surge of adrenaline pushed him further into the knee-high water.

Reid listened for any sign of life. Nothing but the sound of wind and waves crashing on the rocky shoreline. Angling away from the car, he aimed at the passenger window and closed in. *Looks empty.* "Caleb! Talk to me." He heard men behind him. With a quick glance, he saw Sergeant Dulles and at least a dozen officers with guns drawn.

Turning back to the car, he looked inside the windows. "Oh, no." He holstered the side arm. Ripping open the door, he got a closer look at the blood-stained cockpit. No body. Just blood splattered everywhere. "He's on foot!" He turned, pointing for the woods. "Call in the dogs!"

31

In a small interview room at the courthouse, Caleb covered his face with his hands, his elbows resting on an old wood desk. His ears taking in advice. His brain throbbing from reality.

"Mr. Hunt," the female public defender said. "If you don't take the plea bargain for Arson in the Second Degree, you're going to prison for at least ten years. I'm sorry, but there's no way we win a jury trial. Your face is on the surveillance camera in the housing projects—before *and* after the crime." The gray-haired woman adjusted her glasses and waited for his reply.

Caleb sat upright, plopping his hands on the table between them. "I told you. It wasn't me. The tape is blurry." He lied through his teeth, but his conscience was reminding him of the truth. Memories from that night of rage. The sound of glass breaking before the explosion of fire. The shrieking cries of women and children's voices escaping through the shattered window. The galloping sound of three men as they ran past the basketball court, not realizing they were caught on camera.

"You've seen the camera footage." The court-ordered attorney shrugged. "It's clearly you. Plus, they tracked your cellphone there and back to your house. You also have an obvious motive: Retaliation for the assault against you in school." She let out a breath. "There's no way out of this, Caleb.

Unless... of course, you're willing to give up your accomplices."

"No!" Caleb dropped his fist on the desk. "Fuck it. Two years. That ain't shit. I'll take it."

"It's three years." She corrected the young man. "But twenty-eight months if you get good behavior. Then four years of probation. Fifty days of work crew." She let out another deep breath. "I'm glad you came to the right decision. You're doing the right thing. It will straighten your life out. Let's face it, you're going down the wrong path. You could have killed a family of ten."

"You don't understand." Caleb shook his head. "I'll do the time, but I didn't do it."

The public defender let out a short breathy laugh. "It doesn't work like that." She flashed a quick smile. "For the judge to accept the plea bargain, you'll have to, not only accept your role in the felony arson, but you must... show at least *some* remorse."

"What?"

"Yeah, you can't just say I didn't do it," she said, shaking her head mockingly. "But send me to prison. No. The judge has rules to follow. Laws to abide by. He can't grant a plea unless the defendant is self-aware of what's happening. Otherwise, the mentally ill could be manipulated into pleading guilty."

"What about the Alford plea?"

"How do you know about that?"

"I do my research. I can't admit to something I didn't do."

"Mr. Hunt, I would strongly advise not to do that. The judge could throw out the entire plea and make you go to trial." She shook her head. "And I know for sure... I can't win that case."

Caleb sunk his head. "Fine. But I won't incriminate anyone else. And I *won't* admit I set the fire. I was just along for the ride."

The free attorney slid forward a stack of papers. "Sign here."

*****

Four months into his prison stint, Caleb Hunt was in one of five not-too-private showering stalls. Shampoo was fizzing in his hair. While his eyes were closed, the four other inmates using the facility abruptly walked out with heads facing the floor. When Caleb rinsed the shampoo out of his hair and eyes, he noticed he was alone in the room. Not even a guard.

He turned off the shower and wiped the water drops from his arms and chest. Walking out of the stall to find his towel, he jerked to a stop. Three short Asian men were entering the shower area—fully dressed in blue prison garb and prison-issued sandals. Two of them were holding shanks in their hands.

Caleb angled his body, lifting his fists in front of his face. "Back the fuck up!" he barked. "You know what I'm capable of, Kong." With pure adrenaline pumping through his body, Caleb looked past the gang where a guard usually stood periodically, but there was no one there.

"Ain't no C.O. coming to save you," Kong Zang said. "They on the payroll. The cameras are down." He flashed a crooked smile.

Caleb unclenched his fist and shrugged. "Fine. Who wants to die first?"

"You fought well against little kids," Kong said. "Things different now." His head shifted to the swelled-up Asian man next to him with gang tattoos on his arms, chest, and neck. He had short cropped black hair and face that looked flexed.

"Why do you always hide behind your friends, Kong?" Caleb balled his hands into fists. "You scared to fight me one on one?"

Kong laughed. "No. No. You gonna get stabbed, white boy. Again. And then we gonna take turns fucking you till you bleed out." He paused to lift his cleft chin. "Bitch."

"Bring it!" Caleb barked; his wiry muscles were flexing into a wide stance fighting position with his fists up in front of his face. Glancing at Kong's dark beady eyes, he noticed the biggest of the three take a step forward. Caleb took a step back and planted his right foot at the base of the shower stall. He was mentally preparing himself for a knife fight. Swangin.

Kong snapped his fingers and the two short stalky inmates edged forward. They were both gripping homemade knives made from sharpened toothbrushes and duct tape. The bigger of the two lowered the shank, yelling something in another language before blitzing.

Caleb pushed off the shower base and launched an attack on the first belligerent. He grabbed the incoming wrist and tugged down as he charged forward. They slipped to the wet floor and Caleb landed on top. After he dropped a devastating punch on his chin, Caleb paused to grab the wrist of the second man with a swinging plastic dagger. Yanking him to the ground, he dropped a hard blow on his nose. At that moment, Kong pounced like a junkyard dog in competition for a bone.

Caleb was rolling on the floor with Kong. One man was laid out. Grunts and punches were thrown. Caleb was bleeding. The third man rose to his feet and hovered over Kong and Caleb, desperately waiting for an opening to strike Caleb in the neck.

With his back on the floor, Caleb took a hard blow to the eyebrow and his head bounced off the tile. Stars flashed and his vision got blurry. He gripped Kong's shirt tight, bringing him so close he could kiss him. Just as he was about to bite his nose off, he heard a thunderous bark from what he thought to be a man of authority.

Everyone froze. Turned. It wasn't guards, it was three tall and husky Native American men with towels around their waists and tattoos on their chests and arms. One bald, two with long black stringy hair.

"Get the fuck off him!" The biggest of the three ordered with a rising hand.

Two Asians got up. One was on the floor. He was spilling blood down the drain. Caleb slid back against the wall, swooping up the shank that belonged to the unconscious man.

"Turn around," Kong said to the lead Native. "Walk away. We make deal later. You get paid."

"Nah, you walk away," the beefy Native American said. "And we won't smash your skulls into mush."

"You make bad mistake, Arrow," Kong said. "We all black belts." He stuck his hand out and received the other shank from his gang brother. "Last chance. Make deal."

Caleb flinched when Arrow whooped and hallooed a war cry. Stumbling aside, he slipped and fell on his butt, narrowing his gaze on the big man charging forward with great intensity. The man's brothers were right behind them. They steamrolled over the two standing Asians in short manner. They pounded on them relentlessly until they were near catatonic.

Arrow extended a hand to Caleb and lifted him to his feet. "You okay?"

"Yeah." Caleb dropped the shank and staggered slightly. Blood was streaming from his brow, all the way down his arms, and dripping to the wet floor. "Thank you."

"No," Arrow gestured to the shank next to Kong who was curled up and groaning. "Finish the job. We all in this together now. Can't leave witnesses."

Caleb nodded with low eyebrows before crouching for the knife. Kneeling on Kong's side, he rolled him flat on his back. "Kong!" he said, looking at the broken face and red jagged teeth. "You started this in a bathroom. Over nothing. And I'm gonna end this in the shower. Over everything."

"Fuck you, white boy." Kong spit blood and teeth chunks in Caleb's face.

Caleb responded by jamming the sharp toothbrush into Kong's neck and jerking it forward.

*****

At lunch the next day, Caleb was sitting next to Arrow and his posse. Setting down his spork, he leaned closer to his new friend. "Thanks again," he said with a low tone. "I owe you my life. I'm not kidding. I'll do anything to—"

Arrow cut him off with a menacing hand. "I don't know what you're talking about." His voice was low, eyes locked on Caleb. "Guards got paid off. We all good. But I do have a few requests, so listen up. I have ten years left on my sentence. You don't wanna be like me. Never. I'm a different breed. No, you're gonna finish your time. You're gonna learn from me. You're gonna do everything I wish I could do. You're gonna have a second shot at life. I won't. Not until 2017." He paused and dropped a heavy hand on his shoulder. "When I get out, I expect a job waiting for me. That means *you* need to make a success of your second chance. You have to live a peaceful, clean life."

"But—"

"No buts, kid," Arrow said. "With my criminal record and skin color, no one will hire me. I'm unemployable. That's why you're going straight. You owe me a favor, and I expect you to deliver. In return, no one will touch you. Period." He shook his head. "We be running shit up in here. You in or out?"

Caleb let out a breath. "I'm in, but I wanna ride with you. You saw me. I did not hesitate. I'm 'bout it, 'bout it."

"No." Arrow shook his head. "You don't want no part of this life. Trust me. You'll thank me later."

32

Duluth, Minnesota
June 21, 2010

In a black cap and gown, Lerch Black cut through the thick crowd at the Duluth Convention Center. He had just graduated from college, and he was looking for his mom and little sister.

Stopping in front of the concession stand, Lerch adjusted his black glasses as he saw a solid foe from high school with a light-colored dress shirt tucked into dark slacks. "Is that Caleb?"

The man in question turned and looked at him. His dark eyebrows were arching. "You talking to me?" he asked with his fingers touching his well-defined chest.

"You're not Caleb?" Lerch regarded him with a squinting left eye.

"Yeah, I'm Caleb," he said. "Do we know each other?"

"Hey, it's been a long time." Lerch's mustache hoisted on one side. "I barely recognized you either. I just wanted to say hi." He made strong eye contact. "I'm Lerch Black. You don't remember me? Kick-Me boy?"

Caleb's mouth cracked open. "Oh, I remember. You look a lot different." He pursed his lips with a slight nod. "I hope you don't have any hard feelings. My buddies were pretty hard on you."

"The past is history. I probably deserved it."

"Nah, it was harsh. I'm sorry I never stopped it. We were stupid kids."

"I appreciate the apology." Lerch met his eyes. "It means a lot to me."

"So, what? You just graduated? What's your major?"

"Pre-med. But I'm a medic in the National Guard. Probably going to Afghanistan soon." Lerch smiled. "What are you doing here?"

"My friend Denzel just graduated with a business degree." Caleb nodded his head. "I was actually looking for him. I kinda got to go." He let out a breath. "But I appreciate your service. Be safe over there. I heard it's dangerous."

"I'm not going till September. One last summer at home." Lerch smiled. "You wanna go fishing or something? Slaughter some walleye?"

"Look, Lerch." Caleb paused to meet his eyes. "I'm actually glad we had this conversation. I've really been trying to put that life behind me. I just got out of prison. I need to right all my wrongs. You just gave me closure. Thank you."

"Thank *you*," Lerch said with a smirk. "You just gave *me* closure." The muscles in his neck swallowed contempt. "Well, maybe we'll chat again sometime."

"Nah." Caleb shook his head slowly. "Even if I wanted to, I couldn't. You threatened to kill me and my friends. That wasn't cool."

"What do you mean?"

"The list. You passed it to me in English class. I was number six on your stupid little revenge list. I can't forgive that. I'll never forget."

"I forgave *you*."

"How 'bout this. I wish you well. But next time you see me, keep walking. I don't want to go back to prison." He walked away into the throng of men and women. Children and old people. Black and white. Short and tall. All enjoying the peace and greatness of America. A moment in time when people smiled. When people laughed without a worry in the world. An era of calm before the storm.

33

Farah, Afghanistan
July 5, 2012

From inside an armored personnel vehicle, Lerch Black's vacant gaze was locked on the tan boots of a soldier who was sitting across from him. His mind was not paying any attention to the commotion of his unit. It was somewhere in the past. A dark spot with no light. A childhood of abuse and neglect. Walked on by many boots. Stomped on by his own dad.

"Black," Sergeant Rojo said. He was wearing the same attire as everyone else: desert camo fatigues, a helmet, and a rifle crossing his chest. "You okay?"

Lerch leveled his head. "Yes, sir. Just got a lot on my mind, sir."

"We dismount in ten minutes," Sergeant Rojo said, raising his voice three octaves. "I need you to have one thing on your mind, Black: Completing the mission!"

"Yes, sir!" Lerch barked from his gut, sweat rolling down his side.

"Too late to go home to mommy." Rojo barked. "The enemy is on the move! I need your head focused! I'm depending on you to save my life, magot."

Lerch swallowed his pride. *My mommy just died,* he thought, but instead he just nodded. *My sister, too. Train derailment. Benzene spill. They suffocated to death, you asshole.*

When the modified tank on wheels hit a bump in the road, the men inside jerked into each other. They were cruising at twenty-five mph. A long trail of dust followed behind them.

The scorching July sun was cooking the tank and burning the landscape at the foot of the rugged mountain range. As far as the eye could see, there was nothing but dirt and rocks and tall weeds. One road leading to no man's land.

"All right, men," Sergeant Rojo barked. "When the vehicle comes to a stop, I want everyone to—" An earsplitting explosion lifted the armored vehicle in the air and dropped it on its side. A red-hot roaring fire engulfed the exterior of the tank on wheels. Flames were reaching for the sky. Black smoke was billowing inside and out.

Injured men were pancaked on top of each other. Soldiers were screaming in pain. Blood was spraying everywhere from the shrapnel that pierced the plate on the bottom of the vehicle. Men were coughing from the thick cloud of smoke. Gunshots were heard from outside. Tings from bullets reflecting off the tank were continuous. Sustained.

Lerch was underneath several men. He couldn't budge them. "Get off me," he cried, shoving a blood-soaked man in the back. "I can't breathe," Lerch cried. Pushing with all his might, he managed to squirm around him. With his boot, he stepped on another soldier's helmet and ignored his desperate plea for help. Climbing his way over the top of the heap, he trampled on his fellow brothers in arms to the top manhole that was now on the side.

While coughing and gasping for air, he reached for the hatch with ringing in his ears. Lerch spun the lock and cracked it open. Daylight and gunshots welcomed him. He closed it shut and weighed his options: bullets or smoke.

Pushing the hatch open, he quickly crawled out and dropped to the ground. He pulled out his sidearm. Ducking low on the dry sandy dirt in the prone position, he scoped the rugged terrain. Multiple muzzle blasts were coming from the base of the mountain. He judged them to be less than a hundred yards away and closing.

Above Lerch's head, the hatch creaked open and a charred hand stuck out. "Help!" Sergeant Rojo cried from the manhole.

Lerch looked up and met his eyes. He felt something boiling in his chest. "You should have treated me with more respect."

"What?" Rojo coughed out a whisper. He was gasping for air and bleeding from his nose and ears.

Lerch flashed a smile. Grabbing his arm, he pulled him out of the tank and to the dirt. "You always treated me like shit! And now, I'm going to return the favor." He stuffed the pistol up against Rojo's side, and then he squeezed the trigger twice. Each eruption was muffled by flesh.

The sergeant opened his mouth for air. "Why?" he croaked out.

"I already told you." Lerch ripped his dog tag from his neck and whipped it into the manhole. In his next breath, he pulled a grenade from Rojo's vest. Removing the pin, he dropped it in the open hatch of the tipped-over tank on wheels.

"Good luck," Lerch said to Sergeant Rojo and then bolted as fast as he could. Rojo's panicked screams pushed Lerch just out of danger before the grenade exploded. The fiery blast wave shoved him to the ground. Snapping his head back, he saw a humongous flame reaching above the wreck and toward the pale blue sky. Rojo was toast.

Shifting forward again, he crawled away from the fire and toward a nearby boulder. The distraction gave him cover from the cheering terrorists. Gunshots were popping off from the other side of the smoldering heap of metal and charred human flesh. When he peeked his head around the edge of the boulder, he saw figures encroaching on the wreck. Some were as close as thirty yards.

Lerch pulled back and dropped to his butt. He had a moment to catch his breath and think of a plan to escape. A plan to find allied forces. The base was only fifty miles away. He chuckled softly like a lunatic surrounded by abusive staff members with needles filled with Haldol. That was the life he lived until his mom's lawyer proved Lerch killed his dad in self-defense.

At the sound of dogs barking in the distance, Lerch felt a tremor shudder down his spine. The men screaming in Arabic were close. With one quick glance around the stone, he saw a group of terrorists dancing near the tank, shooting their weapons into the smoky air above.

With my luck, I'll get beheaded on TV, he thought, and then pressed the barrel of the gun against his temple.

34

Duluth, Minnesota
April 26, 2026

Caleb Hunt woke up strapped to an old workbench a few feet away from Mars. Their heads were both craning to face each other. He was wearing a dirty white T-shirt and jeans. Black socks. No shoes.

"He said they'd let you go," Caleb said. The cinder block wall behind her reminded him of how naïve that sounded. *No one is getting let go.*

Mars sniffled. "I wish you didn't come here," she said, her voice cracking as the tears ran down the side of her bruised face. "These guys are sick." Her clumped and ratty auburn hair was draped on the bench.

"I wouldn't rather be anyplace else in the world," Caleb said, pursing his lips in a nervous type of smile for the dire situation. The sight of marks on her face made his blood boil. An electric buzz of fear, anger, and love ripped through his body.

The basement door creaked open, and Dr. Beaumont stepped forward in a white lab coat, holding a small rectangular case. Gaytan closed the door behind them. "Oh, Caleb. How touching." He squeezed Caleb's foot on his way to address Mars.

Leaning forward close to Mars' ear, Beaumont lowered his voice to an angry whisper only she could hear. "Caleb is about to endure a great deal of pain." He snapped the box open and set it on the bench next to her neck. "Unfortunately, you won't get to witness most of it." He rose to his full height, pivoting toward Caleb. A syringe now in his left hand. Needle pointing upward.

"Please don't hurt him." Mars cried, her head angling to face Caleb. "He. He never hurt you."

"You're wrong, Mars. Caleb hurt me more than the rest of them." Beaumont paused, turning to hover the needle over her blinking eyes. "Did you know Caleb was my locker partner in seventh grade?"

"No, I didn't." She glanced at Caleb and then returned her glare to Dr. Beaumont.

"Of course not. He wouldn't admit we were once friends. In seventh grade I bought him pop and chips with my lunch money every day. He protected me from at least two bullies. And then...in ninth grade, he sided with Blake and the so-called 'Dangerous crew.' Yes, betrayal hurts more than a kick in the ass. When I saw Caleb laughing as they tormented me every day, it hurt. I remember it like it was yesterday."

"I'm sorry, Lerch." Caleb's voice cracked. "I told them to leave you alone. They wouldn't listen. If I would have tried harder, they would have teamed up on me and kicked *my* ass. I was just a stupid kid... trying to fit in."

"Exactly. You were weak then, and you're weak now. A coward. A stupid coward. All it took was Mars' pinky finger to get you here. You are so predictable. So pathetic, I knew you'd sacrifice everything... for her."

"I-I will," Caleb said, his eyes snapping open. "Just let her go. You can do whatever you want to me."

Beaumont flashed a smile. "I give you my word, I *will* let her go. As long as you complete my mission."

"I'll do anything." Caleb nodded his head frantically. "Please."

"Good. But just in case you change your mind, I'm going to have to pump you full of Succinylcholine."

"What the fuck is that?" Caleb asked, his head cocked in the direction of Dr. Beaumont and the needle. As Beaumont leaned toward him, Caleb's body flinched. His eyebrows low as can be.

"No!" Mars cried. "Please just let us go. My family's rich. We'll pay you anything!"

Beaumont's head snapped to face Mars. "Shut up!" He turned his attention back to Caleb. "The dose I'm about to give you... will put you in a coma for at least twenty-four hours. Hopefully more."

Mars cried. "Lerch! You don't have to do this."

"I like it when you say my name." Beaumont turned to look at Mars, and then he straightened himself to the prize. Looking down on Caleb—and the fear he displayed on his scrunched-up face—he felt satisfied with the moment he'd always craved. And then he plunged the needle into Caleb's arm. Injected the knockout drug. "When I drop you off at the hospital, I don't want you to tell the doctors about the bubonic virus shedding from your body."

"What?" Caleb's head twisted upward, his eyes squinting as he read the truth on Lerch's face. A hot flash of adrenaline flowed through his body and secreted through his pores.

Dr. Beaumont slowly pulled the needle out of Caleb's vein. Turning, he glanced at Mars and noticed her lower lip was quivering as he set the needle in the case. "I'm about to inject a virus into your body." His back was facing Caleb. A new syringe was in his hands. Smiling at Mars, he spun on his heel and carefully raised the needle to eye level.

Caleb was thrashing on the bench. As he inhaled and exhaled his last breaths of air with pure blood, a ragged groan rumbled in his throat.

Dr. Beaumont showed Caleb death, the destroyer of worlds. "What I am holding in my hands is a weapon of war. A deadly mix of Ebola and Corona Virus. It creates a highly contagious Hemorrhagic fever that is not treatable." He laughed shortly, turning to look down on Mars' squinting green eyes. "It's irreversible, but of course, if Caleb told them too soon, they could quarantine the hospital and the city. My dear leader wouldn't like that. They'd come looking for me. They'd feed me to the dogs." He lowered his voice. "I don't want that."

"So, what? You're doing this for money?" Caleb asked with a softy groggy voice.

Beaumont turned, giving Caleb a close-up examination of the bioweapon in a needle. "No, no. Really, it's my pleasure. A wise old imam spared my life. In return, I offered to punish America for its cruelty. Not just its government. But people like you deserve to suffer in the worst possible way." He pointed a trembling finger at Caleb. "You treat people like shit. And so does everyone else. We will never know how much evil goes on in America every day. Every moment. Not just bullied kids. But child sex abuse is ramped in America. My own dad raped my little sister for years. What kind of nation is this?" One of his fists was clenched. "America must embrace the suffering. People will never forget my name: Lerch Black!" With his free hand, he hit his chest twice, shooting his arm out high like one of Hitler's minions.

"You're fucking sick." Mars fought against her restraints.

"Not at all." Lerch swallowed, looking down on Caleb's blank slumbering face. "I'm a doctor." He poked the second needle into Caleb's bloodstream. "I'm in top shape. Physically...and mentally. Caleb is the one who's about to get sick."

*****

After Gaytan rolled Caleb out of the basement on a dolly, Mars sat alone for at least an hour, staring at the chipped lead paint on the ceiling above her head. Her mind drifted off to worry about Caleb, the possible virus, and what they would do to her when they came back. *I have to escape,* she thought, flexing to test the straps. As her body arched, the canvas restraints carved into her skin. Grunting with a beet-red face, she tried again to break loose, and then her head clicked toward the basement door that was creaking open. Her body went limp.

"Mars," Rick Gayton said playfully. "We got the house all to ourselves."

"What do you mean by that?" Mars' breaths were heavy and speeding up by the second.

"Dr. Beaumont just drove to the Twin Cities," Gaytan said. "To drop off your lover in a high population center." He plopped his hand on her thigh. "He won't be back for a loooong time."

"If you don't get your hand off my leg," she snipped. "I'll tell Lerch. He thinks I'm his prize."

"It's Dr. Beaumont." Gaytan said sternly. "But fuck him. I'm sick of him telling me what to do. Using me to do his dirty work." His hand slithered up to her inner thy and... "It's time I have some fun. Roll the dice. See what happens."

Mars jerked her body but the restraints held her tight. "So, you're just gonna rape me?"

"I haven't thought that far, yet." Gaytan exhaled an audible breath and his bushy lip curled upward. "I just like looking at you. Curvy in *all* the right spots." His meaty hand slid up her midsection, stopping on the soft cup of her breast.

She jerked violently and snarled. Gaytan's hand dropped to his side.

"I'm gonna soak this in." He tugged on the longest part of his beard as he undressed her with his eyes. "Cuz I don't think he plans on keeping you alive much longer."

"What do you mean?" She took a few quick breaths. "He gave Caleb his word."

Gaytan laughed shortly. "I heard him. It just doesn't seem like his style. He hasn't let anyone go yet. He's really into patterns." The grizzly man nodded. "He never diverts from his plan."

Mars bit the inside of her lip. "Maybe you should stop him?" Her low sassy voice sounded like someone other than herself. It sounded like a boss bitch.

Gaytan laughed shortly. "He'll probably make *me* do it. He likes to watch. I think he gets off on it. He likes it when I strangle them. But when I drilled a hole in Lee's eye, he looked away. That's when I knew he was weak."

"Why do you let him boss you around?"

"He's the boss," he said with a rumble in his voice box. "But we're a team. He took me off the street. He pays me well." His head cocked to a tilt. "The Iraq war changed me." His eyelids popped open wider. "I kinda like killing bad people." He gave a self-assuring nod. "I've never killed a bad girl though."

"What if I let you fuck me?" Her voice was more than a whisper but softer than a bark. "Would you let me go?"

Gaytan pulled a folding knife out of his pocket, flicked it open with his thumb. "I could fuck you right now. And there's nothing you could do about it." His smile grew to a short laugh.

"You could rape me, but you'll never know what it's like to *fuck* me." She put extra emphasis on the word he seemed to like.

"That sounds real good. But in all reality, if I let you go, I'd have to kill Dr. Beaumont." Gaytan shook his head. "Because he'd find me. He'd wait until I least expect it, and then he'd torture me in the worst possible way. I know exactly how his mind works."

"I'll help you kill him."

"No. I don't like the good doctor very much, but I don't want to kill the man who fed me all these years. You know what I mean? Wouldn't be right."

"Don't you want to hear me moan, Big Boy?"

"I'd rather hear you cry." He poked her in the thigh, ripping a hole in her black yoga pants. Jerking the knife outward, he ripped a tear in her pants, exposing bare white flesh.

"That would be a waste," Mars said in a faint bedroom voice, her hips cocking just enough against her restraints to make it look inviting. "You'll never get another chance with a girl like me. Look at yourself in the mirror. No self-respecting woman wants you."

Gaytan playfully smacked her in the mouth three times. "I like it when you talk in that voice." He looked her up and down. "I just grew an inch." Leaning forward, he reached out and gripped her neck harder than she expected. "Now you're gonna get fucked. Little bitch. Little fucking whore." He squeezed her throat tighter until her face darkened. "You have no fucking options."

When he let go of her throat, she gasped for air and shook her head, coughing. "You can't rape me on the table you stupid piece of shit." She coughed violently but soon continued with a strained voice. "Unbuckle me and bend me over."

"Okay." He showed her his knife. "I'll unstrap you, but if you try to run... I'll gut you like a fish. And then I'll piss on your corpse."

Mars' eyes shifted away from him as he unstrapped her leg restraints. "I won't run. Just let me go after. Please." The canvas ratchet strap fell to the floor and the heavy metal buckle cracked against the concrete.

"I can't do that." Gaytan loosened the next restraint. "This is gonna be a ride I want to take more than once." He laughed softly under his breath. "When I unstrap the last one, I want you to get down... and take off your clothes. Slowly." He softly poked her in the neck with the tip of the knife, just enough to make her bleed a tiny amount.

She gasped as he pulled back.

"You only get one warning." He showed her a close-up of the knife. "I will shove this fucking knife in your throat." He tilted it and gripped it in his hand. "Just give me a reason."

Mars' chest was rising and falling. The last ratchet strap clunked on the floor. "Okay." Her breaths were so fast she was almost panting. The pulse in her ears was drumming the beat of her adrenalized heart rate.

"Get up." Gaytan stood with the knife clenched in his fist and dangling at his side. His breaths were quick and heavy. It looked like he was gritting his teeth.

Mars dropped her feet on the basement floor. Rising tall, she felt every muscle in her body secretly flexing. The flex caused pain and the realization that her right knee was badly bruised. She braced herself with one hand on the workbench. A flake of paint broke off and floated to the floor.

"Strip." His hand tilted upward. "Slow like."

Mars was stalling. Breathing. Blinking. Quaking under the skin.

"Do it!"

Mars peeled off her shirt with haste, and her large firm breasts bounced in her sports bra. "It's not too late. Just let me go, and I'll give you the best fuck of your life."

"Shut up, bitch." He paused, taking in the hourglass figure. "Drop trou, before I slit your throat." He licked his lips.

Glancing down at the buck knife, Mars saw the restraint and the buckle in the corner of her eye. "Let me grab my ankles first," Mars said. "My yoga pants are see-through when I bend over."

"Do it."

With trembling fingers, she bounced on the balls of her feet, creating a distraction with her jiggly breasts. He dropped his jaw. When she noticed his free hand rubbing on his crotch, she spun her body away from Gaytan, whipping her dark auburn hair. Arching her back, she made her knees touch her elbows, and then dropped to a low squat, gripping the end of the strap. She cocked her hips and craned her neck to see the bearded man in a trance shuffling forward.

Springing up like a top, she whipped the buckle forward and connected with Gaytan's face. The heavy buckle hit with the force of a Middle Ages mace, tearing skin and flesh and hair. Misting the air with a spray of blood.

Shrieking in pain, Gaytan fell to his knees, growling like a cornered dog. He dropped the knife and his hands shot to his nose. Blood was dripping through his fingers as he held his face together. "FUCK!" He screamed. "You're dead, bitch!"

35

Khyber Pass, Pakistan
August 7, 2012

Lerch Black was curled up in a ball in the corner of a small rocky cave. His body was trembling uncontrollably. Sweat, blood, and dirt was clotted on his roughly bearded face. He could smell his own filth. And shit.

At the sound of feet walking in the underground jail cell, he covered his head with his hands. Breathing heavily, he hoped they would take him out of his misery.

"Sit up," a man said in English but with an Arabic accent.

Lerch dug his fingers into the dirt and struggled to lift himself to the sitting position. Raising his chin, his blurry eyes studied the aging man with a gray beard and a white turban wrapped around his head. Looking past this man with the white robe, he saw two younger men with scruffy black beards, AK-47s, and earth-toned Arab garb. Looking past the soldiers of radical Islam, he saw a stone wall and closed his eyes to picture his hero one last time before they killed him like the rest of the prisoners of war.

A vision of his sister at ten years old appeared in the black void of his mind's eye. She was begging his dad not to beat him. Standing up to the monster in her head. And then she got smacked to the floor. But she got back up.

If Gretchen could stand up to his dad, he could stand up to this barbarian who beheads infidels on a daily....

"American scum," the gray beard Arab said with a slightly raised voice.

Lerch's eyes snapped open. The dark-skinned man in the white robe was holding a long shiny sword in his hands.

"It is your turn to make video," the imam said. "If you stay still, it will be painless. If you move, I will make you suffer."

Lerch eyed the beautiful sword with the black handle. It looked ancient. Nothing like the cheap China-made sword he had cherished since he was a kid. The sword that once freed him from the predator in his home. "I can help you," Lerch croaked out. Slightly lifting his head, he clenched the muscles in his jaw.

The imam snorted. "You...are infidel. Devoid of light. Your filth is irreversible."

"That's why you fail," Lerch said, swallowing his timidity. "You won't do what is necessary to defeat your enemy. 9-11 wasn't shit." He paused to glance at the frail-looking guards. "You fucking Arabs are weak... and stupid. Americans will own this fucking country for twenty years."

The Arab spit on Lerch. "You have all the watches," he said calmly. "But we have all the time." He gestured to his minions. "Sit him up," he barked out in Arabic. "Roll the tape." He met Lerch's black crusted eyes.

Two men ran up to Lerch. Each man took an arm, violently jerking Lerch to his knees. Holding him erect, they barked orders in Arabic.

The imam lifted his sword high. His guards dispatched, leaving a swaying, trembling, filthy Lerch Black. The imam with the sword walked behind him, slowly turning to face the camera. This time he spoke in English. "The infidel has spilled blood on Arab land." He paused with a cold look into the camera. "Soon, it will be your streets running red with blood. Today…is just a taste. Our target will be your civilian—"

Lerch raised his voice. "I'll deliver smallpox to America!"

A bearded guard jerked the back of his gun forward and rifle-butted Lerch in the side of the head. He went down with a groan and a thud.

"Camera off!" the imam shouted in Arabic, and then switched to English. Turning to Lerch, he saw his prisoner holding the side of his head as blood dripped to the dirt floor. "Why would any man do that to his own country? Surely, not just to save your life?"

Lerch tasted the blood from his finger. "I hate America." Pushing his small frame to a sitting position, his face scrunched up. His short breaths erupted into a low growl. "I want them to die. All of them."

"You're weak. Desperate," the imam said. "You would say anything to save your life."

"The people in America have treated me like shit since the day I was born," Lerch said. "Not just the teachers and the cops and the government, but the people. If you're small, they walk on you. If you're different, they laugh at you." Lerch's gaze met the gray eyes of the old imam. "They need a reality check. They need suffering on a wide scale. They need a surprise. A wake-up call."

"Action speaks louder than words, American pig. I'll put you to the test right now." The imam raised his voice in Arabic. "Bring me the next American pig!"

In less than a minute, two bearded men dragged in a blond-haired blue-eyed man. His desert camouflage uniform was torn and soiled. The American flag had been ripped off. His beard looked like it was rubbed in mud and maybe shit.

The guards dropped him on the ground. The wounded warrior curled up and began trembling in fear.

The imam dropped his sword in the dry, orange dirt. "Prove your loyalty." He stepped back behind his guard whose AK-47 was level. "Off with his head. ISIS delivers slow death. Ten hacks." The terrorist leader shook his finger.

Lerch reached for the sword with no hesitation. His eyes raked the ancient weapon for a long moment, and then they shifted to the imam. His lip started tugging upward.

*****

During the six years of living deep in a cave, Lerch Black gave medical treatment to countless ISIS soldiers and saved many lives. He earned the title of doctor. Changed his name to Dr. Randy Beaumont. He grew a thick black beard. He trained as a soldier. He studied as an intelligence agent. He submitted himself to torture and interrogation training. He pretended to submit to a new religion (Lerch had no God.) Lerch Black even fought in many battles side by side with the Taliban. He killed Americans. Tortured a few. For the first time in his life, he felt accepted and loved by his peers.

And now, after completing his training, Dr. Beaumont was underneath a blanket of darkness, hugging his mentor one last time. Two dusty Toyota SUVs were idling side by side. Beaumont and his gray-bearded leader were standing in between.

Stepping back to face him, Beaumont bowed at the waist.

"Your faith will guide your path." Imam Aziz dropped a hand on his shoulder.

"May the Light be upon you." Beaumont bowed again. "Thank you, Imam. I am forever grateful."

"Thank me with your actions."

Beaumont embraced his mentor briefly.

"Safar sa'aid," Imam Aziz said and kissed his cheek twice.

Turning, Beaumont hopped in the back seat of an SUV. When the door closed, the man in the passenger seat started speaking in Arabic. And then the bearded man in the back seat translated into English:

"If you do not follow orders, we will find you. Feed you to hungry dogs. We will find your family. Friends. We will rape the women... sell children off for a life of servitude."

Beaumont's head nodded slowly. "I fully understand."

The man faced forward. "I don't trust you. Imam Aziz is wrong."

"I don't blame you," Beaumont said coldly. "I look like the infidel. I talk like an infidel. But I hate them more than you. Your caliphate is limited to the Middle East. If you want to bring America to its knees, you need *me*." Lerch raised his tone a notch. "Only *I* can make that happen. Only *I* can fit in... and walk amongst the white devil."

*****

In a tin garage on the Mexican side of the border, Dr. Beaumont's Arab guide handed him a small stainless-steel tube with a smaller glass vial inside. "Shove this up your ass." It was the size of a double A battery, but a little bit longer. "You will see sign... when day of reckoning is upon us. Imam Aziz will sacrifice himself as martyr. It will be all over the news. It could be one year. Or maybe ten. You be ready."

Lerch took the vial and unbuckled his pants. "Anything for the mission." He bit his lower lip and tugged them down around his ankles. He spit on the tube and rubbed it around.

Bending his knees, he sucked in air and then let out a long-strained grunt. Standing tall, he pulled his pants up. Wincing. Breathing heavily, he arched his back and stood crooked.

"No hesitation," the terrorist said. "Good. Peace be with you, brother."

The second terrorist clapped his hand on Beaumont's back. "On judgment day... *you* will become martyr." He nodded his bearded head. "Seventy-seven virgins await you."

"I don't want virgins. I want revenge."

*****

In a subterranean tunnel in Tijuana, Mexico, Dr. Beaumont was in the middle of a desperate pack of migrants marching north toward freedom. Opportunity. Safety. He walked tall when other men were ducking the low ceiling. Squinting his eyes, he smiled at the USA landmark sign nailed to a wooden support beam. "There's no place like home."

Beaumont coughed from the thick, dusty air in the dimly lit tunnel. Spanish commotion and cheers were reverberating off the walls. The pain in his ass drowned out the words he didn't understand.

After about ten minutes, the line of migrants came to an abrupt halt. Jubilant hoots and hollers filled the tunnel as people began climbing a dirt-caked metal ladder. One by one, the men, women, and children ascended. Each person let out a scream of glee. Libertad! Libertad! *Freedom! Freedom!*

Approaching the ladder, Beaumont grabbed the rung in front of his eyes and yanked himself up with haste. Little pieces of dirt fell on his beard but he kept climbing until he was inside the back room of a clothing factory. The daylight beaming through the windows made him squint.

"Escuchar!" A man with a handgun yelled and everyone in the room shut up. "Un coche manejar a Los Angeles."

Dr. Beaumont stood, looking around the room at the people with wide eyes and smiles on their faces. *Why would anyone be so happy to come here,* he thought. *They have no idea what's coming.*

*****

Waiting for the red light to turn green, Dr. Beaumont basked in the hot California sun with his arm hanging out the window of a newer mini-van he stole. A few weeks had passed, and his face was freshly shaven. His hair was short with a gel-slicked part to the left. He fit the part, and his confidence made him look important. The crooked smile on his face said: I hold the future of the world in a safe deposit box at my mom's cabin.

His afternoon peace was interrupted by a pauper on the corner who was holding a cardboard sign next to the traffic light.

"Anything helps," the tall thin man said with a low raspy voice and a friendly wave.

Beaumont shifted his head in the man's direction. "Are you a veteran?"

"Yeah. Served in Afghanistan."

Dr. Beaumont waved inward. "Hop in, I'll get you lunch."

The man nodded, reaching for his bag. His clothes were dark, dirty, and weathered. His beard was gnarly.

When the man dropped in the passenger seat and shut the door, Beaumont hit the gas. "What's your name, soldier?"

"Rick Gaytan." He eagerly stuck out his massive hand and smiled. "Master Sergeant, US Army."

Lerch shook it firmly. "I'm Dr. Randy Beaumont," he said, his straight black hair blowing in the wind.

"Thanks for offering lunch. I'm starved."

"No problem. But why are you standing out there in the heat?"

"The war fucked me up. I can't sleep, so I can't work." Gaytan raised his voice a few notches. "The fucking government says I don't qualify for Social Security. They say I'm able-bodied."

"Do you do drugs?" Beaumont read the stranger's eyes. He wondered if this man could be cured of his affliction, trained to become a capable apprentice on his path of destruction.

"No."

Beaumont put his blinker on. "Do you drink?"

"I've drank enough. Didn't help."

"How would you like a flexible job?" Beaumont angled the car to the right and hopped into the far-right lane.

Gaytan's eyes widened. "How many hours a week?"

"I just need an assistant. To help me with certain tasks." Beaumont turned into the parking lot of a liquor store.

"Like what?" Gaytan asked, his head cocking to eye a college-aged woman with a case of beer in her hands. She was heading toward the near-empty parking lot.

Beaumont parked on the side of the liquor store. As the young woman strutted past them with extra short shorts, Gaytan bit his lip, his eyes following her to her car. Dr. Beaumont smiled at his human weakness and hunger to want something he couldn't have. "The type of job that could help you get a girl like that."

"You got my attention." Gaytan shifted in his seat to face his new friend.

"It's the type of job most people wouldn't have the stomach for."

"If you're a drug dealer, I'm out."

Dr. Beaumont let out a heavy breath. "No, no. I'm not after that kind of destruction. But the job does entail a certain amount of…creativity." His head shifted to get a better look at the liquor store. "I'm gonna rob this place. Right now. All you got to do is drive. I'll split the money with you."

Richard Gaytan's eyes widened. "What about the cameras?"

"This is a stolen car. I have another car waiting. Are you in... or out?"

Gaytan pursed his lips. "I'm in."

Beaumont tugged a three-hole ski mask over his head. "Give me two minutes. Park in front."

36

Duluth, Minnesota
April 26, 2026

Mars swooped low and picked up Richard Gaytan's knife from the basement floor. Jumping backward, she dodged the big man's swipe at her ankles. At a few feet of distance, she looked down at the large man on his knees, blocking the doorway. Gaytan was holding his face as the blood dripped from cuts on his brow, nose, and cheek.

A wicked growl shot out of his mouth.

"Stay down," Mars said. "I'll let you live. Just get out of the way."

"You might let me live." Gaytan rose six feet two inches. When he lowered his hand, it revealed a split-open nose. A gash so big there was a red flap dangling by a few strings of flesh. "But I won't return the favor. That knife ain't gonna do shit but make me mad." He spit blood on the cellar floor between them.

"Stay back!" Mars glanced at the pocketknife and swallowed her doubt.

"I will," he said with a low distorted voice, his head turning to gesture toward the only exit. "I'll wait right here for Dr. Beaumont to come back. We'll see what *he* says." His hand raised and pressed against his nose. Blood was rolling down his arm and dripping on the floor.

"If you don't bleed to death," Mars snickered, "he'll kill you for being so weak and stupid. How are you gonna explain how I got loose?"

"You might be right." Staggering from pain, Gaytan lifted his fists. "So, I'm going to have to kill you where you stand." He spat more blood and took a step closer.

Mars quickly surveyed her surroundings. Just a neat basement with tools hanging on the wall to her right. No visible second exit. The widows were too small. She considered a hammer within reach, but she opted for the knife and squeezed it tighter.

"You look scared, Mars."

"You look... red." She pointed behind Gaytan. "Oh, shit! He's back!"

Gaytan smiled. "You won't fool me twice, bitch." He balled his hands into fists and crept to within five feet of Mars. She had her back against the brick wall.

Mars flexed her body and lowered her stance as an explosion of adrenaline crushed her fear and pain. She screamed a high octave, thrusting forward with her right hand stiff and low. The blade was swinging at Gaytan with her second lunging step. Her forward progress stopped when the blade jammed in his gut and her body slammed against his massive frame.

Gaytan let out an aggravated groan and spit blood on Mars' face. Gripping a handful of her hair, he collapsed to the floor, taking her with him. The faceplant buried the knife fully inside his giant stomach cavity and pinned her half underneath him.

Mars shrieked, fighting to get free from the dead weight. With her face pressed on the cold bloody floor, she felt the grip on her hair loosen. Another jerk and she was free, on her feet, panting above a heap of a man.

As she stepped back to her work bench, she let out a series of heavy breaths. Staring down on the limp man on the floor, she wondered if he was really dead. Her head snapped to the wall, and then she rushed to grab the hammer. Eyes on Gaytan and the growing puddle of blood around him, she sidestepped the workbench she had lived on for so many days.

Her black shirt was crumpled up on the bench. She grabbed it and put it on. *I'm free.*

Stepping toward the door, she stooped low and bashed Gaytan in the back of the head with the hammer three times. The body didn't flinch. She hit him in the spine at the base of his neck. No movement. Satisfied that he was dead, she jumped over his legs and bolted through the door, climbing the steps two at a time. Unlocking the back door, she sucked in the first taste of freedom.

Standing in the middle of a gravel driveway, she spun and saw nothing but trees and darkness in every direction. No car. No lights as far as the eye could see. Just a narrow, wooded path in the dark. Wasting no time, she picked up the pace and briskly followed the unpaved road. A slight hobble developed on her right side. The adrenaline was wearing off, and with it came the return of her knee pain. Wincing, she gripped the hammer tight and limped down the long winding exit to safety. Halfway down the path, she stopped to catch her breath and rest her sore and throbbing knee.

"Fuck that," she barked, huffing and puffing with her hands on her hips. "It could take hours before the cops get here." She heard crickets in the dark and lowered her tone to a growl. "I can't let Lerch get away with this."

While Mars was plotting her revenge, Dr. Beaumont was two hundred miles south, pulling into the Emergency Room entrance in Minneapolis, Minnesota. Jamming the shifter into park, his heart pounded erratically in his chest as he twisted and giggled at the sight of Caleb Hunt and his unconscious body in the back seat. "Oh, you really are the perfect host." he said, sliding out of Blake Connor's Ford Mustang.

Swinging open the passenger side door, he grabbed Caleb's ankles, pulling his limp body out of the car. His head cracked on the concrete and Beaumont couldn't bite back his smile under the N95 mask. Taking a strained breath, he quickly rearranged his features from amusement and excitement to one of fear and pain—playing the part of the Good Samaritan.

"Help!" Beaumont hollered, waving his purple-gloved hands in the air. A pair of goggles was resting on top of the mask. A plain black ball cap was set low on his head.

Two men in blue came rushing out with a stretcher rolling toward him. A female healthcare worker approached Beaumont and studied him from head to toe. And then she took a double take at the goggles and mask.

Dr. Beaumont shrugged. "I'm immunocompromised. Hospitals make me nervous."

The female nurse regarded Beaumont. "What happened to your friend?" she gestured to the lifeless soul being lifted on the stretcher.

"I don't know," Beaumont said, his eyes following the Black Plague as they wheeled Caleb away on the stretcher. "We ate Chinese food, and then he said he wasn't feeling so good. He was holding his stomach before he passed out."

"What's his name?"

"Lerch Black."

"Can you come in and answer some questions?"

"No problem." Dr. Beaumont nodded. "I'll go park and come back. Please help my friend."

*****

Mars Sundean was in the living room of the house, hunting for a weapon bigger than the hammer in her hand. The flat-screen TV on the wall was off. The glass coffee table was empty. The place reminded her of a military barracks. Neat and tidy. Not a cushion was out of place until she pulled the leather couch away from the wall and tipped it over. No gun in sight. The only thing left to check was a cabinet in the corner of the room.

Pulling open a middle drawer, she saw a leather Koran caked with dust. She remembered Lerch talking about a leader. Maybe he *was* a terrorist? Maybe he did inject Caleb with a real bioweapon? Pursing her lips, she closed the drawer and turned around.

With her head on a swivel, she lumbered to the carpeted flight of stairs on the side wall. Grabbing the railing, she pulled herself up to the second floor one step at a time. With three rooms to choose from, she reached for the door on her right and turned the knob. The door creaked and she gave it a push. Hitting the light switch revealed a state-of-the-art tech room with gray desks up against three walls. Two computer screens and a laptop on each desk. Countless black devices, cameras, and little black specks that looked like tiny microphones.

Raising her head, Mars' dry, cracked lips barely moved. "Holy shit," she whispered as her head slowly rolled to view the full collage displaying hundreds of pictures of his victims on the walls: Blake and Caleb at the reunion. Derek Bane at the pool hall. Lee Wallis strapped to the bench. Bob Sturgis and Tarik Brownridge sleeping on a couch in opposite directions.

Pivoting to the other side of the wall, she saw Detective Ford with his kids, and... "Oh my God." Her hand covered her mouth. The entire ceiling was dedicated to her. Some nude. Some in bed with Caleb.

Breathing in through her nose, she turned with a red-hot face, swinging the hammer at the computer screens, shattering the black glass and plastic. Turning the hammer around, she reached for the ceiling and tore down all the compromising pictures of her with the claw. And there on the center desk, in the corner of the room—stood a three-tiered Samurai sword rack.

Mars let go of the hammer and veered to the corner.

Reaching for the long sword on the bottom tier, she grabbed the red and black handle and gripped it tight with both hands. The stainless-steel blade was glistening in the light.

"This will do." She gave a check swing with the sword.

Mars spit on the floor and tiptoed back down the stairs, her eyes and ears straining for any movement. In the back of the living room, a narrow hallway led her to the kitchen and the basement door. Pausing with her hand on the knob, she twisted her wrist, opened the door, and then closed it behind her. Holding the weapon firm against her chest, she slowly hobbled down the steps.

The door was open and Gaytan was already collecting flies. Crossing the threshold, she continued plotting and planning a trap. The pool of blood had been flowing toward the drain under the first bench. Planting both feet in the dead man's blood, she turned and limped to the back room, leaving red footprints behind her. Inside the small storage room, she stepped out of her shoes and kicked them against the wall.

Spinning on her socks, she avoided her footprints and shuffled forward to hide in the darkness behind the furnace, the water heater, and the storage freezer. *Time to wait,* she thought. *And then, I'll end this once and for all.*

*****

Lerch Black opened the basement door with a shit grin. "Oh, Mars. You'd be so proud of your Caleb—" The rest of the words drying on his lips as he crossed the threshold only to find Rick Gaytan in a big contorted heap on the floor. Swiveling his head, his urgent gaze fell on the empty workbench against the cinder block wall. The dark red blood underneath it.

"What the fuck?" Lerch screamed with a trembling voice and two clenched fists. "She's gone!" His eyes followed the bloodstream back to the source, and then he found small footprints next to Gaytan's body.

With fast heavy breaths, his head snapped to study the footprints, his eyes zigging and zagging up the concrete floor. With his heart pounding in his chest, he pulled out his black Glock 30 handgun and slid the top back to put a bullet in the chamber. Creeping close to the wall, he peeked around the corner and cursed in frustration. The storage room was empty. She was gone. But why did she leave her shoes?

"Mars!" He screamed in the doorway, his free hand clenching into a solid fist as he peered down on her bloody shoes. "You'll never escape. I'm in your fucking head!"

When Lerch stuck his head in the room, Mars emerged from the dark area around the furnace, tip-toeing forward with the sword in the ready position, using the moment to take him by surprise. She was three feet behind him when she attacked.

Mars chopped the sword at the meaty part on the back of Lerch's neck. "Die, mother fucker!

Lerch's small frame spun around, and she felt a speck of blood spatter on her face as he crashed to the floor. The gun flew out of his hands and slid into the corner.

Lerch cried out, desperately reaching his hand to cover the gash on the back of his neck. He was squirming on his side with his teeth gnashed together when he looked up at Mars. "I should have killed you in front of Caleb."

Mars raised the sword high and dropped it down on Lerch's leg, his cries fueling her rage and pent-up emotion. He shrieked, reaching for her hand. She overpowered his weak claw, this time dropping the blade on the arm he was using to block the blow to his head. Stepping even closer, she swung harder, this time rendering his cut and broken arm useless.

"Why won't you die!" Mars chopped and screamed again.

Lerch grunted and used his good arm to try to squirm toward the gun in the corner of the room. "Stop!" Blood was dripping from several areas of his body.

Mars stepped on the wound on his leg and rubbed it in. Crouching, she swung the blade low with one hand. The swipe took off several fingers and scratched the hundred-year-old concrete.

Lerch yelped and pulled his hand into his chest. Breathing heavily, he groaned in pain and sucked in air. Twisting to roll over on his back, he used his feet to continue inching closer to the corner and the gun.

With a crazed look in her eyes, she lunged forward, impaling the sword in his gut. Turning the blade sideways, she pulled it out slowly. Mars stepped back and watched Lerch squirm. Listened to him whimper. Gurgle. Cough for air. She heard the rip in his voice with each wheezing plea to stop.

Mars stepped back with the sword in the ready position. The blood was dripping down the blade and rolling on her hands. With short fast breaths, her restless green eyes took in the sight of street justice. *He's still alive.*

Lerch wasn't moving but he was wheezing.

"You deserve what you got." She looked over her shoulder and saw Gaytan in a puddle. "All these tough guys and cops — and it takes little ol' me... to stop you and that *beast* over there."

Lerch let out a soft groan.

"I know you hear me, Lerch." Tears ran down her cheeks. "Where the fuck is Caleb?"

Lerch Black was sprawled out. Face down on his stomach. One leg bent at a right angle. He was still leaking blood like a sieve. But he was breathing. Wheezing.

Looking down at the critically injured serial killer, something caught her eye in the corner of the dimly lighted room. *The gun.* Mars dropped the sword, swooped down, and grabbed the black gun. Holding it in her hands, she tilted it and read the small print on the side of the gun. "Glock 30," she snorted. "That's my fucking gun."

"K-kill m-me." Lerch coughed and spit up blood on his chin. "The pain is too much. You win. I just want to die."

Mars had the gun trained on Lerch. "I should let you suffer," she growled softly, just enough to feel the rumble of hate in her throat.

"Kill me," Lerch whispered. "You'll never find Caleb without my help. He's under a false name."

"Where is he?"

"Will you finish the job?"

Mars nodded slowly.

"Say it."

"Give up the info... and I'll take pleasure in squeezing this trigger."

"Caleb's at the University of Minnesota Medical Center." He coughed and more blood came out. "Downtown Minneapolis. Under the name... L-Lerch Black. Tell the authorities... he has been infected with a m-militarized v-virus called E6C6... 26. They'll quarantine Caleb and staff. Y-you m-might save... t-the w-world."

"That's a good gesture." Mars shook her head. "I'll warn them, but they won't believe me. People don't release bioweapons too often, ya know?" Mars spit on Lerch's face. Picking through his pockets, she found his keys and phone and set them on the floor behind her.

"I wanted to make Caleb suffer." Lerch coughed, and then continued with a faint scratchy voice. "I want to make the whole world suffer. But I changed my mind. I'll be satisfied with just Caleb and the boys."

Rising to her feet, she shifted the gun to his ankle. "I changed *my* mind. I won't be satisfied until I see you... suffer." She squeezed the trigger and exploded a round in his foot.

Lerch found the energy to jerk and scream. The report of the weapon reverberated around the room with his voice.

Mars clacked off another shot. Lerch now had two mangled feet. And then she leveled her arms in the direction of Lerch's head. Crouching in a two-handed stance, the gun trembled in her hands. She breathed in a rhythm with her heartbeat. All of his treachery flashing in her mind. All of what he took away from her. The last sight of Caleb's eyes before the second injection. A memory of her and Caleb laughing before he opened the cardboard box. And that magical kiss on Mars' Island.

She pulled the trigger. A final thunderclap destroyed Lerch Black's head and life. But she hit him again for good measure.

What a mess.

37

Two Harbors, Minnesota
April 26, 2026

Mars was speeding down the road, her eyes growing narrow and urgent as she passed the green mile sign to Duluth. Lerch's phone was pressed against her ear. "I can't calm down," she said with a sharp voice. "They cut my fucking finger off. And—"

"Hold on, hold on," Detective Reid said, interrupting her words. "Where are you at?"

"On the highway by Two Harbors. I'm twenty min—"

"Are you in danger?"

"No, I just killed the serial killer you're looking for, but he already released a—"

"What? You killed him? How?"

Mars stomped on the gas. "Yes," she yelled, one hand on the wheel. "The killer is a fucking terrorist. He just released a deadly bioweapon. He injected—"

"A bioweapon?"

"Yes, fucking let me talk." She paused briefly and continued when she heard silence on the other end of the phone. "He injected Caleb with a bioweapon. He dropped him off at the University of Minnesota Medical Center. Under the name Lerch Black."

"Ma'am, Lerch Black is dead."

Mars shook her head. "No, he's dead *now*. I just put a bullet in his head. Trust me, the virus is spreading every second we argue. I watched him inject Caleb. Call the hospital right now!"

"Okay. Okay. I believe you. I'll make the call."

*****

An obese female hospital worker answered the phone at the reception desk. "State hospital," she said and took a sip from her bottle of pop. At the agitated sound of the voice in her ear, she raised her tone. "Whoa, slow down, sir." She sat upright. "Let me type that name in." She stopped talking and rolled her fingertips on her keyboard. When the person of interest showed up on the computer screen, she dropped her jaw an inch. "We do have a patient here with that name. He's in the Intensive Care Unit. Just to confirm, you said Ebola virus, right?"

Detective Reid was breathing in the phone. "Yes! Quarantine the hospital!"

She hung up the phone and sprung out of her seat. Lumbering to the nearby security guard, she raised her voice. "Stop! Stop!"

The guard in black stopped with a flinch, turning to face her. "You, okay?"

"We have a possible code red," she said curtly, leaning forward with one hand lifting to express urgency. "I just got a tip from a detective in Duluth. Quarantine Lerch Black. Room 665 This is not a drill."

*****

The next day at the hospital, a dark-skinned military virologist in a white Hazmat suit observed Caleb Hunt's vitals inside a large quarantine bubble. His female assistant was standing at his side, copiously taking notes. The patient was in a coma, but he was starting to show symptoms of the virus on his skin.

"I hope we're not too late," Dr. Patel said, looking down on Caleb who was pale with breathing tubes connected to his face. Small red lesions were visible on his arms and neck and there was more growing all over his body.

"There's a chance we just started a major pandemic," she said, looking at the doctor through the shield of her suit.

"I recommended they lock down the entire city and the state," the doctor said. "We don't know when this virus becomes transmittable. Dozens of nurses and doctors came into close contact with him before he was in quarantine. That's problematic."

The physician's assistant put a little bit of Vaseline on Caleb's dry, chapped lips. "There's a chance this virus can't spread until he's symptomatic."

"We'll find out soon enough." Dr. Patel turned and unzipped the exit of the bubble. His assistant walked through the slit in the plastic and he followed her, quickly zipping it up behind him.

"The virus is progressing in the patient," the assistant said. "Seems to mimic the Ebola virus, but it's also attacking his upper respiratory system. I've never seen anything like it."

Dr. Patel let out a heavy breath. "I have," he said. "I helped in replicating its mutation—"

Caleb made a choking noise.

The doctor snapped his head to the bubble and saw Caleb's eyes wide open and darting in every direction. Ripping his tubes out, he expelled a stream of red vomit on his pristine, white gown and blanket.

Dr. Patel unzipped the bubble, entered, and met eyes with Caleb. "Sir, are you okay?" he asked. "Nod if you can hear me."

Caleb covered his mouth with his hand and coughed a few times. "I-I hear ya." He was breathing heavily. "I-I've been infected with a virus. He said it was... uh... uh... it was... E-Ebola mixed with Corona—"

"We know, Caleb," the doctor said. "We're doing everything we can to save you."

"How long have you known about the virus?" Caleb sniffled.

"Twenty-four hours," the assistant said. "You've been in a coma. All of our test results will be back any minute now."

"Fuck the test!" Caleb's arms were flailing. "Lock down this hospital." His voice was strained. Raspy. "Track down every person who left this hospital. The man who did this to me is a terrorist. He works for—"

"Calm down," The doctor rested a gentle hand on Caleb's shoulder. "The hospital has been in quarantine for the last twenty-three hours. Nobody in, nobody out." He paused, touching his chest with his white-gloved hand. "I'm Dr. Patel, and this is my assistant, Dr. Cole. We're from the government. We're here to help."

Caleb tried to cover his dry cough with the crook of his arm. "I-I feel like shit," he said, his bloodshot eyes were filling with tears and spilling over. "Am I. Am I gonna die?"

"Mr. Hunt. Take pleasure that your body will save lives in either case." Dr. Patel nodded. "We've already gained a lot of vital information from you while you were in the coma. Now that you're awake, we can test how you react to different medicines and we can ask you questions. If the virus you are infected with is a direct match with a military strain, we may already have a vaccine."

"Why didn't answer my question." Caleb sniffled and dried his cheeks with the back of his hand.

"Caleb, we just don't know," Dr. Patel said. "You have to stay strong. Keep fighting. You're doing good."

"Don't let Lerch Black get away with this."

"He's dead," Doctor Cole said.

"No." Caleb shook his head. "He's alive. He faked his death in Afghanistan."

"No, sir. We were told your girlfriend killed him." The assistant was nodding her head.

Caleb sat upright, shrugging. "What? Really?"

"That's correct, Mr. Hunt," Dr. Patel said. "Mars Sundean is a hero. She may have saved the world. She's under quarantine in Duluth, but I don't see why we can't set up a phone call."

"That would mean the world to me."

EPILOGUE

Minneapolis, Minnesota
April 28, 2026

From his tilted hospital bed, Caleb smiled at Mars' face on his video phone. "If you wore a Hazmat suit, I don't see why you can't visit me."

"Trust me," Mars said with a warm smile. "I'm coming to see you at the soonest possible moment. I'll do whatever it takes."

Caleb endured a coughing fit. "I-I'm afraid we don't have much time."

"What do you mean?" She pursed her lips. "Other than the sores on your face, you seem fine."

"I feel weak," Caleb said, covering his mouth to cough. "My temperature is 103, my blood oxygen is 85, and my blood pressure is super low." He coughed harder. "And I can tell the doctor doesn't think I can handle the truth."

"You got the best of the best helping you. Trust their judgment. Maybe if you knew the truth, you'd drop dead. Maybe it's best you just fight this virus."

Caleb let out a heavy breath. "I sure hope the virus is contained."

"Me, too," she said. "It's crazy, we survived the revenge list, and now our lives are occupied with this stupid virus. We just can't win."

"At least we still have each other," Caleb said, offering a weak smile.

"Caleb, you risked your life to save me." Mars raised her voice a notch. "Thank you. When you beat this virus, I want you to come home. I'm going to spend the rest of my life trying to return the favor."

"If I survive, I'll always know it was because of my thirst... for you." Caleb paused, shifting his eyes to the breaking news on the TV screen. President Clacher was speaking from the Oval Office. "Mars, check this out." Caleb turned the phone around so the camera was facing the TV.

"... marks another grim day in the history of America," President Clacher said from behind the Resolute Desk in the Oval Office. "Over the past ten years, we've survived nuclear war, we've defeated tyranny, and now, together, we will overcome this Black Plague. Unfortunately, the death rate for this military-grade virus is 100%. It is irreversible. We know this, because, we've had this same virus in our arsenal for decades to deter Russia and China from ever using such a weapon. After World War Three, rogue elements of those countries stole many weapons of mass destruction and sold them off to the top bidder. The good news is... that we have a vaccine... that works. If we quarantine the sick, and vaccinate the rest of the population, we can kill this virus." The president leaned forward and spoke with a hushed whisper. "Do your part. Get vaccinated. Get vaccinated. ... Get vaccinated."

Caleb's head jerked backward. "100% death rate?" he asked with a sinking heart.

"No, no. They don't know that." Mars breathed into the phone. "They're guessing. They don't know how tough you are. You've been shot, stabbed, and beaten. This ain't shit."

Biting back his tears, he looked at Mars on the cellphone screen. "If I ain't gonna make it, at least I got to talk to you, and see your lovely face on video." He tried to calm down her rising upset. "Your eyes still make my heart buzz."

"Aww, Caleb." Mars' voice cracked. "You're going to make it. I know it. I can't fathom any other outcome." She sniffled and wiped her nose with her hand. "Fuck that. I'm coming there. I don't care how, but I need to be with you."

"This hospital is under quarantine."

"I'll rent a fork lift. Get close to your window."

Caleb breathed out a weak laugh. "I don't have any windows." He coughed. "I live in a bubble."

"Caleb Hunt. Me and you are responsible for saving the future of mankind. If it wasn't for us, God knows how many people would die. I'm going to ask to speak to the president. He might be able to make accommodations."

Caleb coughed into the crook of his arm. "That's a good idea. But you don't want to see me like this. I look like a freak."

"Caleb, I love you more than life itself. I love you for who you are, not how you look. Don't you know, I would die... just to get close to you?"

He rested his hand on his heart. "If I die tonight, I'll be at peace... because I finally know you love me."

*****

Mars Sundean marched in the back door of the Minneapolis hospital with two military escorts. They were wearing yellow Hazmat suits with big black badges hanging around their necks. After several checkpoints, they took the elevator to the top floor.

They were greeted by a dark-skinned doctor in a white Hazmat suit. "Welcome, Miss. Sundean," Dr. Patel said. "Caleb is waiting for you."

"Is he okay?" Mars asked with squinty eyes.

"No, ma'am," the doctor said. "I'm afraid his organs are failing him. Follow me." He waved his gloved hand and led her to a ventilated unit specially designed for infectious diseases.

When she entered the white state-of-the-art room, her eyes widened at the sight of Caleb in a plastic bubble with tubes in his mouth. "Oh, no," she worded in her suit mask.

"The breathing tubes are keeping him alive," Dr. Patel said. "Acute respiratory failure. He needs 100% oxygen at all times. But he is responsive if you want to go inside."

"Okay," Mars said softly.

The doctor unzipped the bubble. "I'll give you ten minutes alone with him, and then he'll need to rest."

"Thank you," Mars said, ducking inside the bubble. Looking down at her unrecognizable lover, she burst into tears at the sight of his red skin riddled with lesions on every visible square inch of his body.

Caleb's eyes snapped open and he basked in the glory of Mars' dreamy face and her dark auburn locks of hair on the other side of her protective shield.

"Caleb!" she smiled. "I made it! President Clacher pulled some strings."

He winked one eye.

"I'm sorry you're going through this." She reached for his hand and squeezed it. "I love you so much."

Caleb squeezed her gloved-hand and gazed into her wet green eyes.

"Are you happy I'm here?" Her eyes were locked on his, trying to read his thoughts.

He squeezed her hand tighter.

"I should have never dumped you." She confessed her big mistake that had been weighing heavy on her heart for days. "You were right. I was safer by your side."

Tears rolled down Caleb's cheeks and the light reflected twinkles in his eyes.

"I'll never forget the time I spent with you." She sniffled. "You'll always be in my heart."

Caleb wiped his tears from his irritated skin.

"There's something I need to tell you." She let out a heavy sigh. "I wanted to tell you in person. It's good news." She paused dramatically, her eyes locking with his. "When I was in quarantine, they took a bunch of tests. And uh... um. I-I'm pregnant, Caleb. It's yours."

His eyes expanded.

"I can't wipe my tears," Mars said, choking down her anxiety. "I promise to raise him or her to treat people with—"

Caleb made a gagging noise in his throat, and then his eyes fluttered. A sustained beeping noise sounded and he began convulsing violently. Mars' body shuddered inside the suit, her head shifting to the black monitor on the side of his bed.

Flatline!

"No!" Mars cried. "Help! Help!" She grabbed his limp hand and a current of burning adrenaline pumped throughout her body.

Dr. Cole physically ushered Mars out of the bubble and Dr. Patel entered.

Mars' head craned back to eye Caleb as she was pulled out of the room. When the door shut, Mars was still looking back, but the woman hastily escorted her to a quarantine room on the other end of the floor. The door was closed and locked.

Mars sobbed and let out a loud wail. And then she pounded on the thick window.

At the sound of a knock on the door, Mars jumped to her feet. When the door opened, Dr. Patel entered and closed the heavy door behind him. He had a cold look on his face behind the shield.

"I came to inform you that Caleb passed," the doctor said gravely. "He contributed a great deal of information to science. My data will be studied for decades. Lives will be saved because of his cooperation."

Mars sunk her head and cried. "W-why couldn't you save him?"

"It's a nasty virus," Dr. Patel said. "So nasty it could not have come from nature. Only humans could create and deliver such evil."

"I guess Lerch got what he wanted."

"What did he want?" The doctor's face was twisted behind the shield. "The virus has been contained. Billions of lives have been saved. He failed."

Mars sniffled. "No," she said, shaking her head. "He wanted Caleb to suffer... and die a horrible death."

Did you like my crazy story?

Please leave a review on Amazon and barnesandnoble.com!
That will help me grow.

Thank you!

Other Works of Fiction by Nick Campanella

Path of Affliction

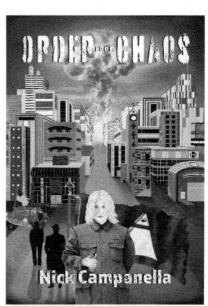

Order From Chaos

<u>Thank you!</u>

About the Author

Nick Campanella is the author of Path of Affliction, Order from Chaos and Devoid of Light. His early years were spent on the hockey rink, and his later years have been spent bouncing from one hard labor job to another—until he found his passion for writing. After ten years of perfecting the manuscript, he is excited to share his book with the world.

Printed in the USA
CPSIA information can be obtained
at www.ICGtesting.com
LVHW090340280224
772984LV00047B/455

9 781970 153477